Thornspell

Thornspell

HELEN LOWE

ALFRED A. KNOPF

NEW YORK

THIS IS A BORZOI BOOK PUBLISHED BY ALFRED A. KNOPF

All rights reserved. Published in the United States by Alfred A. Knopf, an imprint of Random House Children's Books, a division of Random House, Inc., New York.

Knopf, Borzoi Books, and the colophon are registered trademarks of Random House, Inc.

Visit us on the Web! www.randomhouse.com/kids

Educators and librarians, for a variety of teaching tools, visit us at www.randomhouse.com/teachers

Library of Congress Cataloging-in-Publication Data
Lowe, Helen
Thornspell / Helen Lowe. — 1st ed.
     p.   cm.
Summary: In this elaboration of "Sleeping Beauty," Prince Sigismund, having grown up in a remote castle dreaming of going on knightly quests, has had only a passing interest in the forbidden wood lying beyond the castle gates until a brief encounter with a beautiful and mysterious lady changes his life forever.
ISBN 978-0-375-85581-8 (trade) — ISBN 978-0-375-95581-5 (lib. bdg.)
[1. Fairy tales. 2. Princes—Fiction.] I. Sleeping Beauty. English. II. Title.
PZ8.L9474Th 2008
[Fic]—dc22
2008004149

Printed in the United States of America
September 2008
10 9 8 7 6 5 4 3 2

First Edition

To Andrew, who has never doubted.

Contents

The Silent Wood

A boy was lying on his stomach on the topmost tower of a small, square castle, basking like a lizard in the sun. There was a book open on the lichened stone in front of him, and one slightly grubby finger traced the illuminations on the page. Neither he nor the book was supposed to be there at all, but he had slipped away from his many guardians to lose himself in the enchanted world of *Parsifal* and the Grail quest. When he was done with reading, he would simply doze on in the warm afternoon sun or look out, lofty as a falcon, over the world that surrounded the castle.

Even from the high tower it was a small enough world, for the castle, the gardens, and the parkland that surrounded it were contained by a high stone wall. The wall snaked for miles between the park and the white dusty road, and even the local village lay inside the great wrought-iron gates. Sigismund, for that was the boy's name, couldn't remember the gates opening since the day his father had first brought him to the castle, several years before. He supposed they must open sometimes to let his father's couriers pass, and the merchants who brought luxuries from the capital, but he had never seen it happen, not even when he raced to the top of the tower to watch a departing caravan. There was always something that distracted his attention at the critical moment—or the dust in summer, or snow of winter, would be too thick for him to see the gate at all.

Sigismund could lie for hours watching the road and imagining the long leagues to the capital, with all the towns and great houses, woods and fields, along its length. He would daydream of the adventures that might befall a traveler along the way, for there were still tales told of both faie and ogres dwelling in these remoter provinces. Sigismund's tutor, Master Griff, might look down his nose at such tales, but Sir Andreas, the castle steward, would shake his head and say that you couldn't take anything for granted, not in this country. Sir Andreas himself would never say more, but Wenceslas, who worked in the stable and was a particular friend of Sigismund's, said that Sir Andreas's own father had been killed fighting ogres. He too had been the King's steward and led his men against the ogres when they began killing travelers and raiding outlying farms.

This story always gave Sigismund a shiver down his spine, because it was both exciting and sad at the same time. He liked to imagine riding out in the same way when he was older, protecting the people from outlaws and monsters, except that in these daydreams Sigismund always overcame his opponents and set any wrongs done to right. His favorite dream, however, was of the day when his father would come riding back from the endless rebellions and outright wars in the southern provinces. Then, thought Sigismund, his eyes half shut against the sun's glare, they would go adventuring together—perhaps along the fabled Spice Road and into the Uttermost East, where dragons flew like silken banners in the noonday sky and men spoke in strange tongues.

He didn't like to think about what would happen if his father never came back, if he was killed fighting in the south. Sigismund supposed that he would have to return to the capital if that happened and be crowned king in his turn, although he would much rather ride out alone, like Parsifal on the Grail quest. I could be a knight-errant, he thought, and make my own way in the world, as princes used to do in the high days of King Arthur—or the Emperor Charlemagne, when Roland held the pass at Roncesvalles.

"But not crown princes," Master Griff had said on the one occasion when Sigismund voiced this dream aloud.

"You'll find that was only younger sons, even then. The oldest son still had to be responsible and mind the kingdom."

Thoughts of princes-errant and the Grail quest drew Sigismund's eyes away from the eastern road to the great Wood that stretched for league on tree-tossed league into the west. Every sort of tale was told about that Wood: that it was the home of witches and of faie who would lure the unwary down into their hollow hills. Some stories even said there was a castle hidden deep in the forest, although there were as many tales as there were trees when it came to the nature of the occupant.

One story, usually told in whispers, claimed that the hidden castle was the seat of a powerful sorcerer, another that it belonged to the Queen of the Faie, She-of-the-Green-Gold-Sleeves. There were other tales again that made it a lair of dragons, or basilisks, or trolls that munched on the bones of men. Sigismund had asked Master Griff for the truth of it, but his tutor had shaken his head.

"Trolls that munch the bones of men! You're getting too old for such stories, Sigismund." He had squinted out the library window into the enclosed garden below. "All that is known for certain is that your great-grandfather placed an interdict on the Wood, forbidding anyone to go there. But the reason for the ban was never set down, and now even your father's council seems to have forgotten why." He shrugged. "Yet from what Sir Andreas says, no one in these parts has ever broken it."

Sigismund wondered whether this meant that something particularly bad had happened in the Wood during
his great-grandfather's time, so bad that no one wanted to
go there anyway. The old western gate into the castle was
long since walled up, but there was still a remnant of a
road that must have run into the forest once. It was little
more than two rutted and stony wheel tracks now, but
Sigismund had followed it one day, making his escape from
the castle by means of a mossy channel that had once been
the moat, and a culvert under the outer wall. The road did
not go far, petering out into a bridle path within a few
hundred yards of the castle wall, and fading away altogether beneath the forest eave.

It had been very dark and quiet beneath the canopy, a
heavy, listening silence. There was no call of bird or insect,
no whisper of a falling leaf—not even the wind stirred.
Sigismund had felt the fine hairs lifting along his forearms
and up the back of his neck, and taken a step back.

"Wise boy." The voice that spoke was dry as one leaf
skeleton settling on another. Sigismund had whipped
around, but saw nothing until there was a stirring between
two downbent hazel trees and a crone hobbled out. She
must have been gathering firewood along the forest fringe,
for there was a load of bundled sticks on her back and she
had to twist her head to look at him. Her eyes were sharp
and bright as a blackbird's, but sunk into the weathered
seams of her face. Sigismund had thought she looked a little like an old tree herself, knotted and twisted with the

years, although she moved more like the blackbird, coming close to him with a light, hopping step.

She was lame, he had realized then, that was why she hopped. And he stared, half shocked, half delighted, when he saw that she was puffing on a small, flat-bowled pipe. A thread of smoke rose from it, curling into a question mark above the glow of orange embers.

"That load's too heavy for you, Granny," he said. "Let me carry it back to the castle for you, and the stable master will find a donkey to take you both down to the village."

Light and shadow flickered across the seamed face like sun through shifting leaves, and her laugh was a cackle, dry as her first words. "Ye've a kind heart, lad," she said, "for all yer lordly clothes, but don't 'ee worrit about Auld 'azel. I'm used to burdens, born to 'em, 'ee might say." She chewed on the pipe stem, studying him with her head to one side—exactly like a bird, Sigismund had thought, trying not to laugh. "Stay away from t' Wood, though, 'ee should."

"Why?" he had asked. "Why shouldn't I come in here if I want to?"

Her sidelong look was sly. "Does 'ee want? Ye was goin' backward, last I looked."

Sigismund had flushed then, a slow burn in the region of his ears. "I was surprised," he said, with dignity. "That was all."

"Nay," she contradicted him, around the pipe, "wise.

Forest's dangerous t' likes of 'ee, root an' branch alike."
Her voice had changed then, making him think of earth
and moss, and the leaves of years lying deep beneath the
trees. "E'en yer hunt master takes 'is hounds east or south
or north a ways—no' westward, no' into this wood."

Sigismund had drawn a deep breath in, feeling his eyes
grow wide. "So what is in there?" he demanded. "Is it dragons, like they say, or simply basilisks and trolls?"

The crone cackled again. "Nowt simple about basilisks
or trolls, lad, not if ye meets 'em. This wood's no place for
babes, so ye get away back to yon cassle. 'Tis close enough
t' wood for ye, for now."

Afterward, Sigismund was never quite sure how he
found himself halfway back to the castle before he realized that he had even turned around. He could feel the
old woman's blackbird eyes, but he did not look back.
And although he watched for her from his lookout on the
tower, he never saw her trudging back beneath the load of
firewood. Sigismund spoke to Sir Andreas later, asking
him what he knew of a Granny Hazel. The steward shook
his head and said she could have been any number of old
women in the village. He had paused then, pursing his
lips, before adding that he was surprised any village
woman was bold enough to pick up sticks along the forest
eave.

Could she have been a witch? Sigismund wondered,
thinking about the old tales. He puzzled over the encounter

7

for a while longer, until Master Griff gave him *Parsifal* to read and he became immersed in that. But the next time he made his way to the culvert he found a stout metal grille welded across it, and shortly after that the old fruit trees that had grown up against the low north wall of the castle were cleared away. It was no longer possible for an adventurous spirit to exit the castle by either means, and Sigismund had brooded over this wrong for days. It was one of the reasons he had retreated to the high tower with only *Parsifal* for company, for there he could at least look out at the world he was not allowed to enter.

He should have known better than to tell Sir Andreas about the forest, he decided, staring into the heat shimmer of the afternoon, even if he hadn't mentioned how he got there. It was easy to forget how seriously the castle garrison took the interdict, especially those who had been born and raised in the forest's shadow.

Sigismund remained staring straight ahead for some time, his chin propped on his hands and his eyes fixed on nothing in particular, until he realized that there was a plume of white dust rising beyond the crest of the first low hill, away to the east. He sat up, narrowing his eyes against the glare, and thought that it would take a very large number of horses and vehicles to raise such a cloud, even at the height of summer. His second thought was of his father and the huge train of courtiers, soldiers, and servants, with all their attendant baggage, which always traveled with him. His third thought, however, following immediately on the second, was that a king never went anywhere unheralded and his father would have sent messengers on ahead. All the same, the dust cloud signified a large company, which meant someone of note. Sigismund stood up, dusting down his clothes, and decided to investigate.

It was easy enough, in the sleepy heat of the afternoon, to slip unnoticed into the stable and saddle his horse. Even the flies buzzing against the stable window seemed slower than usual, a drowsy backdrop to the day. The bay pony, Mallow, who was not as young as she used to be and getting too small for Sigismund, swished her tail and laid back her ears, just a little, when he came into her stall. Yet despite this initial resistance, she allowed herself to be saddled and led out a side door into the park.

Given the size of the castle grounds, it was some time before they came to the great wrought-iron gates that opened to the outside world. These were locked, as they always were when Sigismund rode that way, but if he reined Mallow alongside and peered through the metal palings, he could see the cavalcade coming down the road toward him. The summer dust spread out behind it in a white haze, smothering the briar hedge in the ditch beside the road.

A pennant flew above the cavalcade, but although Sigismund narrowed his eyes he could not make out the device on the sky blue background—but there was a golden plume on the pennant bearer's horse and gold embroidery on its saddlecloth, which swept almost to the ground. There were lancers too, riding in step, and the bright sunlight danced on their polished breastplates and glittered on their lanceheads. Sigismund stared, surprised by their presence, then reflected that this was a remote corner of the world—and there was the forbidden Wood. A great lord or lady of the court might well think an armed escort necessary.

He wondered, his knee pressed hard against a metal paling, whether the noble visitor was coming to see him, perhaps with a message sent by his father—but again dismissed the idea after brief reflection. He was sure that a message heralding their arrival would have been sent in advance, just as if his father himself had been arriving.

There was a traveling coach behind the lancers, with a sky blue body beneath the film of white dust and great yellow wheels. Another pennant fluttered from its roof, but the device still eluded Sigismund's gaze. It needed a breeze, he thought, to lift the pennant and spread it out for all the world to see. But there were six white horses pulling the coach, with a postilion in a blue coat riding the leader, and these horses too had nodding golden plumes and gold medallions on their harness that gleamed in the sun. They stopped with a great tossing of heads and pawing of hooves when they drew abreast of the gate, and the whole cavalcade behind them, the wagons and packhorses, and a second company of lancers in the rear, all came to a trampling halt.

Sigismund turned Mallow away from the gate, then brought her round again so that he could look directly into the coach, but a servant had already let down the steps and was holding the door as a lady got out. Sigismund stared at her, for she did not seem like a real flesh-and-blood person, but like an icon wrought in gold and precious stones, or someone's dream of a great lady of the court. He felt a little dizzy as she walked toward him and he could hear the buzz of flies from the stables again, a confused, haphazard spiral in his head. The sound of bees along the briar hedge was a slow drone.

The lady's face was hidden by her wide-brimmed hat with its extravagant swirl of white plumes, but Sigismund could see the fall of golden hair across one shoulder. Her dress was of sapphire blue silk, and her gloves were stitched with gold thread and extended halfway up her arms. Sigismund thought, seeing her hair and her graceful step, that she must be young, but when she was close enough for him to see her face, he was not so sure. It was unlined, that face, smiling and very fair, with eyes as blue as cornflowers, but he did not think she was young—not in the way that Annie, who dusted his room in the castle and giggled a lot, was young.

Sigismund swung down from his saddle and bowed, lower than was required from a king's son, and the lady's smile deepened. She held out her gloved hand, touching his fingers through the gate.

"Hello, chance-met stranger," she said, and her voice was sweet and clear as a note struck on crystal. Sigismund blinked.

"I am the Margravine *zu* Malvolin," the lady continued, "and I believe we have lost our way. I am looking for the road to Westwood village, for I have inherited a little castle called Highthorn, which is located nearby."

Sigismund realized that his fingers were still resting against hers and withdrew them. He blinked again, trying to clear the slight buzzing in his head, and waved a hand toward the distant forest. "You are on the right road, madame. The Wood itself lies over there, but the town called Westwood is located some ten leagues further on." He frowned, concentrating. "It has a market square and a town charter, but I didn't know there was a castle there."

The Margravine laughed, a clear tinkle against the sleepy air. "Oh no," she said, and just for a moment she did seem like Annie. "It is not a foursquare castle like this one, and not nearly so large either—just a little jewel of a place with two towers, very graceful and white." She smiled. "More like a pagoda, one would say, with a drawbridge that is always down, and a moat with swans."

A vision of it swam before Sigismund's eyes like a mirage. He could see the swans amidst the water lilies, both floating on the still water. "I should like to go there," he said, and meant it.

The Margravine reached her gloved hand through the gate and tapped Sigismund, very lightly, on the cheek. Her voice was tender, almost caressing. "Of course you would, and why not? It is the most beautiful place in the world." She withdrew her hand and placed one fingertip against her lips, casting down her eyes in apparent thought. When she looked up again it was swiftly, catching Sigismund's eyes with her own. They were like a blue pool at the heart of a quiet wood, he thought—you could drown in them.

There was something about that thought, the recollection of a wood that was not just quiet but still as death, that made him draw back. It was so hot that it was difficult even to breathe, but he could hear shouts and the thud of horses' hooves in the distance, telling him he had been missed. The Margravine appeared to hear it too, for the cornflower eyes looked past him as if she could see the riders coming.

"Ah well," she said, and the caressing note was back. "Perhaps another time." Her eyes lingered on him. "But then again, perhaps not. I will give you a talisman, just in case."

She drew off her glove and slid a ring from her finger, three strands of yellow gold woven tight around a blue jewel. The jewel made Sigismund think of water in the hot stone courtyards of the south where he had spent his early years: royal blue beneath a web of light.

"A gift," the Margravine said, "to remember me by." And she laughed her tinkling laugh.

Sigismund shivered as his fingers reached for the ring. He thought that a cold wind must have sprung up or a cloud covered the sun, and he looked around, brushing a hand across his eyes to clear them. He saw someone through the blur of sweat, standing in the long shadow cast by the gate. For a moment Sigismund thought it was the crone, with her head twisted up beneath her load of sticks. But then his vision cleared, and he realized that the silhouette was in fact slim and very straight. It was hard to see through the sun's dazzle, but Sigismund had an impression of bare dusty feet beneath a ragged kirtle, centered in the pool of shadow. A village girl—but what, he wondered, would she be doing outside the gate?

He wiped his eyes again and tried to focus, but the girl had vanished. The Margravine did not seem to have noticed anything, but she started slightly as a flock of sparrows rose up, out of the ditch, and darted between her outstretched hand and the gate. The ring dropped sparkling into the dust, and Sigismund thought the lady frowned—but then she was smiling again as she stooped to pick it up. For a moment she stared down at the blue jewel in her hand, her gaze searching, intent, before she shrugged and turned away.

The thudding hooves were louder now and very close. Sigismund could hear voices calling his name, but he did not turn or call back to them, just stared at the Margravine as she stepped back into her blue and yellow coach.

"Until later then," she said over her shoulder, as the plumed hat dipped through the door. A gloved hand waved in farewell. "We will meet again. I am sure of it."

He was still standing there, staring after the coach, when Sir Andreas and the guard galloped up. The cavalcade did not seem nearly so long as it had before, and the last lancers were just disappearing around the bend in the road as the castle horses slid to a halt, sweating and blowing from the speed of their run.

"Who was that?" Sir Andreas demanded, quick and sharp. "Did anyone speak to you? What did they say?"

But Sigismund could only shake his head. His tongue felt too swollen for speech, and the buzzing of the flies was louder and more frenzied than before.

"He seems dazed," the guard captain said. "It must be from the sun, coming out in this heat without a hat."

"Or gloves," Sir Andreas said, frowning, for a horseman always wore gloves.

"It's alright," said Sigismund, enunciating each word with great effort, "my hands are quite cold." And he slumped to the ground at their feet.

The Enchanted Sleep

Everything after that was a blur of anxious voices, with someone calling for a wagon to be brought from the village, or a hurdle if there was no wagon to be had. Sigismund could hear the quick to-and-fro of voices above his head and the thud of hooves galloping away, but a darkness had come between him and the day. After a time even the voices faded, and his body felt as though it was burning up. He couldn't remember being brought back to the castle, whether by wagon or horseback. He only knew that the next time his eyes cleared he was in his own bed, with people whispering somewhere beyond his line of vision.

"Not sunstroke," one voice said gravely.

"This may be beyond our powers," said a second, unknown voice. Then Master Griff said something about a message being sent to the King at once. He sounded tense and unhappy, and someone else cursed, a pithy expletive that made Sigismund want to smile.

Sir Andreas, he thought, before he drifted away again into a shadowy, indistinct realm remote from his body. He tossed and turned on the bed, now hot and now cold, now pushing the blankets away, now shivering beneath the piled-up covers. Sigismund was aware of crying out and having bitter medicine poured down his throat, but the fever did not abate. Even when his vision cleared, as it did from time to time, he still felt as though he was floating somewhere above his body. He could see the topmost tower through the window of his room and sometimes he drifted beside it, close enough to touch the lichened stone. He saw, from this lofty height, that there was a fire burning in his room, but he felt cold anyway. He tried to call out but his throat was dry, and his skin felt as though someone was tapping at it with blunt nails. It made his body feel heavy, even while his mind floated beside the tower.

The next time he opened his eyes it was night, with only firelight illuminating the room, and someone was leaning over his bed. Dark wings of shadow flared on either side of a featureless face and Sigismund tried to draw back, to call for help, but only a croak came out. A hand touched his forehead, cool as water in a summer brook, while the other rested on his wrist. "Be still," a voice said, cool as the hands, and then: "Drink this."

Sigismund shook his head and twisted, but the cool hands were firm and combined with the voice to make him drink down something that was smooth against his swollen throat, refreshing rather than bitter. It pulled him back into his body, enough to see that the dimly lit figure by his bed was a woman, not some creature out of nightmare. He still could not make out her face, but her voice was like a thread of silver in the firelit dark, bidding him sleep.

"Can't," whispered Sigismund, and put out a hot, dry hand, grasping at her wrist. "Who are you? Did Sir Andreas bring you here?"

He thought she smiled. "I am here," she told him, "that is what matters. And if you lie still and close your eyes, I will tell you a story to help you sleep." Her cool hand rested lightly over his own. *"Once,"* she said, *"long ago but not so very far from here, there was a small but happy kingdom. . . ."*

The silver voice went on, weaving itself into Sigismund's dreams and telling him how the King and Queen of that happy land had one daughter, who was both blessed and cursed at her naming ceremony: blessed with many gifts and virtues, but cursed by an evil faie to prick her hand on a poisoned thorn and die on her eighteenth birthday. Everyone present had wailed and lamented, but at the last minute another faie stepped forward and converted

18

the curse of death into one of sleep, an enchanted sleep that would last for one hundred years. And so it had come to pass. On the day that the princess turned eighteen a thorn did pierce her hand, and she fell into a deep sleep. And all the great palace, from her royal parents to the lowliest kennel boy, slept with her. A great hedge of thorns grew up around the sleeping palace, and the wild forest around that, pressing in close on turret and wall—and so it would remain until the hundred years were up and the chosen prince came to break the spell.

"A brave prince and true," the silver voice said, "for only one who is courageous and true of heart can dissolve that spell. And the faie do not die, so the one who cast the evil spell lives on, still pursuing her wickedness and her grudge against the sleeping princess."

In the morning the fever had gone completely, but so too had the woman with the silver voice. Sir Andreas shook his head when Sigismund asked who she was and said he must have dreamed her—there had been no woman here that he knew of. The castle apothecary had come at one stage, with his assistant, but that was all. Sigismund wanted to protest, but he had only the haziest recollection of what the woman looked like. It was her cool, firm hands that he remembered, and her voice, telling him the story of the princess in the wood. And he was sure, because it fitted with the interdict and the other stories, that the wild forest that had grown up around the enchanted palace must be the same Wood that he looked at every day from the castle.

This thought stayed with Sigismund throughout the long, slow weeks of his recuperation. He would lie in bed and think about the view of the forest, its vastness, and how it stretched into the mist of distance. Despite all the stories, he had never seen any sign that there might be a castle hidden in its midst, not even a glimpse of the topmost spire of some tall tower. Now, however, he found himself haunted by the tale of the enchanted sleep. He would daydream about it while the summer heat swam in the languid air, and wonder what it would be like in a castle where everyone was asleep—and had been sleeping for close to a hundred years.

It would be very quiet, Sigismund thought, and very, very still. No fly would buzz or bird sing, fluttering from tree to wall. No horse would stamp or swish its tail in the stable, no dog would bark. He wondered too about the birthday feast set out on the long tables, and the guests gathered in their finery. Would the dust of years have settled on the food until it shriveled and disappeared, or did the enchantment keep it as fresh as the moment it was first set out? And what of the guests? Were they sleeping in their chairs, in the same position as when the enchantment fell, or had their heads fallen forward onto the table?

The atmosphere would be eerie, Sigismund decided,

and not a little sad, with that whole glowing, beautiful gathering fallen, between one breath and the next, into the magic sleep. He could picture it all in his mind: the King and Queen on their golden thrones with pages and ladies-in-waiting sleeping around them, while courtiers leaned against walls or sprawled on the floor. The only person he could not visualize was the princess herself. Every time he tried to imagine her, he saw a spiral staircase instead, with its wrought-iron balustrade winding up, and then up again, into a shimmering golden mist. But there was never any sign of the princess, or what lay at the top.

It was very odd, Sigismund thought, almost as strange as the idea of a whole palace falling asleep at all. He found it hard to imagine his own gray castle falling into an enchanted sleep, especially when he listened to its bustle. People were constantly going in and out of its many doors, pursuing all the work that kept the household running: the food growing and preparation, the cleaning and dusting and laundering. Servants called out to each other, clattering up and down stairs, banging doors open and closed and jeering at the men-at-arms, who of course jeered back when they were not drilling in the courtyard or patrolling the walls. It would take a very powerful spell indeed, Sigismund thought, to make a whole castle fall asleep.

He said as much one afternoon when Sir Andreas came to visit him. He was feeling drowsy and the words were out of his mouth before he realized their implication. "Now who," the steward said, "has been telling you stories of a sleeping castle? Was it the lady you met at the gate?"

Sigismund frowned with the effort of remembering the lady at the gate. It all seemed hazy now, lost somewhere on the far side of his illness, but he remembered her eyes and the sweetness of her voice. She had tried to give him something, he recalled, remembering how it flashed and glittered as it spun into the dust. He thought there might have been someone else there too, and the image of bare brown feet beneath a ragged skirt surfaced briefly in his mind. A shadow, perhaps, watching from the hedgerow, but Sigismund could recall no more than that. He sighed.

"I don't think so, but I can't really remember her very well. It was the other lady, the one who came when I was sick."

"And what lady was that?" Sir Andreas asked. His voice was calm, but his eyes had narrowed.

Sigismund stretched out one arm and let his hand drift down the plastered wall, watching the fall of shadow beneath it. "You said she must have been part of my fever dream, but I don't think she was. She had cool hands, and she gave me something to drink that made the fever go away."

"Did she now?" the steward said. "And you're sure that she was the person who told you this story?"

"Mmmm." Sigismund looked up and was startled by the intensity of Sir Andreas's gaze. "Is something wrong?" he asked.

"I'm not sure," Sir Andreas replied. "Tell me more about this lady."

So Sigismund told him, while Sir Andreas leaned against one post of the four-poster bed and watched him closely. He would nod occasionally or ask a question, but Sigismund thought he seemed more thoughtful than worried. "Interesting," he said at last. "But may I ask you a favor, Sigismund? If you meet this lady again, even if you just dream of her or think you have been daydreaming, will you let me know at once?"

"She seemed kind," said Sigismund, feeling that some defense was required.

The steward's expression softened. "She may well be. But all the same, I should like to know."

"Alright." Sigismund continued to watch him. "And the other lady, the one on the road?"

Sir Andreas's face hardened again. "I don't want you to talk to anyone beyond the gates. Will you promise me that too, Sigismund? Not anyone!"

"Alright," Sigismund said again, taken aback by the rasp in the steward's voice. "But I would like to know why."

Sir Andreas sighed. "It's because your father has enemies, and they're not all in the southern provinces. That's why he sent you here after your mother died, so that we could keep you safe. But this is a strange part of the world, and there are things that live and walk here that folk in the cities and the central provinces would scoff at. Not everything that's strange is ill disposed, but you never know, and that's why the gate is there—and why I want you to prom-ise me to stay away from it. Even," he added, "if there's something out there that you feel you just have to investi-gate, or you think it's Master Griff, or me, or someone else you know, calling to you from the other side."

Sigismund studied the back of his hand where it rested against the plastered wall. "You're talking about magic," he said, and his voice was small.

"I'm talking about being careful, that's all," Sir Andreas replied. "It's a strange part of the world, as I said, and we can't afford to overlook that."

"No," said Sigismund. He does mean magic, he thought, with a little thrill of excitement, but he doesn't want to come right out and say so in case it alarms me—or because I might say something to Master Griff. He walked his hand up the wall again, studying it as though fascinated by the detail of muscle and skin.

"It was a sad story though, about the sleeping princess. Do you think it could be true, perhaps even the reason for the interdict?"

"No one knows the truth of the interdict and the Wood anymore," Sir Andreas said, "not even me, and I am your father's steward here in the west. It may be that my father knew, but if so he died without passing the informa-tion on."

Shortly after that, Sigismund dreamed of the en-chanted palace for the first time. In the dream he was walking along silent corridors and halls, through courtyards where even the fountain water hung glittering in midair, and up long flights of stairs. As he walked he would open doors and peer into quiet rooms, and he had a sense of urgency, as though he was looking for someone or something just out of sight. The sleeping princess, he thought, when he woke and remembered the dream, but although he had the same dream several times after that, he never found her. Everyone else was there, exactly as he had imagined them after his illness, but the princess was always concealed, always just out of sight or hidden around the next corner.

Sigismund never met anyone in these dreams or spoke with them, so he told himself that they were outside the scope of his promise to Sir Andreas. He repressed the suspicion that Sir Andreas might not agree, reassuring himself that they were only dreams and therefore harmless, spun out of the tale that the lady with the silver voice had told him.

Then one night the dream changed. This time he was not inside the palace, but standing in the forest, staring at a vast, twisting hedge of thorns. The sky overhead was dark, and Sigismund was filled with doubt and a sense of danger. Thunder cracked in the distance and lightning severed the sky, illuminating the sword in his hand. It was long and straight, with a white gleam along the edge of the blade and a jewel, red as blood, set into the pommel. The sword was as compelling a presence as the hedge of thorns and Sigismund could sense its power, like lightning in his hand. It was important in some way, he knew that too: that was why it was in the dream.

The next dream was dark as well, and the power of the storm and the brooding oppression of the forest had grown, but there was no red and white sword in his hand. Sigismund was shaking with cold and kept circling the hedge of thorns, looking for a way in, but there was none to be found. And this time there were voices in the darkness, shrieks amongst the treetops and slithering whispers in the hedge that made him start at every shadow. He wanted to escape from the dream and wake up safe in his own bed, with a candle close at hand, but he was trapped in the menacing dark.

When light did come, it was in a blaze of carnelian and gold, like the winter sun coming up over a stark horizon. It filled Sigismund's dream, banishing the darkness and the whispering voices, and he had to fling up an arm against its brilliance. There was someone at the heart of the light, he thought, squinting against the dazzle—a man on a horse pacing toward him out of the ball of fire. The horse was red, and light rippled like water on the rider's mail shirt and gleamed on his metal coif as he leaned forward, gazing down at Sigismund. A corona flared and flickered around the spiked helm, and just like the woman with the silver voice, Sigismund could not make out any details of the rider's face.

"So," the horseman said. His voice was light and pleasant; it reminded Sigismund of bees humming on a summer day. "It is good that we meet, but dreams like this can be dangerous. We will have no more of them for now."

He straightened and made a brief, imperative gesture with one gauntleted hand. The light followed the movement, spiraling around horse and rider like a comet and pulling Sigismund forward, into its burning heart. He wanted to cry out as the woods spun away from him, to ask who the horseman was, but as is the way with dreams, no words came.

"Soon," promised the summer voice, amused, and the comet swept between them. The next thing Sigismund knew, he was waking up in his own bed, with the castle bell ringing out a new day and Annie twitching his bed curtains aside, her face bright with excitement.

"Time to get up, slug a bed!" she cried, then dodged his well-aimed cushion, giggling. "No, truly—Sir Andreas says to come downstairs at once, because our new master-at-arms is here. He just rode in with the dawn."

Balisan

There was a red horse standing in the courtyard. Sigismund could see it from his window as he dressed, and he peered out at it again from the landing above the main hall. The red mare looked taller, seen close up, with a flowing mane and tail, and was more finely built than the destriers ridden by Sir Andreas. There were golden tassels on her bridle, and the leather on her saddle was embossed in scarlet and gold. Sigismund stared, for usually only warhorses were given such lavish harness. The mare lifted her head as if sensing his gaze and stamped one foot against the cobbles, a small, emphatic sound.

The hall was dark, despite a few shafts of sunlight that turned the dragon banner of Sigismund's family to fire.

The banner hung down from the ceiling, and Sigismund could see the remains of breakfast set out on the long table beneath it. Sir Andreas was standing on one side of the wide stone fireplace, facing a slightly built man of middle height who had his back to Sigismund; Master Griff sat at the table, his expression thoughtful. Sigismund hesitated in the doorway, trying to gauge the mood of the room and to take in as much detail as possible before the newcomer became aware of his presence.

Sir Andreas, Sigismund thought, seemed uncertain. He was frowning down at a paper in his hand, and he had run a hand through his dark, gray-flecked hair so that it stood on end. "It's unusual," the steward said, "for the King not to have sent word ahead to tell us you were coming."

The newcomer was wearing a long, mail shirt that caught the scanty light as he shrugged, gleaming red one way and gold another, the metal scales rippling like a serpent's skin. "He said the matter was urgent," the man replied, "and he knew I would travel faster than any courier."

"Urgent," Sir Andreas began, looking up from the paper, then he saw Sigismund. "Ah, Sigismund," he said. "This is Balisan, whom your father has sent to be master-at-arms here—both for you and for the castle garrison."

Sigismund advanced into the room as the newcomer turned and bowed, pressing both hands together before his heart in a gesture that Sigismund had never seen before.

His eyes widened as he saw a round helmet, with a mail coif and spiked crown, resting on the table beside Sir Andreas. "Sir Balisan?" he inquired, bowing.

"We do not use such titles where I come from," the master-at-arms replied. "Balisan will do."

Was it the same voice? Sigismund wondered. It was an even tenor, with a sibilant emphasis on each word but without the resonance of his dream, and he could not be sure. He studied the newcomer's face instead, noting the smooth golden skin and high cheekbones beneath long, almond-shaped eyes. The right cheekbone was flattened by a white scar and the man's eyebrows flared upward, giving his expression a sardonic cast. Sigismund found it hard to decide on the color of his eyes—tawny as a cat's was his first thought, but he amended it to bronze after a second glance. They were almost the same color as his hair, and the whole impression was of a figure cast in rich metal, except that this Balisan was alive.

Sigismund had never seen anyone like him before and he looked at Sir Andreas for guidance.

"He has your father's writ," the steward said, and held out the paper. Sigismund took it, but continued to study Balisan.

"You don't look like one of my father's men," he said.

Balisan smiled. "I am from the Paladinates, which lie to the east of your father's kingdom."

Sigismund's eyes widened, for those lands were famous

for their hero-knights. There were even reports that some of the knights were sorcerers as well as warriors, although Master Griff scoffed at this.

"Are you a paladin then?" Sigismund demanded eagerly. What he wanted to do was ask whether or not it had been Balisan he met in his dream, but he dared not, especially with Sir Andreas listening.

"Sigismund—" Master Griff began, but Balisan checked him with a gesture.

"Some have called me that," he said, "although it is not a word I would use to describe myself. But I have some knowledge of arms, and of the forces and powers that contend in this world, and your father believes that I may be of use to you."

Sigismund looked at the paper, which was written in his father's hand and bore his seal. "You are welcome then," he said slowly. "Although I hope you won't find it too dull here."

Balisan shrugged, as if to say that the dullness or otherwise of life was not something that concerned him. He spent the rest of the morning speaking with Sir Andreas and Master Griff about the daily round of castle life, then rode the circumference of the park on his red mare. Sigismund could see them from his aerie on the high tower, circling the length of the wall, and he wondered again about the resemblance between this new master-at-arms and the horseman in his dream. It seemed too close

31

to be coincidence, especially when the rider had said that they would meet again soon.

It's uncanny, thought Sigismund. He's uncanny.

He brooded over this conclusion for some time, then must have slept as the heat grew, for he woke with a start to find the shadows lengthening and the trapdoor creaking open. He sat up, staring as Balisan's head and shoulders emerged from below. It was unusual for anyone to follow him up here, but given the dream he was not entirely surprised that the new master-at-arms would seek him out sooner rather than later.

"So this is where you hide," Balisan said. He swung himself the rest of the way up and walked to the parapet, looking out. "And this is the great Wood."

There was something in the way he spoke that imbued the Wood with power and mystery, and Sigismund shivered. "It's under the interdict," he said. "No one's allowed to go there."

"No," agreed Balisan. "That time has not yet come." He looked around, the tawny eyes studying Sigismund. "Do you *want* to go there?"

Sigismund hesitated. "It would be an adventure. And it would be good to know the truth of all those stories, and whether there really is a castle, and who lives there."

Balisan looked out over the green sea that was the Wood. "Truth," he murmured. "Now that *would* be a powerful quest. But perhaps you would like to show me this castle first?"

Sigismund hesitated again. "Why not Sir Andreas?" he asked. "He's the steward."

"But you are the prince," said Balisan. "It is your castle, and in that sense I am your guest."

"That's true," Sigismund agreed, and decided that he quite liked the idea of showing Balisan the castle. The man seemed friendly, and so far he had not roared and cursed like the captain of the castle guard. His manner, like his speech, was mild, and this realization made Sigismund bold. "Was it you in my dream?" he asked.

"Yes," said Balisan. He said nothing more, just continued to look at Sigismund, who swallowed.

"Is that why my father sent you?" he asked. "To protect me from dreams?"

Balisan nodded. "Amongst other things. Sir Andreas was worried, and your father thought that my abilities might be useful here. But I will also teach you the arts of war."

"Amongst other things," Sigismund said, holding his look.

Balisan met it without any change of expression. "Given the dreams," he replied, "yes."

Balisan, Sigismund found, wanted to see everything, from the topmost tower where they stood, to the cellars and armory in the castle foundations. Sir Andreas came with them into the cellars and showed them the little-used chambers on the upper levels as well, where doors had to be unlocked and then locked again behind them.

The steward left them when they went outside, and at first Sigismund enjoyed showing off the stables and barracks on his own, but it was harder to understand Balisan's interest in the herb garden, or the little orchard between the kitchen and outer walls. He studied the grille across the culvert and the trees that had been felled to keep the wall clear, but he made no comment until they reached the sunken garden. There was a lilac walk there and the leaves provided a green fretted shade, although the flowers were long since done.

"Who planted this?" asked Balisan, looking around.

Sigismund frowned, trying to remember. "This was the first moat once, when the castle was just a single tower. But Sir Andreas says that most of the garden was laid out by my great-grandmother, and I think she planted the lilac walk as well."

"Ah," said Balisan. He seemed amused, for some reason that Sigismund could not fathom. "A farsighted lady. That would have been around the time of the interdict?"

"I suppose," said Sigismund, not seeing that it mattered. "There's a mosaic in the middle, which is quite nice. I've always liked it anyway."

The mosaic formed part of the bricked circle that was the center of the lilac walk and depicted a girl dancing, with lilac blossoms falling from her upraised fingers and strewn beneath her lilting feet. There were lilacs twined through and around her white gown as well, and crowning the dark fall of her hair, although her face was turned away. Sigismund thought there was a joyful feeling to it, like the return of spring after a long, cold winter, and Balisan seemed to like it too. He squatted on his heels and studied it for some time.

"Interesting," he said after a while. "Do you know who this is meant to be?"

"Master Griff says that she's the spirit of spring," Sigismund replied, "but no one knows for certain."

"No?" said Balisan, his tone making it a query rather than agreement. He moved on without asking further questions, but Sigismund overheard him later that evening, talking with Sir Andreas in the garden beneath the library window. Their voices floated up clearly to where he was sitting in the window seat, reading a book.

"The King said you were worried by something the boy told you, about a woman who came to him when he was ill?" That was Balisan, with the slight sibilance to his speech, while Sir Andreas's reply sounded troubled.

"It might have been a fever dream, but if not, then she must have passed every ward between here and the park gates to get in. And they are powerful protections."

"Perhaps." Balisan's tone was thoughtful. "But neither ward nor wall will keep out what is already in."

Sir Andreas was silent. "What are you suggesting?" he asked at last. "Whoever the woman was, she did not belong to either castle or village, and it is four generations now since the wards were established. No one could hide themselves for that long and remain undetected."

Sigismund sensed Balisan's shrug. "You may be right," he said. "And if she did cure the boy, there may be no cause for worry."

"Anyone approaching him like that, without our knowledge, worries me." Sir Andreas sounded unhappy, and his voice sank to a murmur. Sigismund, openly listening now, thought he caught the words *his mother*, but could not be sure.

"I agree." Balisan's voice remained clear. "Particularly since we know that one luring spell has already slipped through and retained enough potency to draw the boy to the gate."

Their voices moved away then, and although the word *lucky* drifted back, Sigismund heard nothing more. He sat as though turned to stone, his book forgotten, unable to think of anything but the words *wards* and *luring spells*. Sir Andreas had already hinted once that magic was at work, and Balisan had openly admitted that he had first met Sigismund in his dream, but this—

"It's real," Sigismund whispered, "which means that the story of the sleeping castle is probably true as well." His heart was beating like a marching drum, but when he tried to remember events at the gate his head became filled with buzzing, like flies trapped in a hot window. There were a few fragmented images, of blue eyes and a tinkling voice and a point of light like a blue star, sparkling into the dust, but the buzzing grew louder when he tried to pursue them, and pain lanced behind his eyes.

He pressed his hands against his lids and heard a harsh whisper out of his childhood in the Southern Palace: *"They say it was poison that killed her, although no one knows how, or why."*

"I heard it was a curse that withered her soul." The second voice was a man's, speaking low.

Sigismund shook his head, trying to clear it, but that only made the pain and the buzzing worse. He groaned, rocking forward, and the book slipped to the ground.

A lean hand reached down and picked it up, while the other rested on his bent head, and both the pain and the buzzing subsided. "This is a consequence of your dreams," said Balisan. "Dreams allow you to explore other planes, but they can also let others work their will against you— and your enemy is powerful." He handed back the book.

Sigismund took it, blinking up at him. "No one's ever told me that I have an enemy," he said, indignation warring with his disorientation. "Is it the same person who killed my mother?"

Balisan squatted on his heels so that they were eye to eye, and the curved tip of his scabbard clinked softly against the floor. "You are not supposed to know about that," he said. "Your father forbade it, because he wanted you to have the chance of a normal childhood once he brought you here."

"I didn't know until just now," Sigismund replied. "There was a buzzing in my head, and then pain, but through it I heard voices, courtiers whispering in the Southern Palace when my mother died." He looked away, out to the pink and bronze of the sunset sky, with darkness gathering behind it. "I must have overheard them at the time, but didn't remember until now."

"That may be a consequence of the dreams as well, bringing old fears to the surface." Balisan stood up, his eyes thoughtful as they rested on Sigismund. "I know you will have questions, about your enemy and your mother's death. But first we need to return to the lilac garden."

The lilac garden? Sigismund wondered, bemused. He wanted to demand why, but the disorientation from the headache made it easier to go along with the master-at-arms for now. And it was pleasant in the evening garden, with the day's warmth lingering in the bricks and the first moths dancing in the shadows.

Balisan paced the length of the lilac walk, and then back again, while the twilight deepened and a half-moon glowed yellow above the garden wall. He stopped on the edge of the brick circle and studied the shadows of tree and flower, while Sigismund shifted from foot to foot beside him and wondered what the master-at-arms found so fascinating about this place. It was just a garden, after all, where Sigismund had run and played a hundred times. He could hear frogs calling from the pond, and soon the crickets would start their nighttime chorus.

He straightened, determined to ask what they were doing here, but at the same moment Balisan turned his head. There was a glimpse of white further down the walk and a flutter of movement, soft as the beat of a moth's wing. Sigismund stared, and thought the white might be the sweep of a skirt or a mantle trailing across the bricks, but he couldn't think of anyone in the castle who would come here at this hour. A moment later, a spray of overhanging green was lifted back and a woman in a white dress stepped out onto the circle of bricks.

It was the woman from his illness, Sigismund was sure of that, although she seemed younger, with dark curls piled on top of her head and falling in a cascade down her back. There was a pattern of leaves and flowers sprigged lightly across her white skirt, just as in the mosaic, but her expression was grave, her eyes dark as she looked at Balisan. The master-at-arms bowed low, pressing his palms together before his breast.

"I felt your coming," she said. Her voice dropped, clear as silver, into the stillness of the dusk. "And you use both eyes to see with. I have dwelt here for close to one hundred years now, but you are the first to suspect my presence."

"I see the lines and threads of power," Balisan replied, "whether hidden in nature or the works of human beings.

But I was also looking for you, since you revealed your presence when you cured the prince."

The lady turned, a glimmering through the dusk, and smiled at Sigismund. "And you are quite well now, I think?"

There were no great ladies in the castle, and no other women as beautiful and graceful as this one. Sigismund felt shy and intensely curious at the same time. He bowed, a little clumsily compared with Balisan. "I am," he said. "Thank you. But who, or what, are you?"

The lady's smile had a great deal of sweetness in it, but the gravity returned swiftly. "I am called Syrica," she said. "I wait and I watch—over those who dwell in this castle and the Wood that is your neighbor. My purpose is to thwart the lady you met on the road."

"The Margravine *zu* Malvolin?" Sigismund asked. The name slipped from his tongue as easily as if he had never forgotten it, and this time he remembered her blue eyes smiling at him and the tinkle of her laughter.

"Yes," said Syrica. "She is my enemy, as she is yours. She will do you harm, if she can."

"She has already tried," said Balisan. The hum that Sigismund remembered from the dream was back in his voice.

Syrica looked at him and nodded. "The wards held her out—just. But I did not think she would act so openly. She took me by surprise."

"Not only you," said Balisan. "She has been clever, stirring up trouble in the south and keeping all eyes focused there, on the strife against the King."

Sigismund looked from one to the other through the half night. "But who is this Margravine?" he asked them. "What does she want?"

"She is of the faie, as I am," Syrica told him. "But she desires power and dominion in this mortal world and has set her heart on the Kingdom of the Wood, since the palace there is built on a place of great power."

Sigismund drew in his breath. "So she must be the faie in that story you told me when I was ill?"

"She is," Syrica replied. It had grown so dark that she was little more than a cloud of white on the far side of the brick circle. "And I am the one who thwarted her, converting the spell of death into the enchanted sleep. I have waited here and watched since then, hidden out of sight and mind for the hundred years to end. For the one you call the Margravine will never accept the undoing of her spell or let the magic run its course undisturbed. She will try and turn events to her purpose again, either by ensuring that the princess never wakes, or that the chosen prince will be a puppet serving her will."

Sigismund took a deep breath as memory flashed, followed by a searing image of a blue jewel extended to him by a fair, slender hand. He had reached out for it through the iron bars of the gate, but something had gone awry—a cloud of sparrows had risen up, out of the ditch, and the jewel had spun to the ground. He shook his head as the memory slipped away again. "But I still don't understand why she is my enemy?"

"She hates all human rulers and their kingdoms." Syrica's reply was soft. "But she works against your House in particular, because your great-grandfather placed the interdict on the Wood. She feels that it has buttressed my spell and helped keep her from the kingdom she desires." The soft voice paused. "And you, Sigismund, will come of age in the hundredth year of the enchanted sleep. This means that you, more than any other, are likely to be the chosen prince."

There was silence beneath the lilacs. A breeze riffled leaves and hair, whispering of the leagues of wood it had wandered through, but Sigismund remembered the absolute stillness beneath the trees. And he heard Auld Hazel telling him to keep away—*for now*. Sigismund shivered, feeling a mixed sense of excitement and danger, and wondered if this was how Parsifal had felt, riding forth on the Grail quest.

He forced his mind back to the present. "And the Margravine knows," he said slowly. "That's why she tried to give me the ring."

Syrica nodded and took a step toward him. "No faie spell is ever certain once the magic has been set in motion. But the Margravine and I are both tied to this spell. We know its terms and how the magic is likely to work itself out. And in one respect, at least, the magic is specific: the chosen prince is the only one who can undo the spell. So she will want to make sure that you serve her will before that day comes." She traced the outline of his face with gentle fingers. "You are related to the Margravine through your mother, whose own mother was a *zu* Malvolin. But it will not save you, unless you become her puppet." The silver voice was sad. "It did not save your mother when she would not raise you to serve the Margravine's will."

Sigismund turned away so they could not see his expression. He had only just learned that his mother had been poisoned, and now Syrica was saying that it was because she had defied the Margravine *zu* Malvolin to protect him. Sigismund shook his head, and counted every shadow on the moon's face until the tightness in his throat eased. When he turned back, both Balisan and Syrica were watching him.

"So is that why both of you are here?" he asked. "To keep me safe?"

"In part," Syrica said. "But this place too has power, in a small way, and it has allowed me to remain hidden all these years, holding the threads of my counterspell intact." Her face turned, pale, toward Balisan. "And you?"

"I am here for the boy," the master-at-arms replied, without hesitation. His voice was resonant, sure. "The King sent for someone out of the Paladinates and I am kin to his House, although at some remove."

To Sigismund's surprise, Syrica laughed. "Is that it?" she

43

asked, amusement shimmering in her voice. But there was a remote expression in her dark eyes, as though she was looking at something beyond the lilac walk and the castle walls. "I doubt the Margravine will have any success trying the wards again, now that you are here."

Balisan bowed. "So do you come into the open now, or remain hidden?"

Syrica shook her head. "The Margravine is stronger than I am—and the only way the spell can be undone before the hundred years are up is to kill me. If she finds me she will certainly try, which is why I have stayed in hiding—and only acted when there was extreme need," she added, with a glimmer of a smile for Sigismund, "to save you from the Margravine's ill-wishing." She looked back to Balisan. "It is vital that my presence here continues to remain secret, even from the King and his steward."

Balisan bowed again, his palms pressed together. "As you wish," he said, "so shall it be. You will reveal yourself when the time is right. Meanwhile, we shall not do anything that would draw attention to your hiding place."

They waited as the white figure faded back into shadow, leaving them alone in the night. Sigismund wanted to ask why Syrica was so sure that Balisan's presence would keep the Margravine at bay, but something in the quality of his companion's silence daunted him. He waited, this time without fidgeting, until the dark figure beside him stirred.

"Farsighted," Balisan murmured, as though thinking aloud. "And patient as well, to maintain such a vigil. All the same," he added as they walked back to the castle, "even allowing for the lady's presence, I think I will continue to ward you against dreams."

Lessons

Sigismund lay awake for a long time that night while the events of the day chased each other through his head: a master-at-arms who could walk in dreams and who spoke openly of magic, a faie hidden within the castle walls—and another who was his enemy because, like Syrica, she believed he was the prince who would undo the hundred-year sleep.

"And I want to," Sigismund whispered to the night. It was the sort of quest he had always dreamed of, like those pursued by Parsifal and Gawain and the rest of King Arthur's knights. But gradually his thoughts turned to his mother. He had been so young when she died that all his memories of her were blurred, and now he found it impossible to call up a recollection of her face or voice. Had she been kind and beautiful, like Syrica, or grave and formal, like his fading memories of his father? In his heart Sigismund felt sure that she must have been like Syrica, only less remote.

They say it was poison that killed her. Again the whisper out of childhood memory, overlain by Syrica's voice, soft and sad in the twilit garden: *It did not save your mother when she would not raise you to serve the Margravine's will.*

Did she know? Sigismund wondered again, staring into the night. Did my mother know that defiance would mean her death? He rolled over, punching the pillow into a new position. She must have been brave, Sigismund thought, and felt his throat close. He wished he could remember her face.

He thought he might lie awake until dawn, mulling over everything that had happened and been said, but tiredness crept in and he fell into a heavy sleep. He woke to early sunshine filtering through the faded rose of the bed curtains with their pattern of briars worked into the brocade with heavy silver thread. Sigismund reached out and touched one of the flowers, studying his safe, familiar world through half-open eyes. Annie said the bed curtains were shabby and old-fashioned and should be replaced, but Sigismund liked them. Sometimes, when he lay close to the fabric, he could smell the faintest hint of rose perfume, like a memory of summer caught in the weave.

This morning the elusive drift of rose mingled with the sunshine and when Sigismund closed his eyes there was a

47

flash behind them—a sharp image of bare, scratched legs and a flock of sparrows rising from a thorny ditch. He groaned and rolled away from the memory, wondering what the day would bring. He suspected that his life was going to be a great deal busier, as well as considerably more interesting, with Balisan here. But Sigismund couldn't help feeling trepidation as well, because now he knew he had an enemy, one who had brought about his mother's death.

"Not just your mother's," said Balisan, when they met again later that morning. They were in the room immediately below the roof of the topmost tower, which Balisan said would do for their studies together—when they were not on the roof itself or in the castle's training hall. The tower room was large and pleasant, with windows that looked out to the four winds and the ladder to the roof fixed against one wall. Sigismund noticed that there was already more furniture than there had been yesterday, and that the whole place had been swept and dusted clean.

"You can breathe up here," the master-at-arms said, going from one window to the other. "More importantly, we are out of everyone else's way—as you have already discovered for yourself."

Sigismund thought that sounded promising, because he was full of questions: about the Margravine and Syrica, the power of dreams, and what, exactly, Balisan could teach him. He was also eager to know why his father had chosen Balisan to protect him, and if it was mainly because the

Margravine had caused his mother's death. It was at this point that Balisan held up a hand, checking the tumble of his words, and told him that it was not just his mother's death that could be laid at the Margravine's door.

"There are many," he continued, "who whisper that your line must have been cursed, for every generation has seen fewer of those born into your family survive to have children of their own." He was taking books out of a bag as he spoke and stacking them on a long table set in the center of the room. They all looked old to Sigismund, with dark leather bindings and illuminated lettering down the spines. "It has not all been poison and daggers in the back, although there has been plenty of that, but there have been many accidents—too many, people whisper, for the ill luck to be solely chance. Belief in a curse has grown so strong that your father had difficulty finding any princess or noblewoman who was willing to marry him."

"Except my mother," Sigismund put in. He was sitting cross-legged on a stone window seat and could see the green Wood and a patch of wind-feathered sky.

Balisan glanced up from one of the books. "I wonder," he said softly. "I suspect she may not have been willing at all, if she knew anything of the Margravine and her plans, which later events suggest she must have done."

Sigismund frowned. "Are you saying that the Margravine *engineered* the marriage?" His voice came out taut and a little too high.

"I consider it quite likely." Balisan placed the book on the table and this time Sigismund could read the title: *Of Faie and Their Ways.* "Think. Why was your great-grandfather able to place an interdict on the Wood so powerful that it has never been broken, not even by the Margravine?" Sigismund shook his head, uncertain, and an expression that could have been exasperation crossed the master-at-arms's face. "It would take more than a royal decree scratched on parchment to keep that one out. There is power in your family line, Sigismund, an ancient bond to the land itself."

Sigismund leaned forward. "Like the king in the Castle Perilous, the one Parsifal heals on the Grail quest?"

"Something like that," murmured Balisan, weighing another book in his hand. It was the largest yet and Sigismund eyed it uneasily, wondering exactly how much he was going to have to read.

"So why, if the interdict's so powerful," he asked, "haven't we been able to fight back against the Margravine? Why have so many of my family died?"

The bronze eyes held his, cool and level as a blade. "Like all human aptitudes, the talent for power does not necessarily appear in every generation. You are the first to inherit it with any strength since your great-grandfather's time, although so far it has only manifested as visions and dreams." He put the heavy book down and pushed it along the table toward Sigismund. "But even without the power of your inheritance to call on, your kin have not bent to the Margravine's will. She has been trying to gain the same control over your House as she has over the *zu* Malvolin, but each generation has resisted her wiles."

"So she killed them instead?" whispered Sigismund. "Is that what happened?"

Balisan nodded. "That way there would be fewer to stand against her when the hundred years are up. And it is possible, probable even, that she engineered the marriage between your parents in order to have a greater chance of controlling you."

Sigismund drew a deep breath in. "So that's why my father sent for you when Sir Andreas wrote that the Margravine had been here."

The master-at-arms nodded again. "Yes. The old secret of the Wood has been passed down from king to king— and he would very much like you to be your own person, and to live to grow up."

An image flashed across Sigismund's mind, a vision of his father sitting in a drafty campaign tent with the lantern light flickering over piled maps and reports. He recognized Sir Andreas's seal, stamped in wax on the top-most scroll, and saw the bitter set of the King's mouth. Then the tent flap stirred, lifting on a gust of wind, and Balisan stepped through.

Sigismund shook his head and the vision cleared. He frowned at the spine of the book that Balisan had pushed toward him, tilting his head to one side to read the elaborate script: *Coats of Arms and the Codes of War: A Guide.*

"But that's heraldry," he said, a little indignantly. "I've already begun learning that with Master Griff. I thought you were going to teach me the arts of war, and how to protect myself from the Margravine."

Balisan slanted an eyebrow upward, in a way that made Sigismund feel like a small child crying for sweets. "I am," the master-at-arms told him, "but both these things require training and discipline. You have fallen easily into the way of dreams, but without knowing what you were doing or what dangers lurked there. That must be remedied. But," he added, nodding at the tome in front of Sigismund, "knowledge too is a form of power, and when you know that book you will know the colors and emblems of every noble house in this kingdom, as well as the alliances they represent. You will be able to tell friend or enemy at a glance, even in the heat of battle, simply by reading their coat of arms. And that," he said, turning to look out over the Wood in a way that forbade further questions, "is a beginning."

As the next few days slipped into weeks, Sigismund began to wonder if his expectations of a more interesting life had been misplaced. The only new practice that Balisan introduced was getting Sigismund to meditate at dawn and dusk on the roof of their tower, or in the chamber below if it was raining. The master-at-arms claimed that it was a routine followed by all the hero-knights of the Paladinates: it taught them to become fully aware of both the detail and totality of their surroundings, without being distracted by either.

"A paladin must become indivisible from all things," Balisan told Sigismund in the first dark predawn, "just as he is one with the blade he wields."

Secretly, Sigismund thought the meditation was more about endurance than awareness. He would sit cross-legged and straight-backed in the center of the tower roof and try to rise above the jangle of his thoughts and the heat or cold of the air. But there were times when he wanted to yell at Balisan and tell him that he was a prince and didn't have to do this, even if it was part of knightly training in the Paladinates. But that would have meant giving in, and Sigismund was not prepared to give in.

So he gritted his teeth, persevering, and occasionally, as the weeks passed into months and autumn into winter, there would be a moment when the cycle of his breath seemed one with the wind or the first light glimmering on stone. But it was only ever a flash, and then the moment would be gone.

The best thing during this time was that Balisan took over Sigismund's training in weapons—the lance, sword, and dagger, the long- and crossbows, and the harquebus. They spent most afternoons in the training hall or practicing archery at the castle butts with the other men from the castle, because the use of weapons, Balisan told him, must become second nature. If you had to think about your next move, then it was already too late. This at least Sigismund understood, because he had heard it from Sir Andreas and other teachers since he was old enough to pick up his first sword. So he didn't complain when Balisan made him repeat every exercise until he felt his feet and hands could have moved on their own, without his eyes or mind to guide them.

To underline this point, Balisan would make him train blindfold while guards attacked from different parts of the hall. Sigismund had to rely on his other senses to detect when an attack was coming and from which direction. At first he found this as frustrating as the meditation, but after a time he began to feel as though the air itself was coming alive around him: he could detect the shift and movement of its currents as much as hear an attacker move.

Sigismund was good with all weapons, but Sir Andreas and the off-duty guards would often come to watch his training and agreed that he had a gift for the sword.

"And although that is important for any knight," Sir Andreas observed one afternoon, "it may be vital for a prince who has enemies."

It was late, and only he, Sigismund, and Balisan were left in the training hall. The day had been hard as iron and their breath smoked on the chill air.

"Because they might try and mob me in battle?" Sigismund asked, placing his sword back on the weapons rack.

Sir Andreas rubbed at the stubble along his jawline. "Yes, although that is why princes and generals have honor guards in battle—to protect them against that sort of thing. I was thinking more of a challenge to single combat, since no knight sworn to the code of chivalry, not even a crown prince, can refuse such a challenge."

"It is a time-honored way of disposing of an inconvenient enemy," Balisan said softly. "To refuse is to be branded a coward, and no knight will follow a man with that reputation."

"But, of course," Sir Andreas added, "murder disguised as single combat only works against an inferior swordsman." He clapped Sigismund on the shoulder. "So that's why it's fortunate that you have a gift!"

By the time Sigismund had been training with Balisan for a year, his natural ability had lifted to a higher level. The sword felt as much a part of him as his hand or arm, and he absorbed new cuts and moves as though he had been born knowing them. He found too that he could read an opponent's body without conscious thought, knowing what they were going to do almost before they did it. This could have been simply repetition and unrelenting practice, but Sigismund did wonder if the meditation might also be having an effect. But gift or no gift, he could never best Balisan, no matter how hard he tried.

"Not yet," the master-at-arms said, when Sigismund finally expressed this frustration. "But the time we have spent together is nothing compared to the years I have spent training and fighting with swords." The bronze eyes were calm as they met Sigismund's. "But there is no room for such feelings when you face an opponent. Frustration, anger, fear—they are all distractions that will kill you if you hold on to them, more deadly by far than any enemy. You must let them drain out of you like water through a sieve, until there is nothing left: nothing except you and your antagonist."

Sigismund nodded, for they had been through this before and he understood its importance. He was considerably less enthusiastic, however, when Balisan insisted that he learn how to clean and repair his own armor and weapons, and mend his horse's harness as well.

"But I will have squires to do that," Sigismund protested, "and grooms."

Balisan's left brow flared higher, his sardonic expression pronounced. "And if your squires are killed? Or you become separated from your followers and have to depend on yourself to survive? What will you do then?"

Sigismund shook his head, having no answer for that, but he wished there were a few less things that Balisan considered essential for a king's son to do well. He learned to be glad of the times when his lessons covered the training and care of hawks, or hunting with hounds, so that he could escape into the sunshine and fresh air, galloping his new horse with the castle hunt. Balisan never hunted with them, but Sigismund would see him sometimes, standing on top of the high tower and looking out over the park and surrounding countryside.

"Never misses owt," said the Master of the Hunt the day he tracked Sigismund's abstracted gaze to the small distant figure on the castle pinnacle.

"Doesn't sleep either, from what I've heard," said Wat, one of the younger huntsmen, tossing back his shock of yellow hair. Like his cousin Wenceslas, Wat had been a friend of Sigismund's since the King first brought him to the West Castle—so Sigismund knew that Wat was immensely proud of his hair and had practiced the toss until it became second nature, especially around Annie and the other maids.

"And that red mare of his," Wenceslas put in. "If she was any more knowing she'd talk!"

No one paid much attention to that, though, because Wenceslas loved stories of animals that could talk. He had them from his Gran, he said, and Sigismund thought he must have caught the storytelling gift as well, for the groom could hold the entire castle spellbound. He had a bench outside the stable where he sat and whittled on the long summer evenings, while the horses gazed over the half-doors of their boxes and the castle folk drifted out to listen.

Sigismund joined them whenever he could, and sometimes Balisan listened as well, although he came and went like a cat and stood so far back in the shadows that most of those present didn't realize he was there. Sigismund always knew, although he was never quite sure why. Perhaps it was another of those little shifts in the air, or perhaps it was simply the amount of time they spent together, but his awareness of the master-at-arms's presence had become like a sixth sense. And Sigismund noticed that the horses would always stir when Balisan arrived, but otherwise there was only the shift and gleam of his eyes to betray his presence—for those who knew where to look.

Wenceslas's favorite stories involved both horses and hounds, like the fabled Bran and Mifawn, as well as pigs that talked and birds that granted wishes—if you could catch them—and the shy, sloe-eyed witches who spun their magic in the deep woods. He knew numerous tales of people stolen away into Faerie mounds, only to reappear years or lifetimes later, and all the sagas of past kings and heroes. His voice would sink as he spoke of magic swords and high deeds, faithless friends and noble enemies, and loves that were greater and more passionate than those found in the everyday world. Beasts crept into these tales too: unicorns with enchanted horns and dragons that could change their shapes and walk in the human world to aid or oppose heroes. Needless to say, it was these high tales that Sigismund loved best.

He found it strange, thinking about Syrica and the sleeping princess, that he might have become part of such a story himself. His everyday life seemed so ordinary, compared to Wenceslas's legends, that Sigismund wondered if he could have fallen asleep that afternoon in the library and imagined everything that happened afterward.

"Did I imagine it?" he asked Balisan one night when the storytelling was done. "I mean, you haven't taught me any magic yet, and everything here is as dull and ordinary as ever." It had been a particularly long and tiring day, and despite the storytelling he was feeling rather cross.

Balisan was standing in shadow again, but the torch in the wall sconce cast a halo around his head. "Is it?" he asked, and the hum that Sigismund remembered from the dream was back in his voice. "Some would say that both this castle and the great Wood that is your neighbor are far from ordinary. And it is not everyone who has a faie concealed in the middle of their garden."

"I suppose not," Sigismund mumbled, but he was thinking of Sir Parsifal and the Grail quest, and dragons that wore the shapes of men. Speaking with a dragon, he thought, now that's what I call real adventure. "They say there are still dragons in the Uttermost East, but you don't hear any recent stories about them here—not like Sir Andreas's father fighting the ogres."

Balisan's cat eyes gleamed at Sigismund through torchlight and shadow. "A dragon is the symbol of your House, is it not?"

Sigismund shrugged. "Master Griff says that half the world uses dragons as an emblem, because they denote power and ambition in the human world."

"Master Griff is correct, of course," said Balisan. "But if

you asked him, he would also tell you that the crown prince of this kingdom has always been known as the Young Dragon."

Sigismund's eyes widened. "I've never heard that before! I wonder how it came about—do you think there's a story behind that too?"

Balisan smiled at his eagerness. "There is a story behind most things, Sigismund. You could probably find out what this one is if you look in Master Griff's library."

But that, thought Sigismund, would mean poking around in dusty books when there were far more interesting ways to spend his spare time. It was harvest again in the orchards and fields, and the castle hunt was out almost every day after game to smoke or salt down for the winter. Sigismund galloped after deer and hare with Wat and Wenceslas and felt the rush of his horse's speed blow all thought of books and lessons out of his head.

He still liked the feeling of looking out over the world and continued to meditate on the tower roof well into autumn. The days grew shorter and the nights frosty, and it was on one of these nights that the shift came. Sigismund felt his breath deepen, tuning itself to the slow turn of the earth and the answering wheel of the stars. His bones grew heavy, as though sinking into the stone of the tower and the roots of earth beneath it; his mind was the murmur of the trees in the forest, reflecting the distant glitter of the sky. Energy flowed through and around him, and his whole being reverberated, like a note struck on a great bell.

The energy was a tapestry: the flicker of small animals in field and hedge, the warmth of kitchen and hearth fire, the laughter, arguments, and grumbling of people going about their lives. Sigismund could see larger currents as well, woven through the physical fabric of the castle and its grounds. He sank deeper into the ebb and flow of his breath, expanding to encompass that larger pattern—and felt another mind looking back at him.

"You!" he exclaimed, tumbling back into his everyday reality on the tower roof.

"Me," agreed Balisan, swinging himself up through the trapdoor. He was silent, looking down at Sigismund, who stared back, his eyes wide and the cold air burning in his throat.

"I saw you," he whispered. "Your mind, looking into mine."

"Yes," said Balisan. He knelt on one knee so they were eye to eye. "That is the beginning of seeing. Now you can begin to learn."

Lines of Power

They went up onto the tower roof every night after that, and Balisan made Sigismund practice sinking into the power flow until it became second nature. They would sit opposite each other, their breath clouding the air, but no matter how far Sigismund extended his perception, he was always aware of Balisan's eyes, watching, following. Their gleam became like an opponent's blade, something to be eluded. Sigismund tried to let his awareness dissipate, the same way he let his emotions drain away when he picked up a sword. He curled into ground mist, became one grain of gravel amongst the many lying on the riverbank, and crept through roots and leaves in the castle garden.

He came back into himself in a white, clear dawn and

looked out over a world in which every line and angle was etched in frost. Balisan sat opposite him, unmoving as the stone, his eyes dark, aged bronze. Sigismund felt a little like stone himself, filled with the long night's silence. He stretched, cautiously, and Balisan smiled.

"That was well done," he said. "You swam away from me like a fish disappearing into a dark river."

The hand Sigismund lifted felt heavy as stone; his hair crackled with frost as he pushed it back. He shook his head. When he spoke, his voice was a pebble, cast into the chasm of the new day. "Is that what my power is?"

A bird called from somewhere in the garden below, a single sweet trill. Soon there would be another and then another after that, and the castle would begin to wake up.

Balisan's reply was considered, grave. "Your family's power is rooted in the land and has developed out of love for it, becoming an affinity for the energy that runs through earth, air, and water. But you can also draw on that power, using it to make a shield or barrier, as your great-grandfather did with the interdict. And you have the ability to walk in your dreams, which lets you visit places beyond the limitations of your physical body. It is a skill that served your ancestors well, especially in the early years of the kingdom, when roads were few and travel difficult."

Sigismund stretched, enjoying the feeling of muscle and sinew within the layers of his jacket. "Evasion and shielding," he mumbled, yawning. "But what about attacking?"

Balisan shook his head. "It is not the way that your family's power has developed. It might be possible for you to learn such skills, but it would require many years studying the darker aspects of sorcery." He paused, his eyes tawny in the first light of the sun. "But I do not think that is your path, Sigismund."

"Oh," Sigismund said, trying not to feel disappointed. "But what about weapons of power? Like Excalibur or the belt that Sir Gawain won from the Green Knight? In all the stories they enhance the wearer's power."

Balisan's mouth twitched. "They do. But such artifacts are rare and very hard to find, not least because they may not wish to be discovered. And depending on who made them, or why, they are often unreliable." His smile became sly. "I can lend you a book on the subject, if you wish."

Sigismund shook his head, and the smile deepened. "You are quite right," Balisan said. "There are more important things for you to learn."

He gave Sigismund the book anyway, but began to teach him the names of the stars and how they shifted to match the seasons and the turning of the earth. They continued to go up to the roof every night, even when autumn became winter with its snow and ice. And on the night of midwinter, the nadir of the year, Balisan explained how the conjunction of certain stars and planets could open gateways and reveal paths into different realms of existence.

"You must memorize them all," said Balisan. "But the plane closest to us, the one we know best, is the realm of the faie, which we call Faerie."

Sigismund blinked, feeling the wind's chill through his heavy coat. "But I thought that the faie belonged in this world—like Syrica and the Margravine?"

It was a clear night, and Balisan's head was dark against the white blaze of stars. The moon was bright enough that Sigismund could see when he shook it. "The faie have been crossing over into this world—and others—since the beginning of time, and they love it and have power here, but it is not their realm. But there are places where the planes overlap and the fabric of both dimensions is woven so closely together that no gates or powers are needed to cross over—from either side."

Sigismund frowned, trying to absorb what he was hearing. He supposed it would explain some of the more fantastic elements of the old stories, like Faerie mounds and the castles full of monsters and wonders discovered by knights on the Grail quest. Then he remembered his dreams of the sleeping castle and the dark forest outside it, full of strange sounds and unseen things stalking him, and shivered.

"My dreams?" he asked. "Did they take me into Faerie too?"

Balisan shook his head again. "Not in a physical sense,

but dreams are another way of bridging the gap between realms. And the palace you dreamed of is a beachhead, one of those strongpoints where Faerie and the mortal world have always overlapped. Dreaming of it opened you up to the powers and forces present in both worlds—and some of them are not benign."

"The Margravine," Sigismund whispered.

"There are others," said Balisan, "but because of her designs on the Kingdom of the Wood, it is never far from her mind."

Sigismund leaned his arms on the cold stone of the parapet and thought about that. He tried to remember what Syrica and Balisan had said in the garden, about the Margravine desiring power in the mortal world. "But why not just take it by using her faie powers or bringing a host from Faerie? Why did she have to kill the princess?"

"Because despite their power, the faie are still bound by laws." Balisan's reply was measured. "One of the most binding forbids open war between the faie and humans in this mortal realm. So those faie who desire power here must work through mortal agents, and one of the more popular means has been to marry the rulers and heroes of this world and influence events that way. Some, depending on their disposition, have done this to achieve good, but others have acted solely for their own ends." He paused, glancing up at the night sky, then down at Sigismund. "The Margravine tried to marry the King in the Wood, but there is old faie blood in that line and he was not fooled by her wiles. To make matters worse, from the Margravine's point of view, he then married a woman from another family with strong links to Faerie. The Margravine feared that any children born to them would threaten her—which is why she decided that the princess had to die."

Sigismund frowned at the black shadow of the Wood. "But," he said slowly, "wouldn't Faerie law have prevented the Margravine from working a death spell against the princess?"

Balisan shrugged. "Every law has loopholes, especially for those who wish to overturn them. Given the inheritance of both the King's and the Queen's family lines coming together, the princess is at least half faie—and there is nothing that prevents the faie warring against each other. And because the palace is built on one of the places where Faerie and the mortal world overlap, the Margravine was not obliged to cross over to work her magic. So technically she was not using her powers in this world, even though the effect was felt here."

It was Sigismund's turn to shake his head, half impressed, half appalled. "That was . . . clever."

"The Margravine is clever," Balisan said. "Fortunately for the princess, she was not the only one. Many knew of the Margravine's ambitions with respect to that kingdom, but only Syrica foresaw the opening that the strength of the princess's faie heritage would give her. She was able to undo the worst of her opponent's spell and bar her from the castle and the Wood at the same time. But the Margravine can still use the realm of dreams to watch over it from a distance. She is like a spider at the center of its web and will always know when something has disturbed the outer edge."

Like me, thought Sigismund, remembering his last dream, the one that Balisan had banished. The winter night seemed cold and forbidding, and Balisan's presence was stern. There were still a few lights in the castle and village below, but otherwise the whole world lay hidden in darkness. It was mysterious, and full of powers and forces that he did not know but must learn to deal with if he was to survive. He frowned. "But Syrica said that the magic is not certain."

He turned, catching Balisan's nod. "That is the nature of faie power. They love games and contests, even when matters of great importance are at stake. So although the core elements of a spell may be fixed, the rest is left to work itself out in its own way. And once the contest begins all the faie involved are bound to its terms." He paused, and when he spoke again, Sigismund could hear the smile in his voice. "It is of great importance to the faie, but not something that human sorcerers readily understand."

No, thought Sigismund. "Although Syrica did say that only the chosen prince can undo the spell. Apparently the magic is specific about that." He tipped his head back, counting the stars again. "But will I ever be strong enough to do it?" he asked, half under his breath.

Balisan's hand rested on his shoulder, a reassuring touch. "We already know that your family's power does not bend easily to the Margravine's will. And the more you develop it, the less ability she will have to influence you, despite the faie blood you have inherited from her." His clasp tightened briefly. "She will see that inheritance as a weakness, but the flow of magic is always two-way, so the opposite is also possible—it may enhance your capacity to resist her."

Sigismund thought about that and also about what Syrica had told them in the lilac garden. "But the Margravine is still powerful," he said finally. He studied the calm profile beside him. "Aren't *you* afraid to be standing in her way?"

"No," said Balisan. "I am not afraid of the Margravine *zu* Malvolin."

He sounded very certain, but his tone was flat, a sign that Sigismund had already learned meant that he would get no more answers on that subject.

In time, Sigismund learned to see and follow the lines of magic that ran through the world, to recognize the places where the fabric of reality was thin and others where it was thick with power. He knew now that the Wood was dense with it, and even the West Castle rested on its own small shimmer of magic. By the time another autumn came and went, he could merge his awareness into the energy flows around him as easily as he picked up a sword. It became easy for him to see the barrier that was his great-grandfather's interdict and he also learned that it had no power over him.

"In part because your power is drawn from the same source," Balisan told him, "but also because the interdict is linked to Syrica's counterspell—and you are the chosen prince. That is why you were able to step under the forest eave and speak with the witch of the Wood."

"Auld Hazel," murmured Sigismund, and smiled, remembering the flat-bowled pipe and the blackbird stare. In a way, he thought, that encounter had been a beginning, although he hadn't realized it at the time. Shortly afterward he had met the Margravine, and then Syrica, and begun to dream of the sleeping palace and the dark, menacing forest.

With Balisan at his side, Sigismund also began to re-enter the realm of dreams. The inner mind, the master-at-arms explained, never fully slept, so the sleeper could still remain aware while in the dream realm—and connected to the world of power that surrounded the dreaming body. It was simply, he added, ignoring his pupil's groan, a matter of training and practice, building on the first meditations that Sigismund had learned. But despite his groans,

Sigismund applied himself to this as well and learned to step into dreams through conscious choice, and to assert his awareness whenever a dream crept up on him unsought. He would have liked to return to the enchanted palace and perhaps see the sleeping princess this time—but despite the increasing strength and scope of his dreams, he could never find it again.

Balisan only shrugged when Sigismund asked him why. It was spring again, one of those days of mild skies and the first green like a mist over Wood and fields. "The Margravine may be walling you out. Then again, the palace is built on one of the strongpoints between this mortal world and Faerie. It may have reasons of its own for not letting you in, quite aside from any spells and counterspells of the faie."

Sigismund wondered how Balisan always knew so much about the interface between the mortal world and Faerie, but the master-at-arms shrugged again when he asked. He was reading in one of the deep armchairs in the library and did not seem disposed to answer questions.

"I read books," he said pointedly, when Sigismund pressed him, "and it is one of the branches of learning that the Paladinates specialize in. Hero-knights like Gawain and Parsifal, whom you used to esteem so much, need to know about such things."

Sigismund scowled, watching him turn a page. He had begun to study the dispatches sent by his father and these had drawn his attention to the wider world. They were full of the troubles in the south, which dragged on year after year, bleeding the kingdom of soldiers and gold, and made Sigismund feel restless and cooped up. He scowled at Balisan for a moment longer, then flung himself down onto the window seat and frowned out into the sunlit garden. When he finally turned around, it was to find Balisan watching him, one eyebrow raised.

"I'll be fifteen soon," Sigismund said, answering the unspoken question, "and I've lived here over half my life. Surely it's time I rejoined my father?"

Balisan laid the book aside. "There are many," he said, "who will seek to strike at your father through you."

"But that will always be the case," Sigismund pointed out. "Besides, I'll still have you, won't I?"

"For a while," Balisan replied, "but not forever." He smiled at Sigismund's expression. "Even masters-at-arms must give way to other companions when a prince grows up. But I will write to your father and see what he says."

The King, however, had just embarked on a fresh campaign in the south, and he wanted Sigismund to stay where he was. It was winter before he sent word that the rebels had finally sued for peace, and spring again when the next messenger came. This man was mired from head to foot in mud, but his smile gleamed as he handed Sigismund his father's letter.

At last, thought Sigismund. The writing danced before his eyes, but he forced himself to read the message through before turning to Balisan. "My father writes that he will be returning to the capital before the first of summer and bids me join him there." Sigismund shook his head. "I'll be sixteen by the time I arrive."

"Obviously," said Balisan, without even a hint of a smile, "we had better leave at once."

In the Royal Palace

The Royal Palace was a vast maze of stone built on a rock overlooking the great river that ran through the heart of the kingdom. In his first few weeks there, Sigismund was disoriented by the sheer size of the place and bewildered as to why even a palace should need quite so many levels and hallways and doors, all opening one onto the other. He was sure there must be rooms that no one had penetrated for centuries, and the whole place was filled with a cool ancient smell. Master Griff said it was because the rock the palace was built on had its feet in the river below, but Sigismund felt sure that the smell came from years of layered memory, all held in long corridors where the sun never shone.

It did not help that his father was not there to welcome

him. Implementation of the peace agreements in the south had taken longer than anyone expected, and the King was still detained in the southern city of Varana, famous for its twisted spires. It was possible, the chamberlain told Sigismund on his arrival, that he could be there until the winter—but in the meantime a suite of rooms had been made ready for the prince in the old part of the palace.

Why the old? wondered Sigismund, who would have preferred the new wing, with its many windows that looked west over the capital. The old part of the castle was all narrow twisting stairs and doors that were a hand-breadth thick, banded with heavy iron. The apartments set aside for him were pleasant enough, but somber, with dark wood paneling and curtains of dull crimson velvet. The curtains at least gave it an air of richness, although the furnishings were sparse, and fires were lit all year round to warm air chilled by walls of spear-deep stone.

There was an elongated golden dragon, with an enigmatic carnelian eye, inset above the fireplace, and Sigismund saw the device repeated throughout the old palace. It was worked into the stone above doors and hearths, carved into the backs of wooden chairs, and graced old banners, some faded with age, that were displayed on the walls.

"Those banners look as if they'd disintegrate if you touched them," he said to Balisan, when they had been there a week. "And you can tell the old palace was a bastion once. Look at the thickness of the walls, and these arrow slits they call windows!"

"That was why the original castle was built here," said Balisan, "to control the traffic up and down the river, and the pirates that preyed on it. There were raiders too, out of the north, who would travel upriver as far as the channel was navigable."

Sigismund ran a hand over the stone. "But that was a long time ago. Things are more settled now, at least in these middle parts of the kingdom."

"A thousand years," Balisan replied, holding out his hands to the fire. "But it is tradition that the crown prince resides in the old palace, settled times or not."

Tradition, thought Sigismund, could be decidedly un-comfortable, and he missed the easy familiarity of life in the West Castle. It didn't help that he had ridden ahead with Balisan and Master Griff, to be sure of arriving before the first of summer, and that Wat and Wenceslas and the rest of his West Castle household were still following with the baggage train. It was a long road and they would be moving slowly, so Sigismund did not expect to see them before midsummer at the earliest, or even—remembering the condition of the road—summer's end.

He had begun to suspect, however, that the old infor-mal life and the rough-and-ready companionship of guards and serving men such as Wat and Wenceslas would not be permitted in the Royal Palace. The chamberlain was responsible for court etiquette and insisted that the distinction between the nobility and within the different ranks of servants be observed. Even Master Griff had been housed in a distant wing of the palace. Sigismund only saw him for lessons now, and the chamberlain's etiquette required that the tutor depart as soon as the lesson was over.

"Wait until your father is here before you start changing things," Master Griff cautioned when Sigismund protested. "But I imagine he will have his own plans for you, including friends of your own age from the families of the great nobility. Who knows, he may even give you a governorship over one of the provinces, to begin your apprenticeship in ruling."

"When he gets here," muttered Sigismund, but he unfolded his arms and tried not to look or feel so disgruntled.

Balisan was the only one of Sigismund's former companions who remained close at hand, for although the chamberlain tutted at first, and then protested more vigorously, the master-at-arms had still taken over the suite of rooms next to Sigismund's.

"At least until his father returns," he said, and the chamberlain's protests withered as he turned away, unable to meet that unblinking gaze.

Sigismund was glad to know that Balisan was close, a familiar face amongst the many respectful but unknown courtiers and servants. It made him feel safer too, in this dark cool pile of stone with its empty corridors and many doors. It was easy, in a place so thick with shadow and memory, to remember that his mother had been poisoned at the Margravine's instigation and to look hard at the new faces around him.

Balisan was silent for some time when Sigismund told him of his uneasiness within the palace. They were standing on the walls, with the great sweep of the river below them on one side and the red and gray roofs of the city crowding away on the other. Sigismund had wanted to walk the palace perimeter, but it had proved to be an exhausting business and he was ready to stop for a while and take in the wider boundaries of this new world. He could see a cluster of roofs on the far side of the river, but mostly it was tilled fields, dotted with trees, that stretched to a blue line of hills.

Sigismund found the openness of everything a little dizzying after so long in the small, walled castle hemmed about by the great Wood. He supposed he would get used to it soon enough, but he was less sure about the blank, courteous expressions worn by everyone in the palace. "Masks," he said, leaning over the stone parapet.

"And you," said Balisan, "must learn to look for what lies behind them. That is part of what it means to be a prince—but we both need to remain vigilant until we know this court and its ways better." His eyes had darkened to antique bronze as he spoke and Sigismund realized, with a mixture of relief and fear, that he was not alone in disliking the atmosphere of the palace.

It was, he decided as the weeks passed, a very self-sufficient world, with gardens and shops, smithies and stables, all contained within the perimeter of the palace walls. There was no need for the servants or courtiers to go out into the city and few of them did, so that the palace was as shut off, in its larger way, as the West Castle within its walled park.

Was it because his father had been in the south so long that the court had closed in on itself? Sigismund wondered. Or had it always been that way, with the sovereign and those closest to him cut off from both the capital and the rest of the kingdom? It occurred to him that such isolation would have made it easier for the Margravine to stir up rebellion in the south.

But masks or not, these people were part of his new life and he would have to find a way to learn about them and begin to make friends. Sigismund was not sure quite how to go about that with strangers who must all be treated with a degree of caution, if not outright suspicion, but he pushed aside the fear that it might prove an impossible task. He would not, Sigismund decided, leaning his elbows on the parapet and looking out over the wide, deep river, allow that to be the case.

The very next day, he met Flor.

Sigismund was alone in the palace fencing hall, because the man hired to teach him the new art of duello had not turned up at the appointed hour. He had spent some time waiting and then more time exploring the hall, which was large, with a gleaming sprung-wood floor. There were mirrors down one wall, so that you could study yourself while training and correct faults of style or execution, as well as life-sized practice dummies at one end of the hall. At the other end a series of large windows opened out onto a stone terrace, so that the whole space was airy and filled with light. There were orange trees in tubs on the terrace, and a flight of steps led down into a garden with clipped box hedges and gravel paths, which reminded Sigismund of his early years in the Southern Palace.

The fencing master, like his art of duello, also came from the south, and the style of the hall might have been designed to make him feel at home—in which case, Sigismund reflected, it was churlish of him to keep his prince waiting. The chamberlain, in particular, would not be pleased, since he had spent some time explaining to Balisan how this instructor was the finest master of "the art" in the kingdom. Balisan had simply inclined his head, apparently unimpressed that an Italian fencing master had found his way to the capital, while Sigismund tried not to smile. But he had been pleased, all the same, when Balisan agreed that he should learn this new style of swordplay, which was much in vogue amongst the younger nobility.

"Although," the master-at-arms had said, "I wouldn't like to rely on it in battle."

Nor I, Sigismund thought now, picking up a training

foil and trying a few experimental passes. The blade was light and flexible, but he could not imagine it making much impression against armor and suspected that a knight's broadsword would cleave it in two. But he knew that the rapier, as it was called, was increasingly being used for individual combat and duels of honor, dispensing with the need for heavy armor. It would be deadly in that context, Sigismund judged, making a test cut against one of the dummies. He stepped back—and then turned as he caught movement in one of the mirrors, expecting to see the fencing master and receive an apology for lateness.

Instead he saw a boy of about his own age standing in the doorway. He was taller than Sigismund and of slighter build, with a narrow, high-boned face, hair the gold of a newly minted coin, and dark blue eyes beneath arching brows. He stood with an air, and there was a fine, yellow silk lining to his velvet cloak, and jewels in the hilt of his dagger. He was smiling as Sigismund turned, and his expression was half mocking, half friendly.

"Hello," he said, and strolled into the room, letting the door close behind him with a thud. "I can see you've never used a rapier before, or a training foil either, for that matter." His gaze was interested, taking in every detail of Sigismund's clothes and appearance. "You're new here, I take it—just up from the country?"

"In a manner of speaking," said Sigismund. He put the foil back on the rack. "But you're right about the sword. I've yet to learn this new art of fencing."

"If you're staying," the newcomer said, "then you'll have to join our lessons with the Conte Vigiani. He's the finest master in the city."

The name was Italian, but Sigismund was sure that it was not the same one that the chamberlain had mentioned when announcing that a fencing master would be coming to the palace. He studied the boy before him, liking both his friendliness and the humor that glinted in his expression.

"I would like that," Sigismund said, and held out his hand. "I'm Sigismund, by the way."

The boy extended his own hand, but raised his eyebrows at the same time. "Not *that* Sigismund?" he asked. "The crown prince we've all been expecting for so long? No one said that you'd actually arrived. I'm Florian Langrafon," he added, clearly remembering his manners, "but everyone calls me Flor."

Sigismund confirmed that he was indeed *that* Sigismund and had been in the palace for several weeks. Flor whistled, clearly surprised. "I wonder why the chamberlain's keeping you such a secret? I can't see any possible reason for it myself, but the man does love his etiquette and ritual. Or perhaps—" He broke off, glancing sideways at Sigismund as though some new thought had struck him.

"Yes?" Sigismund inquired, but Flor looked troubled.

"I'm probably not supposed to say anything, but I wonder—I suppose it's possible that he believes in the curse."

"The curse?" Sigismund echoed, curious to hear what he would say.

Flor's uneasiness increased. "Some people say your family's cursed. You know, because of your mother, and both your father's brothers dying when they were children. I think there were a lot of tragedies in your grandfather's time as well. The whisperers say that's why the King never remarried, because no woman would risk the curse, and so now you and he are the last of your family line. The chamberlain absolutely forbids it to be spoken of, of course, claiming that it's the King's will." He made a face. "So I'll get in trouble if you tell anyone that I mentioned it."

"It's alright," Sigismund said. "I won't tell anyone." He didn't consider it necessary to say that Balisan had told him long ago, although he could see how the existence of such a story might affect the atmosphere in the palace. But none of this was Flor's fault, so Sigismund pushed the matter aside and tried to remember what he knew of the Langrafon family instead. They came from the southeast, if he remembered Balisan's lessons in heraldry correctly, but had never been drawn into the rebellions that racked the provinces further south.

"So when do you have your fencing lessons?" Sigismund asked, changing the subject. He sat down on a bench along the wall while Flor perched at the other end, folding his arms across an updrawn knee.

The Conte Vigiani, it turned out, came to the palace three times a week, and Flor was sure that the fencing master would have no objection to Sigismund joining their group. "In fact, I know he won't, because my family brought him here originally, to teach me." Flor stretched gracefully. "I've been learning for a couple of years now, so I'm the Conte's most advanced student. But I'm sure you'll pick the art up in no time," he added, his smile friendly.

He shook his head when Sigismund asked about other Italian fencing masters in the city, and said that he had never heard of any.

"Someone's swindled the chamberlain, you'll see," he said, when Sigismund explained about his lesson. "He'll have presented false credentials, obtained an advance on his fee, and be halfway to the border by now. But Vigiani is good, the best in fact, and a nobleman as well, so there's nothing to worry about."

From talk of fencing, their conversation turned to Flor's life in the palace, which was similar to Sigismund's routine in the West Castle but without so many lessons. Flor pursued the same training in the arts of war, heraldry, and the hunt, but he laughed when Sigismund mentioned Master Griff's lessons in philosophy and law, mathematics, history, and languages. "You may have to learn that stuff," he said, "since you're going to be king, but I'm a lighthearted second son. My sole duty, besides serving my King, of course"—he nodded at Sigismund—"is to find and marry a great heiress. So the only other lessons I pursue are dancing, a little practice on the lute, and the fine art of dalliance."

"But when you marry this heiress, what then?" asked Sigismund, laughing and protesting at the same time. "Won't you have to manage the great estates she brings with her?"

Flor shrugged. "Isn't that what stewards and factors and even chamberlains are for? Who knows, the heiress might even want to manage her own fortune, if I'm really lucky. But that's all a long time away, fortunately, since no one at court gets married off before they turn eighteen. And for now, my main aim is to have fun." He got to his feet, lithe and lazy as a cat. "It's not so easy for you, of course."

"What is not easy?" asked Balisan from the door. He had opened it so quietly that neither of the boys noticed, and now they both jumped. Flor, Sigismund noticed, studied the master-at-arms carefully, but remained quiet while Balisan watched them both, one eyebrow raised in question.

"Balisan," he said, standing up, "this is Flor—Florian Langrafon. He was saying that it's easier for him to have fun than me. He thinks I have too many lessons."

"Does he?" Balisan's tone and expression were neutral. "You appear to be short one today."

Sigismund explained that the fencing master appointed by the chamberlain had not turned up, and Balisan raised his eyebrow again, but only very slightly. He seemed more interested in Flor, who bowed in response to his salute and answered a few questions about life at court.

But he made no objection when the two boys arranged to meet again.

"Is this Balisan your bodyguard?" Flor asked Sigismund the next afternoon, as soon as they were comfortably established on the stone terrace. He proffered the bag of apples that he had brought to share. "He looks like the engravings of infidel warriors out of the eastern lands. And his sword is like the ones that they use too, shorter than ours and curved at the tip."

"He's from the Paladinates," Sigismund said. "Although he's not one of the hero-knights," he added, as Flor turned to him with quick interest.

The other boy looked disappointed, but after a moment his face cleared. "All the same," he said, "there's something about him. I should not like to take him on, lessons from an Italian fencing master or not."

No, thought Sigismund, but Flor had already moved on to what they should do with their afternoon, suggesting a game of tennis or hunting in the woods and open fields across the river from the city.

Sigismund quickly learned that his new friend pursued all forms of sport with enthusiasm and skill but was passionate about the hunt. "It gets you out of the palace, for a start," Flor told him, "and the city too. I don't know about you, but they both make me feel hemmed in—like being kept in a hutch."

Sigismund agreed about the palace, but was less sure

about the city. The chamberlain still disapproved of his leaving the palace at all, but Balisan thought it would be good for Sigismund to see and be seen, and the King, when appealed to by letter, agreed. *"The people must learn to know their prince,"* he wrote by return dispatch, *"and their prince them, as much as seems prudent."*

Prudence, Sigismund found, meant being accompanied by a detachment of palace guards at all times, and Flor and at least some of his new friends usually insisted on coming along as well. It made everything very formal, but at least Sigismund got to ride through the main streets and see the two great markets with their color and noise. He liked to observe the teeming life of the docks as well, where river barges discharged people and produce from throughout the kingdom. But Balisan shook his head when he asked to explore the narrow twisting wynds where the silversmiths and armorers had their premises, or the backstreets where the new printing presses operated.

"Stick to the open thoroughfares for now," he said, "where your guards can see while still letting others see you. The printers and smiths can climb the rock to the palace and bring their wares to you."

Flor still thought exploring the city was poor sport, but he enjoyed the way a small crowd gathered wherever Sigismund went and the blessings that many of the older people in particular would call down upon their heads. "Although all this is no more than your due, of course," he told Sigismund one afternoon when a group of apprentices gathered as they rode past, cheering for the Young Dragon.

Sigismund raised an eyebrow. "Even," he said, "if they don't know anything about me yet, other than my name?"

Flor laughed. "You're their prince, Sigismund. That's all these commoners need to know."

Sigismund looked at him, thinking that even the common people might expect something more of those who ruled them than just making a fine appearance. He kept this view to himself, however, content for the moment to get to know Flor and his companions, who quickly became his own. Flor was the natural leader of their group, not just because of his easy manner and physical aptitude, but also because he had already fought and won several duels.

No one had died, he assured Sigismund, laughing when asked about these passages of honor. "I know the King forbids dueling—but what can you do when someone throws down the glove of challenge? Honor demands that you pick it up."

But all the young men were passionate about sport, including games of chance in the evening. They would sprawl before the open fires with cards or the dice box, a glass of wine at every elbow—and like Flor, they sympathized with Sigismund over the round of lessons that Balisan and Master Griff insisted be maintained.

Sigismund noticed, though, that their noisy commiserations always died away when Balisan came within earshot. There was something in the turn of his head and the expression in those tawny eyes that checked even those who regarded a master-at-arms as just another class of servant.

They were arrogant, Sigismund thought, observing their behavior, but there was no doubt that their companionship, particularly that of Flor, made his summer in the palace a great deal more pleasant than it would otherwise have been.

Sigismund's West Castle followers finally arrived at the tail end of summer, but it was as Sigismund had suspected: they were all housed in the outer circle of the palace, in a maze of stables, kennels, and mews. The easygoing West Castle ways were frowned upon by the chamberlain and palace servants alike, and it was difficult for Sigismund to even see the people he had once spoken with every day. He still practiced archery with Wat and Wenceslas, but he could see that they were unhappy. The palace servants made it clear that they despised the newcomers, and they mocked their country accents and manners. It made Sigismund angry, but there was little he could do without major changes to palace etiquette, and as always Master Griff cautioned patience.

If only, thought Sigismund, my father would return—for if he does not come soon I will start making those changes myself, regardless of what anyone thinks.

But the business that detained the King continued into

the autumn, and Sigismund began to wonder whether he would ever stand in the same room as his father again. They had not been together since the King brought him to the West Castle for safekeeping, and the only memory Sigismund had from that time was of a stern, formal man in armor, with a short beard and a deep voice. The beard had been golden, he thought, or brown gold, but he could not recall the color of his father's eyes or any other detail of the face above the beard.

There was a portrait gallery in the old palace, which contained a picture of the King as a young man, and Sigismund found himself visiting it with increasing frequency as the months passed. He studied the portrait with the intensity of a scholar deciphering some ancient codex, and wondered what he and his father would find to say to each other after being apart for so long. It even occurred to him, one gray autumn afternoon, that they might not like each other at all.

That would make things difficult, Sigismund thought, frowning up at the portrait. He went to stare out the narrow window at the end of the gallery. The day had been particularly bitter, with everyone agreeing that winter was just around the corner, and the garden below looked dreary and neglected. It reminded Sigismund of the sunken garden in the West Castle, except that it was laid out in the neat borders of a herb parterre rather than a lilac walk.

The sky was gray as iron when he stepped outside, the wind snatching at the last leaves in fitful gusts and tossing them to the ground. The earth was dark and bare, and most of the herbs had died back to brown, withered clumps, although the rue bushes were still green against a sheltered wall. Sigismund bent and plucked a sprig, rubbing it between his fingers, and shivered as the wind gusted again, swirling brown leaves around his head.

He turned away, kicking through a deeper drift, and saw that there was a girl standing beneath the bare crown of an elder tree. A sparrow fluttered into the branches, followed by another, and then a third, until there was a small flock of them preening and fluttering their feathers above her head. Her chemise and skirt, brown as the sparrows, blended with the dreary colors in the garden, but Sigismund was still surprised that he hadn't noticed her before.

She looked like a servant, he thought, a girl from the scullery or laundry, with the ragged hem of her skirt stopping a few inches clear of bare brown ankles. Her feet were thrust into the wooden shoes worn by the lower servants and her hands were scratched, her hair a snarl of brown curls. She had a leaf caught above one ear and was looking at him sidelong beneath a tangle of dark lashes—a shy look, he decided after a moment, rather than sly.

"Who are you?" he asked. "What are you doing here?"

The girl pointed to her mouth and shook her head, and after a moment he guessed that she must be mute.

"All the same," Sigismund said, a little disconcerted, "I don't think you should be here. You'll get into trouble if anyone finds you."

It did not occur to him that he had already found her; he was more concerned with how she had found her way into the garden in the first place. Until now, he had thought that the only access to this particular plot was through the corridors and formal rooms of the old palace, but he didn't think that a kitchen girl would be permitted to come that way. He almost smiled, thinking of the chamberlain's outrage, but the girl shook her head and pointed to the herbs.

"You were sent for the herbs," Sigismund said, his expression clearing. "Although that still doesn't explain how you actually got in," he added under his breath.

The girl seemed to understand him, even though she could not speak herself. She drifted along the path in a cloud of brown leaves, the wooden shoes making no sound on the beaten earth, and stopped where the castle wall curved away from the garden. The brown hand pointed, and Sigismund saw that there was a narrow door set into the wall, just out of sight of the gallery window.

It would be concealed from every other window that looked down into the garden as well, and Sigismund wondered what Balisan would think about that. He was not sure he liked the idea himself, given the ease of access from the herb garden into the old palace. The door was ajar, and when Sigismund peered through he saw a narrow lane winding between high walls. Weeds were sprouting through broken cobbles and a variety of castle refuse had clearly been abandoned there over a period of years.

"Is this the way you came in?" he asked, but the girl had drifted away and was standing by the clumped rue, the sparrows pecking and darting at her feet. She was still watching him, though, with the same sidelong look, wisps of hair blowing across her face.

She reminded Sigismund of someone; he felt the memory would come if she only turned her head another way or shifted the position of her body. "I wonder what your name is?" he asked, taking a step toward her.

Her smile was small and crooked, but it lifted the gravity of her expression and let a flash of mischief in. She raised one finger, indicating herself, then pointed to the herb growing against the wall and then back at herself again.

"Rue?" he asked, and she smiled. It was not quite a yes, Sigismund thought, watching her expression closely, more of an indication that he could call her that. She would answer to it, but he would have laid a wager that Rue was not her true name. He knew what Flor would have said if he was there, which was that there were more important things to wager over than the names, true or otherwise, of serving girls. "Wench" or "you" would be good enough for Flor, if he called her anything at all.

The thought must have acted like a summoning charm, for Sigismund heard Flor's voice calling out to him from the gallery. A moment later he appeared on the steps, his golden hair bright against the dullness of the day.

"Oi, Sigismund!" Flor said, and then paused, his eyes narrowing. "I thought I heard you talking to someone?"

Sigismund looked around, but the girl must have fled as soon as she heard Flor's voice. "There was a kitchen girl here," he said, "gathering herbs. But I think she took fright when she heard you."

"Here?" Flor looked as though he had just smelled something unpleasant. "I'm surprised the lower servants are permitted to even come here—she should've known to take herself off as soon as you appeared." He shook his head. "A kitchen wench, presuming to talk to her prince!"

"She was mute," Sigismund said, a little shortly. "So it would be more correct to say that I was talking to her." But it occurred to him that she had not seemed at all afraid; she had stayed until Flor called out. "Were you looking for me?" he asked, changing the subject.

"I was," said Flor, with a mock flourish, "and am. Firstly, to tell you that there's been word that your father is finally on his way here. Apparently he and his retinue have already reached the Whitetowers. But more importantly, there's to be a big boar hunt in Thorn forest the day after tomorrow, and we're all going—wouldn't miss it for anything! You should come with us, if your guardians will let you out of their sight."

Sigismund hesitated. "I'd love to come," he said, "but how long do you think we'll be away? I want to be here when my father arrives, perhaps even ride out to meet him."

Flor scuffed at a clump of withered herb. "We should be able to do both," he said, as though it was completely accepted that he would go wherever Sigismund went. "The Whitetowers are only a week's journey on a good horse, but the King's progress will take longer. Royal cavalcades always move slowly, and everyone along the way, from the great lords to the mayors of every tin-pot village, will want to address him." Flor rolled his eyes and Sigismund grinned. "The boar hunt shouldn't be more than two days in total, so even allowing another day to ride back, we'll still be in plenty of time to meet your father. And," Flor added, by way of further inducement, "my family has a hunting lodge in Thorn forest, so we'll have plenty of home comforts, none of this roughing it in the woods."

Sigismund thought that he wouldn't have minded camping out if the weather had been a little milder, but he would enjoy getting away from the palace and seeing the Langrafon hunting lodge. It would be an opportunity for Wat and Wenceslas to prove their skill as well. "Alright," he said, feeling the first thrill of excitement. "So long as Balisan agrees."

"He can come too," said Flor. "There's plenty of room at the lodge."

"Balisan never hunts," said Sigismund, "or not that I've

seen anyway." He almost laughed outright at Flor's expression and grinned when his friend demanded the how and why of such an unnatural situation. "He says that he only hunts when he's hungry, and he hasn't gone hungry since he took service with me."

Sigismund was a little surprised, all the same, that Balisan did not oppose his going. "The King's son must be seen to hunt," was all the master-at-arms said. "And it is time for the other young men to see that you are able to stand on your own feet—and are not tied to me or anyone else in your father's household by leading strings."

"That would be good," admitted Sigismund, who had noticed Flor's comment about guardians. He made a face. "Although the chamberlain will insist I take guards with me. As if they'll be much use once we're all spread out, following the hunt."

"The chamberlain will be thinking of your royal consequence," said Balisan. "But I hear this boar is notorious, a powerful and vicious quarry. So don't push to be first spear at the kill. Leave that to the royal huntsmen and those with more experience of hunting boar."

"But—" began Sigismund, knowing that Flor would undoubtedly push, and he didn't want to hang back either. Still, not being first spear didn't mean that he couldn't be in the forefront of the hunt. He shrugged, thinking that the royal huntsmen were likely to be best placed to make the kill anyway, and changed the subject.

Balisan frowned when Sigismund told him about the door opening into the herb garden and the narrow path between the palace walls. "This place is a warren," he said, but seemed unconcerned when Sigismund mentioned the presence of the serving girl.

It was Flor who raised the subject again. He and Sigismund were sorting through their weapons for the hunt and Flor had picked up a heavy bladed dagger, turning it this way and that to the light. "About that dumb wench," he said abruptly, "the one in the garden earlier. The chamberlain says he has spoken to the royal cellarer, but she doesn't know of any mute girl in the palace kitchens."

Sigismund felt a frown settle across the bridge of his nose. "Why did you mention it to the chamberlain at all?" he asked.

Flor looked up from his careful scrutiny of the dagger. "You can't just have servants coming and going as they please in gardens used by the high nobility. The wench needs a lesson to remind her to keep to her place."

"I think," Sigismund said, his voice level, "that was for me to decide."

The dark blue eyes widened. "Surely you're not angry, Sigismund? Must I overlook it when others slight you, just because you don't have a proper care for your dignity? And the girl's only a serving trollop. She'll be thick-skinned as well as thickheaded."

Sigismund shook his head. "My dignity hasn't been slighted because a serving girl was in the herb garden, Flor," he said.

Flor was frowning too now. "I can't believe you're taking this wench's part against me!" he said.

"I'm not," said Sigismund. "I'm taking my part against you, because I think you should let me decide when my dignity's been slighted or one of my servants needs to be punished."

Flor slammed the dagger back into its sheath. "Alright!" he began, then shrugged, looking at Sigismund again and shaking his head. "Well, I'm not going to fall out with you over a serving drudge, not with our first boar hunt together coming up. We need to focus on what's important here."

Sigismund decided not to reiterate that he thought the matter of the serving girl was important. He guessed that he would have to make a similar point with Flor again, and sooner rather than later, but for the moment he was prepared to agree that the boar hunt should be the focus of their attention. Flor was whistling when he departed an hour later and seemed to have completely forgotten their brief dispute. The boar hunt, he said, was exactly the kind of adventure they needed before the King and the full formality of the royal court descended on their lives. Sigismund agreed that it would be good to be active. Privately, he thought that it would help take his mind off the mixture of excitement and uncertainty that he felt at finally seeing his father again.

Some concern for the girl Rue must have remained, however, for that night he dreamed that she was back in the herb garden—but bound to the elder tree by long cables of thorn. There was a band of them, black and barbed, woven tightly around her mouth, and Sigismund could see blood on her lips. She turned her head and met his eyes, or would have, except that there were thorns sprouting out of hers.

Sigismund stepped back and the blind head moved from side to side as though in warning or denial, and a hoarse, protesting sound came out of her gagged mouth. He took another step away and her arms came up as if to hold him there, but in the dream her hands were gone and what she held out to him were severed, bleeding stumps.

The Boar Hunt

Sigismund told Balisan about the dream in the dark predawn, when he was making his final preparations for the hunting trip and eating a breakfast of cold meat wrapped in bread. Balisan was standing with the toe of one booted foot resting on the fender, one arm on the mantelshelf, and the rose and copper light from the fire gave his face an almost demonic cast. His eyes gleamed bronze as he looked at Sigismund.

"And yet you felt no sense of another power, seeking to draw you out?" he asked.

Sigismund shook his head. "I couldn't detect anything. It was probably just a nightmare, except that it seemed so real. I wondered if it could be a warning of some kind?"

"About the girl?" Balisan asked. "Or the hunt?" He

picked up a book from the mantelshelf and handed it to Sigismund. "It is a treatise on boar hunting. Master Griff found it in the palace library and thought it might be useful."

Sigismund stuffed the book into a saddlebag without looking at it. "It seems unlikely that the girl and the hunt could be connected in any way." He buckled the bag closed, frowning. "It was probably just a dream . . . and I was worried about what Flor had done and what might happen to the girl because of it."

A log in the grate collapsed and Balisan nudged it back into the blaze with his toe. "Flor Langrafon takes the prerogatives of nobility seriously," he murmured.

Sigismund nodded. "Too seriously, but he's a good friend and generous to a fault in other matters." To those of his own order, he added silently, but it seemed disloyal to say so aloud. "He paid all Ban Valensar's gaming debts recently, which were considerable—but Ban's grandfather, the old Count, had sworn that he would not bail him out if he incurred such debts again. Apparently he feels that he has plenty of other grandsons and can afford to disinherit one."

"Uncomfortable for Ban," observed Balisan. "And now, of course, he is in Flor's debt."

"It's not like that." Sigismund picked up his second saddlebag. "The money was a gift. Flor was very clear about that; there's no expectation of repayment." He cast a quick look at Balisan, who was studying the play of the flames with absorbed interest. "So you don't think I should give up this hunt? You see no reason why I shouldn't go?"

Balisan looked up, the flicker of the fire in his eyes. "Because of the dream? No. In any case we agreed in coming here that it was time for you to live in the world, and that includes going on hunts. So go, Prince Sigismund."

Sigismund went, and the eastern horizon was already a pale slash as he stepped out into a courtyard milling with men, horses, and dogs. There would be huntsmen with a local pack at Thorn, but every hunter present had his own favorite dogs at heel, and grooms with spare horses for the chase. There was a company of guards as well, their horses drawn up in two neat rows. One of them, sitting just behind the captain, carried a pennant with a red and gold dragon on it—the symbol of the royal House.

Sigismund spotted Wat and Wenceslas by the gate with his own spare horses and went over for a quick word before a horn sounded, calling the company to order. Then Flor beckoned him to the head of the column and they clattered out through the palace gates as rose feathered the sky. To avoid the congestion caused by farm carts already heading for the city markets, they took a steep, winding path down the palace bluff to the river and were ferried over to the other side. From there they followed a country lane for some distance, joining the main road east as the sun cleared the hills. The winter rains had not yet come, so the road was dry and would soon be dusty, but for the moment the dew was still heavy in the grass and surrounding hedgerows.

Sigismund's heart lifted with the sun and he found himself noticing little things: a dew-beaded cobweb hanging from a hedge, the song of a thrush as they clattered past a walled orchard, and the grace of tree branches without their summer veil of leaves. He inhaled deeply, feeling how good it was to be outdoors and part of even such small wonders after being cooped up in the palace for so long. Someone behind him began to whistle a marching song from the northern provinces, and one by one the riders took up the lilting tune.

At first the country on either side of the road was cultivated and closely settled, with many farmsteads and small villages set amongst orchards and ordered fields. The settlements grew sparser as the morning wore on, and they began to ride between low rounded hills dotted with oak and chestnut trees. It was pleasant country and the travelers they met would call out greetings and good luck for the hunt, for the fame of the Thorn boar—and the havoc it caused—had spread far beyond the boundaries of the forest.

It was not until late afternoon that Sigismund had his first view of the forest. They had just crested a low rise and their company was spread out across the road and the grassy slopes on either side. The hills ahead were higher and thickly wooded, the canopy so dark a green it looked almost black—although that, thought Sigismund, was probably the fading light. Clouds had been building up for some time and gave the forest a forbidding look.

"It wears a more friendly face in sunshine," said Flor, "but Thorn forest has always been rough, wild country, teeming with game. I hunt here as often as I can."

"And the hunting lodge belongs to your family?" Sigismund asked as they moved off again, falling into file along the road.

Flor made an airy gesture with one hand. "Langrafon cousins, several times removed, but we've always had free run of the place, which is just as well. The village inns around here provide rough fare and rougher accommodation—the fleas are legendary."

Flor's description of the forest as rough, wild country proved accurate as the road brought them closer. The hills rose up steeply, shutting out the sky, and the trees in the forest pressed close together, tangled into each other and the undergrowth at their feet. It reminded Sigismund of the Wood that adjoined the West Castle, except that this forest was full of bird noise and he could hear running water in the distance. Sigismund thought it was pleasanter up close than from a distance, and he enjoyed the last league or so of their ride beneath the forest eave, although the one village he saw in the distance looked poor: a narrow straggle of cottages amongst the trees, with only a few stony fields.

Flor nodded when he mentioned this. "The soil's poor here, so most of the villagers make their living as woodcutters or charcoal burners, and turn hunter as required."

"Or poacher," said Adrian Valensar from his other side. Adrian was another of the numerous Valensar grandsons. There were four altogether riding to the hunt, including Flor's friend Ban.

"They hang if they're caught at that game," said Flor, "or lose a hand, if the Master at the lodge is feeling lenient. The game, like the forest, belongs to the Crown, so they might as well steal directly from the King's purse."

Adrian shot a quick, sidelong glance at Sigismund. "But honest or dishonest, I've heard they're all keen hunters. We'll probably have every able-bodied man in the forest out with us tomorrow."

The sun was sinking by the time they rode into the cobbled yard of the hunting lodge, which was a foursquare wooden building with a squat tower on one side. Stables, kennels, and storerooms were ranged around the walls, and there was already a large gathering present, all eager for the next day's hunt and to meet their prince. Sigismund suspected that the accommodation would be crowded, but he had no time for further reflection as those waiting pressed around him. For the next half hour he was kept fully occupied, shaking outstretched hands and acknowledging eager greetings.

Flor was in his element, calling out names and greetings in his most open manner and bringing forward those he considered important. These were all, Sigismund gathered, members of the lesser nobility that occupied the small manors in and around the forest fringe, most of them held directly from the King.

"Bluff hearty types, but loyal," Flor told him later, when they finally reached the relative quiet of the tower, where only Sigismund was to have a room to himself. "A few hail-fellow-and-well-mets, and they'll be your men for life. The chamberlain knows that," he added, "and will have made sure that word of your coming was sent ahead."

Sigismund grinned and shook his head at the same time. "Cynical," he said, but Flor shrugged. He was standing just inside the door to Sigismund's room, and although he was dusty from the day's ride, the spark in his eyes was undiminished.

"Realistic," he said, without apology. "And why withhold what costs so little yet buys you so much?"

"You see what I mean?" he whispered later, under cover of the noisy feast. There had just been a prolonged series of toasts to Sigismund's health, then to that of the King, and the drinking and toasting looked set to continue until the night was old. Flor grinned when Sigismund mentioned this. "They're hardheaded as well as hard living," he said with a shrug, "but they'll still be up before dawn for the hunt. Constitutions like iron," he added, and took a deep swig from his own mug.

They were still drinking and shouting when Sigismund left the hall, and he was not even sure that anyone noticed his departure. It was quieter in the tower, but although he took Master Griff's treatise out of his saddlebag, he returned it unopened. Instead he lay awake with his hands behind his head, listening to the sigh of the wind in the forest. It was rising, and Sigismund heard rain spatter against the shutters, suggesting that it would be cold, damp work the next day. There was the occasional burst of revelry in the yard or on the stairs outside his door, but gradually the lodge grew quiet and he fell into a deep, dreamless sleep. He was awake and dressed, however, before the first fist pounded on his door the next morning.

The lodge and its yard were full of men eating breakfast, or checking their hunting gear and the harness on their horses. All the previous night's revelers were there, eager for the hunt despite their excesses, and there were others who had come in with the dark hours. Most of these latecomers were on foot, hunters from the surrounding villages who looked lean and shaggy as wolves in the torchlight. They squatted on their heels by the open gate and around the perimeter of the yard, speaking little and keeping their eyes on the ground, or watching the milling hounds. But Sigismund felt their quick, covert stares whenever his own eyes turned away, and he guessed that these men too were keen to see their prince.

Wenceslas was holding Sigismund's first mount, a tall brown hunter, and had two more on a lead rein. He and the other grooms would follow the hunt, but at a distance to avoid getting caught between the hunters and their quarry. "Where's Wat?" Sigismund asked, and the groom nodded toward the hound pack.

"Outside the lodge with your dogs. Highness," he added, with a quick look round at the guards and other grooms. "Most of the hunters here have brought their own hounds to swell the pack. Wat says yours will run with the others once the hunt is up, but he needs to keep them under control in the meantime."

Sigismund nodded, knowing that dogs were often the first casualty of a boar hunt once they brought the savage quarry to bay. "They say this boar has killed men," he said abruptly. "Have you heard the same story?"

Wenceslas nodded. "It's been hunted before and killed two men, crippling a third—all experienced hunters. It's attacked villagers too as they walked the forest paths."

Sigismund looked at him, remembering the groom's stories about mystical beasts. "Unusual behavior," he said, "even for a wild boar."

"Perhaps." Wenceslas was cautious. "But sometimes an arrow or a spear barb left in the flesh can drive a beast mad when it's been wounded in a previous hunt." He hesitated as Sigismund put his foot in the stirrup, then spoke again, low-voiced. "But be careful of this beast, Sigismund. It's not just that it's savage, it's huge as well, and very fast. And there are strange tales told about this forest. They say there are places in it where the sun never shines and more than just savage beasts dwell."

Wenceslas did not say demons, but Sigismund had heard those tales too. He leaned down from the saddle and clasped the groom's shoulder. "I'll be careful," he promised. "Tell Wat to take care as well, when you see him."

He saw Flor by the gate and lifted a hand in greeting, but the golden youth was frowning as Sigismund rode up. "Your servants are remarkably free with you," he said. "It does not look well."

Sigismund felt his eyebrows lift in imitation of Balisan's stare, and Flor broke off, as if realizing he had gone too far. "I'm sorry," he said, "but one can't help noticing—and people do talk, you know. You are the King's son, after all, and need to give more thought to your consequence." He did not add "and that of your friends," but the words hung in the air and Sigismund knew that Flor was completely serious.

"It's my consequence," he said mildly, since he did not feel any need to explain his friendship with Wat and

Wenceslas. He looked around at the yard and the milling excited dogs, and then up at the graying sky. "Surely we'll be on our way soon?"

Flor smiled and returned some light remark, and a moment later the Master of the hunt blew a long blast on his horn and they were away, streaming east through the forest. The wind was blowing strong and cold as the day broke with high, flying clouds, but it was dark and sheltered between the trees and at first there was plenty of talk and laughter as they rode. The local hunters ran in silence, keeping pace with the horses, and everyone fell quiet as they approached the country where the black boar laired. The only sounds then were the panting of the hounds, the thud of hooves, and the chink of metal on saddle and bridle.

The boar, thought Sigismund, would hear them coming from miles off.

They stopped at the village where the boar had last been sighted, and the headman told them it had come into the fields in broad daylight, uprooting crops and goring one of the men who had tried to drive it off. The villagers had tracked it, although at a safe distance, and would show the hunters the boggy country where it had gone to ground.

The country into which they led the hunt was wild and bleak, with low rocky hills and marshy ground between them. It was more open than the rest of the forest but still choked with low-growing brush, and the going looked difficult. "It'll be ground work at the end," Flor predicted. "The boar'll be able to go to earth here, in terrain where no horse can follow."

"*If* it goes to earth," Adrian Valensar muttered. "From what I've heard, it's more likely to come after us."

It was some time before a hound caught the boar's scent and bayed, a great belling cry, and then the rest of the pack gave voice and hunting horns wound on every side. The wind stung Sigismund's eyes to tears and the thunder of his horse's hooves echoed the blood pounding in his veins. He yelled with the rest as the hunt caught first sight of the boar, but then fell silent, concentrating on keeping his horse on its feet in the difficult terrain.

The boar ran, heading for the roughest brakes and the dark unbroken line of the deep forest beyond. The hunt surged in pursuit, but as the hours passed and the boar kept on, apparently tireless, both men and horses began to drop behind. Sigismund changed horses when the brown began to slow, then pressed forward again, but he began to doubt as the day lengthened and the cloud cover thickened, fearing that the boar was going to outrun them after all. Their numbers had dwindled significantly by now, so that fewer than half of those who had set out were still following when the boar crossed into the deep woods. Sigismund was impressed at how many of the local hunters had kept up with the horses, tireless as the wolves they resembled, even if they had been able to take shortcuts through the rougher country.

He looked around as they passed beneath the trees and saw Flor, his face a grimy mask as he grinned and raised a hand in salute. Sigismund suspected that his own appearance was little better, and Ban Valensar was muddied from a fall, although he was still riding. His cousin Adrian, however, was amongst those who had fallen behind.

The Master's horn sounded up ahead and there was a change in the timbre of the hounds' cries. Flor yelled something, but it was borne away beneath pounding hooves and the blast of Ban's horn as he blew it in reply. Sigismund was sure that the boar must have been brought to bay at last and that the huntsmen would be going in for the kill. As if to confirm his suspicions, the hounds' cries became frenzied, then broke off in a confusion of baying and shouting. Horns were sounding from every side as he came out of the trees and into a long glade—and saw the black boar charging toward him. It must have doubled back, and although there were hounds harrying it on either side, they were unable to bring it down.

Sigismund's horse stood straight up on its hind legs, screaming, while Flor and Ban fought to turn their mounts away from the boar's charge. A hound darted in, but the boar twisted its head, a quick sideways toss, and gored the dog on a bloodied yellow tusk before hurling it away.

The whole incident was over in a split second, barely checking the boar's rush toward Sigismund.

He had his horse under control now, but there was no time left to get out of the way. He could see the boar's eyes, red and furious as it bore down on him, and its size and ferocity gave credence to the forest demon stories. It was hard to believe that a mere spear blade could kill such a monster, but Sigismund struggled to hold his frightened horse steady and prepare his spear for the thrust. He was vaguely aware of Flor and Ban bringing their horses around again, but they were not going to be in time to affect the outcome, and he didn't want to think about what would happen if his thrust failed.

A hound burst from the brush and came at the boar from the side, and then two more were racing to join it. Sigismund recognized them as his own three—Bran, Joyeuse, and Mifawn—all named for Wenceslas's hounds of legend. He caught the yellow blaze of Wat's hair, sweat-stained now, as he came out of the brush behind them. The huntsman's horse looked close to foundering, but he had his spear ready and was closing on the boar, not willing to leave it to the hounds.

The boar must have seen the new threat for it spun, slashing at Bran who leapt away, then sidestepped Mifawn to charge straight for Wat. Joyeuse leapt for its throat and caught an ear instead, holding on gamely, but was tossed aside by a shake of the powerful head and yelped as she

113

connected with the earth. She scrabbled to her feet and streaked in again to join her comrades, who were trying to gain purchase while avoiding the lethal tusks.

Wat's horse was holding steady, and Sigismund could see the young huntsman's narrowed eyes as his spear thrust down, aiming for the boar's heart. Then a dog and Wat's horse screamed at the same time and both were down. Sigismund couldn't make out which dog was hurt as he forced his own horse forward, but the other two were still on the boar and Wat seemed to be pinned beneath his flailing horse. His spear had missed the boar's heart, and the enraged beast shook the dogs off and turned on the huntsman. Wat was struggling to get his knife out, but it must have been pinned beneath the horse as well. Sigismund was close, so close, but knew he was not going to get there in time.

Wat's horse saw the looming head and bloody, curved tusks of the boar and screamed again, kicking to its feet as the dogs leapt in—and then a squealing, snarling melee of boar and dogs rolled over Wat where he lay on the ground. Wat screamed too, and for a moment Sigismund froze. His horse snorted and he recovered, holding it steady with his knees and a hand of iron. He raised his spear, waiting— waiting for the moment when the boar would fight free of the dogs, would begin to turn—and then he thrust down with the full power of his arm, deep into the beast's heart.

The boar did not die immediately but continued to thrash and twist on the spear while Sigismund tried to lift it off Wat's body. There were more men and dogs there now and a great confusion of noise and shouting. One of the forest hunters thrust his spear through the boar's eye, finishing it, while others dodged in to pull Wat's body clear. Sigismund dismounted and dropped to his knees beside him, looking a question at the man who was bending over the wound. It was one of the landholders from the forest fringe—Sigismund remembered him from the previous night's feast—and his expression was grim. He met Sigismund's eyes and shook his head.

The boar's tusk had carved a deep half-moon gash up through Wat's stomach. Sigismund could see the dark blood welling up and the gray, slick glisten of intestine. Wat's eyes were closed, his breathing shallow, and there was a bubble of blood at the corner of his mouth. Sigismund took his hand between both his own, recalling how the yellow-haired boy had been working in the kennels when he first came to the West Castle, and as a huntsman after that—yet he was no more than a year or two older than Sigismund himself.

"We killed the boar," Sigismund said, speaking as slowly and as clearly as he could, hoping Wat would hear him. "You and I between us, with the hounds."

Wat's lids lifted, but his eyes were dark. "Missed . . . my stroke," he whispered. "Hounds?"

"All well," Sigismund told him, although he was not sure if that was true. His hands tightened over Wat's. "I owe you my life, Wat. The boar would have been on me before I could master my horse if you hadn't drawn him off."

Wat's lids fluttered again, but his voice was fainter. His legs and arms were twitching, much in the same way, Sigismund thought uncomfortably, as the boar had convulsed on the end of his spear. He had to lean close to hear what the gray lips said: "Bal'san . . . said stay close . . . feared . . . treachery."

Sigismund almost wished it had been treachery, rather than the sheer ill fortune of a wild boar fighting its way clear of the main hunt when they thought it brought to bay. He squeezed the cold hand between his. "You did well, my friend," he said, and forced himself to look at the welling wound again and meet the hard sympathy in the squire's face.

"I don't think it'll be long, Highness," the man said, keeping his voice low. "There's no way to staunch this blood."

No, thought Sigismund. He saw that the boar was already being trussed onto a spear for the journey back and the hound pack had been drawn off, but most of those present were watching him, waiting. He could see the hunt's Master, gnawing at his lip, and Flor and Ban standing together with Adrian and the others who had arrived

116

late. Looking past them, he saw Wenceslas standing with the spare horses, Bran and Joyeuse pressed against his legs. Joyeuse was licking at a bloody gash down one shoulder and Mifawn was nowhere to be seen.

Sigismund released Wat's hand and stood up, calling Wenceslas over with a jerk of his head. "Best say goodbye," he said, low-voiced as the squire.

It was a somber journey back to the village, with Wat's body wrapped in a cloak and tied over the back of his horse. Mifawn was dead too when Sigismund found her, killed in the last struggle with the boar. The Master had pressed him to take the boar's head back to the capital, in honor of his killing stroke, but Sigismund had replied that the trophy wall in the hunting lodge seemed more appropriate, given that so many of the forest folk, both noble and common born, had participated in the hunt. His words were greeted with approval, and Flor clapped him on the shoulder and murmured something about diplomacy, but the truth was that Sigismund didn't want the head. The beast had been a rogue that needed killing and he had killed it, but at the price of Wat's life. A head on a trophy wall could not even begin to compensate for that.

The clouds rolled in and covered the hilltops as they rode back, and the day faded swiftly. They had brands to light if the darkness grew too thick beneath the trees, but the local men agreed that it would rain before morning, and everyone was eager to push on and reach the village before full night came.

"And at least," said Flor, riding beside Sigismund the first time the terrain allowed, "there is something approximating a road from the village back to the lodge, not like this trackless country."

"It's rough," agreed Sigismund. He had been aware of that when the pursuit was on, but it seemed so much worse now that they were making their way back, weary, hungry, and cold. He tried to concentrate on picking a safe path and to keep his thoughts away from Wat, but the memories kept returning, especially the way the young huntsman would toss his yellow hair and flirt with Annie during happier days at the West Castle. Mifawn's death too was a dull ache in Sigismund's heart, and he wondered what Wat had meant about Balisan suspecting treachery. Why would the master-at-arms have let him come on the hunt, if that was really the case?

"That was a fine thrust that killed the boar, worthy of a prince!" Flor said, as their horses sidetracked around a large clump of brambles. "But I thought you were done for when we galloped into that clearing and the boar charged straight at you."

"I was lucky," Sigismund replied, trying not to be short. "But I wouldn't have stood a chance if Wat hadn't drawn the boar off."

Flor nodded. "It was well done," he agreed, "especially for a servant—although no more than his duty, of course." He whistled a snatch of tune.

Sigismund shut his mouth hard to avoid saying something that he would regret. It was a struggle to hold his anger down, and he wondered how Flor could dismiss any man's death so lightly. He was glad when the trees pressed in too close for anyone to ride more than single file, and even the chill thrust of the wind suited his mood. The gusts had a knack of finding their way through both cloak and coat, and they stirred up dead leaves in the open spaces. A cloud of them blew in front of Sigismund when he was nodding in the saddle, jerking him awake, and for one startled moment he thought he saw the girl Rue in the swirl, but when he blinked and looked again, she was gone.

They lit the brands before they reached the village, in the open boggy country where they had first flushed out the boar. The Master said that it would stop the column breaking up and people straying from the path, but it was not long after that when Sigismund began to nod again. The fiery stars of the brands blended into one long serpent, twisting its way across the heath. It was like riding through a dream where even the air had substance, and Sigismund's mind slipped in and out of a haze of physical and mental weariness, overlain with grief.

He only came fully awake when he realized that his horse had halted before two tall wrought-iron gates, set in a high stone wall. He thought he could make out formal lawns through the palings, and the dark bulk of what looked like a very small castle or a large hunting lodge. It was full night, however, with the moon half hidden in cloud, so he could not be sure of anything except that he was completely alone.

The House in the Forest

It was clear, Sigismund thought, that his horse must have turned down a side path without anyone noticing. But at least it seemed to have brought him to a place where there would be food and shelter, and people who could send a message to the hunting lodge or set him on the right road. It might even be home to one of the forest squires who had been on the hunt, although it was larger than he would have expected and appeared to be made of stone rather than wood. The formal garden, with its creeper-covered walls and box hedges, suggested a home rather than a lodge in intermittent use, and Sigismund suspected that the whole scene would be charming by daylight. But right now he was more concerned with the lantern burning over the door and the fact that the gates opened at the touch of his hand, swinging silently inward.

Strange, Sigismund thought, hesitating, but he was tired and had no idea where he was. He shivered as the wind plucked at his clothes with cold fingers and could see no choice but to wake whoever lived here and ask for help. He urged his horse forward, then stopped again as the gates clicked shut behind him. The shadows cast by the hedges lay in black blocks across the ground, and everything was very quiet. No dog barked to announce his arrival, but he thought he heard a rustle in the hedge, and a moment later something shrieked from a dark corner of the garden. An owl swooped by on heavy wings as both Sigismund and his horse jumped.

Just an owl, thought Sigismund, letting the horse walk forward again. I must be tired to jump at that.

There was a twisted metal ring set into the foot of the stone stairs at the entrance to the house, and a heavy wrought-iron knocker on the door itself. Sigismund tied his horse to the ring before mounting the steps, then brought the knocker down with a sharp rap. He waited, listening, but there was only silence, so he rapped again. There was another pause, and then he heard footsteps inside the house and the sound of bolts being drawn back. A moment later the door swung inward, letting a shaft of yellow light out into the night. Sigismund raised a hand against the brightness, but he could see the dark shape of a man, half concealed by the door, and a wide, tiled hall beyond.

The man made a gesture, indicating that he should enter, and Sigismund stepped forward, still blinking against the light. He opened his mouth, to say who he was and ask for help, but was stopped by a chime of laughter from the end of the hall. Hands clapped together as he hesitated, and a woman stepped forward, her hair gleaming gold in the lantern light. Her eyes were sapphire as she smiled at him.

"Welcome to my house, Prince Sigismund," said the Margravine *zu* Malvolin.

Sigismund whirled to run, but the door slammed shut in his face. The man guarding it smiled out of an all-too-familiar face. "I wondered how long it would take you to get here," said Flor Langrafon. "And such a long ride too. Surely you can't want to leave so soon?"

Sigismund stood very still, watching him. "It's customary for guests to be invited," he said, forcing himself to speak calmly, "and to leave at will."

Flor's smile deepened. "We did extend an invitation," he said, "to your horse, which accepted like a lamb while you dozed on its back. As for leaving . . ." He shrugged. "How churlish to refuse my grandmother's hospitality out of hand."

Sigismund turned, looking from Flor to the Margravine, and saw that armed men had appeared in every doorway that opened off the hall, all of them clad alike in plain dark clothes. "I take it then," he said, speaking to the Margravine, "that you are Flor's grandmother?"

Her smile was a deep curve, the blue eyes limpid as she came further down the hall. "Grandmother," she said, with a pretty shrug, "or great-grandmother, or great-great—I have forgotten. Just as you seem to have forgotten our talk, just a few years ago, when I promised that you should visit me here one day, in my castle of Highthorn."

Sigismund stared at her, taken aback. "I remember now," he said, and did. "But your castle is in the west, far from here. This house is in the forest of Thorn."

"Is it?" she asked softly. "But whether in Thorn or the west, you are in my house now—and not everything here is always as it seems."

Sigismund glanced around, and remembered Balisan telling him about places where mortal ground overlapped with the Faerie realm. He felt the burn of a slow anger: against himself for letting grief and weariness dull his senses, against the Margravine for having trapped him, and against Flor—but he would not think about Flor, not now.

"You brought me here against my will," he said, keeping his voice even. "Why?"

The Margravine shook her head. "Hard words, Prince Sigismund, not the language of those who should be friends." She was still smiling faintly as she scrutinized his face. "And it is of friendship that I wish to speak, and matters of common . . . interest. But I can see that you are tired. You should rest now, without fear, for you are my guest and will be housed as befits a prince."

"A guest," Sigismund asked, not moving, "or a prisoner?"

The Margravine held up one white, slender hand. "Such an ugly term, Prince Sigismund. We will talk again when you are rested, and then my hospitality may wear a fairer face." She extended the hand to Flor. "Come to me, my dear, when our guest is safely bestowed."

Flor came forward and bowed over her hand, then sketched a second, mocking bow in Sigismund's direction. "My grandmother's servants will show you to your room, Prince." He smiled as though at some secret joke. "And you needn't worry about imposing on our hospitality. This house is larger than it looks from the outside, much larger. It's easier to find your way in than out."

Sigismund stared at him, his eyes hard and level, but Flor had already turned to give orders to the dark-clothed retainers, who closed around Sigismund and led him away. The room in which they left him was as comfortable as the Margravine had promised, with rich hangings and a bright fire burning on the hearth. It warmed the whole room and there was food on the table, but Sigismund did not touch it. One of the first things that Balisan had taught him was that he must never touch any food or drink offered to him if he was ever a guest, or prisoner, of the faie.

A quick glance around the room showed him his

saddlebags lying on the table, and their contents appeared untouched. Sigismund almost smiled when he saw Master Griff's treatise on boar hunting but pushed it aside for the last of his bread and cheese, packed that morning for the hunt. He devoured it before trying the door, which was locked as he expected, and peering behind the hangings. But there were no windows concealed there, just dark wood paneling from ceiling to floor.

No way out, thought Sigismund, so what now? He sat down on the bed and rested his dusty head in his hands, trying not to think about Flor's betrayal, or how long it would be before he was missed and the hue and cry went up.

But I must find a way to escape, he told himself, not just rely on Balisan to come looking for me. How will he find me anyway, if this is one of those places that lie between the different planes of existence? Perhaps, he thought with a shudder, no one will ever find me, no matter how long or hard they look. I have to assume that I'm on my own.

This realization made him get up and go around the room again, but he still couldn't find any way out, except through the locked door. Tiredness hit him, solid as a tree branch, and he yawned, feeling as though his face might crack. He needed to sleep, regardless of what the Margravine intended. But Sigismund caught himself before he dropped straight down onto the bed. He did not know whether or not the faie portion of his blood had made him more susceptible to the Margravine's trap, but he knew he needed to try and connect his awareness to any aspect of the mortal world that was part of this place.

Sinking into the familiar practice lightened his fear, and as Sigismund's awareness extended, he realized that his guess had been right: this was a place where the planes overlapped. As his mind cleared further, he heard the familiar deep hum that he recognized from his own world, and the shift and flow of its energy weaving through the alien fabric around him. Sigismund let his mind sink into that flow until it coiled in and around him like a serpent, and he felt secure enough to relax into sleep.

If he had thought about it at all, Sigismund would have said that he would not dream in this place, it was too unsafe—but he found himself in a dream so clear that he might as well have been wide awake. In it, he was drifting through the Margravine's house and he discovered that Flor was right: it was far larger on the inside than it had appeared from the gate. He could hear music and the sound of laughter in the distance and he made his way toward it, coming out into a wide hall. The roof was so high that it seemed lost in shadow, but a second glance up, into those shadows, showed the outline of leaves and branches, and a few stars peeping down.

Sigismund shook his head and worked his way around the perimeter of the room. There was a sweet, wild tune playing and a merry whirl of dancers in the middle of the hall, but it was hard to bring them into focus. They were half corporeal, half shimmering light, and he received an impression of jeweled coats and floating sleeves, with fire-fly sparks where eyes and fingertips should have been. There were long tables set back against the wall, heaped with glowing food, and these seemed more solid, as did the somber, plainly clad servants standing behind them. The only other beings that Sigismund could see clearly were the Margravine and Flor, seated side by side in golden chairs, on a dais above the dancing.

He drew further back into shadow, watching their golden heads bent close in talk, then drifted toward them through the layers of his dream. He was deeply curious, but also afraid that the Margravine might look up and see his dream persona. Sigismund did not want to think what would happen then. The Margravine, however, did not look up; she kept her eyes fixed on Flor.

"It was a pity," she was saying, "that he killed the boar. I was enjoying the havoc that it caused, and it could have proved useful later."

Flor bowed his head. "The servant intervened and the prince took the chance that the melee offered him. Forgive me if I have failed you in this, Grandmother."

A white finger tapped on the chair arm, close to his hand, and the blue jewel on it glittered like a star in the torchlight. "I was not pleased . . . but still, it drew him out, away from the palace and his protectors there, as we hoped it would. That at least was well done, grandson of mine—and now he is here and the imposter in his place, so I am disposed to be lenient." She smiled, and the hand lifted, patting his cheek. "You have come to know something of this prince these past weeks. Do you think he will prove apt to our purpose, or will he test our powers of persuasion?"

Sigismund expected Flor to shrug and return a light answer, but instead he frowned. "I'm not sure. He doesn't say much, but he watches what goes on around him and you can see him weighing it all up. I think he could prove stubborn."

The Margravine lifted her wineglass, studying the contents as they shifted in the light. "The worse for him then," she said, and shrugged. "I will not let some grubby whelp, sired of the beggars this world calls kings, stand between me and my right. Nor will I tolerate those renegades who sully the very name of Faerie with their pathetic attempts to thwart my purpose." She brought the glass to her lips and drank, her lids half veiled. "I have waited," she said, "but soon, very soon now, they will regret opposing me."

Flor leaned forward, his expression avid. "Give me the word," he said, "and I will hunt them down for you, each and every one."

The Margravine smiled. "When the time is right," she

said, "you will get that word. But not now. First we must enlist this princeling in our cause."

Sigismund watched Flor scowl as the lady hummed, her long white fingers tapping out the same wild rhythm that the dancers moved to.

"Why do we need him at all?" Flor demanded. "He stains the honor of your line, just as his mother did, and I can detect little of your power in him. And he has only just begun to train with Conte Vigiani in the fencing hall, so I would have no trouble killing him. Surely doing away with him and his House would be the best course?"

The Margravine glanced at Flor beneath her lids, a sweetly sleepy look, but Sigismund thought he glimpsed something wilder and darker in her eyes. Flor must have seen it too for he drew back a little, and her smile became thinner, almost cruel.

"Oh," she said, "but he does have power all the same, a power of his own. You can see it in his eyes, if you know what to look for. Fortunately for us, his line have grown blind to what they are, which makes him a useful tool, fit for my purpose." The sweetness of her laughter tinkled out and she drained the glass, tossing it to the ground.

The glass shattered as Sigismund took a step away, and one of the servants standing against the wall raised her head, staring straight at him with Rue's face. Sigismund fled, back through the dream to the room where his body slept, but he could not break the connection to the servant

130

girl's eyes. Even as he retreated, she followed, stepping out of the hall and into his room.

"You!" Sigismund exclaimed, unsure now whether he was waking or sleeping. "What are you doing here? And who are you?"

She looked half starved, he thought, as she crossed to the table where the saddlebags lay. There was a hollow, pinched look to her face and bruises on her arms and legs. Her clothes, if possible, were even more torn and ragged than before. But her smile, as she drew out the treatise on boar hunting and showed him the herb pressed between its pages, was a little sly.

"The rue?" he asked, meeting her eyes. "Is that how you followed me here?"

She smiled, nodding, and he noticed how beautiful her eyes were, despite the dirt and the tangled hair. They were large and dark, with gold flecks in them, and they slanted in her face—a little like Balisan's, thought Sigismund, staring into them, or a faun's. There was a smile in them now, glimmering somewhere far down, like sun in water, but sadness too, like the darkness of a pool where the light never falls. Sigismund pulled his own eyes away with an effort.

She must be a faie too, he thought, one of those helping Syrica. And she must know her life is in grave danger simply by being here.

"Can you help me escape?" he asked urgently. "Is there a way out that you can show me?"

She considered him, the smile fading, before pointing: first to herself, then to his forehead and eyes, and finally at each of the four walls in turn. Sigismund stared, not understanding, and saw his own frustration mirrored in her expression as she repeated the action.

"If only you could talk," he began, but she lifted her hand, still and intent as some wild thing. There was a sound, a slithering in the walls as though something alien was moving there. Rue took a step away, her dark eyes strained as the noise grew louder. She took another step, and then a third, and disappeared. The last thing Sigismund saw was her eyes, lingering on his, and then they too vanished as an unseen force shoved him out of sleep and into tense, wide-eyed wakefulness.

The room he had been given was utterly dark; there was not even a reflected glow from the fire. It was silent too, and it occurred to Sigismund that even without windows he should be able to hear some sounds from the outside world, just as he had in the hunting lodge the previous night. He stared into the darkness but his eyes could not pierce it, and after a moment he sat up and reached for his coat. This at least was where he had left it on the foot of the bed, but he had to grope for his boots and then for the saddlebags on the table. The floor felt cold and rough beneath his feet before he pulled the boots on, despite a recollection of piled carpets, and he got a splinter in his finger from the tabletop. It had been smooth before, he thought, pulling the jag of wood out. He stretched out a hand to the wall that had been hung with velvet cloth and touched rock and bare earth.

So, thought Sigismund, not a palace after all. Or perhaps the Margravine spun an illusion so I would not realize that I had been drawn into her dungeon? It explained Flor's smile, he supposed, but not how to get out—and what had Rue meant by pointing to herself, then to his eyes and forehead and the four walls? He wondered if she had seen the walls for what they truly were, even in his dream, or whether she too had been taken in by the Margravine's illusion.

The stone beneath his hand rippled and he snatched it back, but the slithering noise had begun again. Sigismund stood as still as the darkness, listening, the saddlebags clenched hard in his other hand.

"You will need to pay the blood price for this one." The voice was a hiss on the surface, a deep rumble underneath. "He is kin, of a sort. I can smell it in him."

Sigismund strained to pinpoint the direction of the voice but was disoriented by the blackness all around. A second voice spoke, cool and disembodied, but he recognized it instantly as Flor's. "What sort of kin? He is my kinsman too, through his mother, but our line has no connection to yours."

"Distant blood," said the first voice, and Sigismund thought he detected cold humor in the tone. "You will have to pay me gold for shedding it."

133

"It may not come to that." The chill in Flor's voice had deepened, as though he too detected the humor and suspected it was directed at him. "My grandmother believes that he will make terms with us."

"Your grandmother is powerful and farsighted, and those from the world of light do not like to be trapped beneath the earth." The humor was open now. "This boy may be willing to agree to much once he sees the full extent of the darkness that surrounds him."

"Perhaps," said Flor. "But continue to keep close watch. He must not escape."

Sigismund waited, but no one else spoke, and he did not hear the slithering sound again. Who besides Flor is watching me, he wondered, and why can I hear them, even though I'm awake? And what does the Margravine want?

He was sure that he would not like any bargain she had to offer and that the Margravine would not let him leave her house unbound, no matter what he agreed to. Yet even in her own house the Margravine could not see that he was already using the power that Balisan had said was part of his inheritance—and nor could she detect his dream presence. And Flor and whatever creature he was talking to had not realized that Sigismund could hear them.

Perhaps, he decided, standing up and beginning to pace the room, I am not so powerless after all, not the pawn that the Margravine thinks me.

He turned on his heel, frowning as he remembered Rue's strange pantomime. She had been trying to tell him something, but what? Sigismund stopped, his head bent and his arms folded hard against his chest, trying to think it through. "The Margravine as good as told me that this is one of the places where Faerie and the mortal world overlap, when she said that the house I entered was Highthorn. And this room is bound by illusion—" He stopped abruptly, realizing that he was thinking aloud and that the unseen watcher might hear him.

Illusion and overlapping planes of reality—if I'm right, Sigismund thought, his eyes wide, I should be able to just walk out. He shook his head, finally guessing what Rue must have meant when she pointed to his eyes, his forehead, and then the four walls. If he could see with the mind's eye, then he could depart his prison in any direction and follow the earth's energy flow back into the mortal realm.

If, thought Sigismund, his fingers fumbling with the saddlebag strap as he tried to remember what Balisan had said about the conjunction of stars and planets with the earth. He pulled out the treatise on boar hunting and searched for the sprig of rue pressed between its pages. He let his breath out on a long sigh when he saw that it was there, just as it had been in his dream when Rue opened the book. The sprig crumbled a little between his fingers, releasing the faint dry aroma of the herb. "Rue," he breathed, scarcely more than a whisper, and a line of pale light gleamed in the darkness.

Sigismund looked into the light, watching it widen until Rue stood there, smiling through her tangle of hair. Her face lifted, just as it had in his dream of the Faerie hall, and she extended a hand to him, beckoning.

"Come." Sigismund was not sure whether he had imagined the whisper or not, but he reached out a hand to meet hers. There was no touch of fingers, no warmth, but a force tightened around his hand and drew him forward, into a wall where the substance was no longer stone, but fluid. He swam his way through and into the long, low-roofed corridor on the other side.

Substance and Shadow

here was a howl like a great wind rushing through the earth and a clangor of blowing horns. Rue fled, a pale glimmering down the corridor, and Sigismund followed. The corridor twisted and turned, with flights of stairs up and down, and sometimes Sigismund was uncertain whether he was running through rock and earth or a dark twisted wood that reached out to clutch and trip. He focused his awareness as Balisan had taught him and found it helped separate illusion from substance on either side. Mainly, however, he concentrated on staying on his feet and following Rue.

The howling was louder now, baying at their heels, and Sigismund could hear voices in it, crying and cursing after him as the walls alternately closed in, then drew back. The pursuit would catch up soon, he thought, unless Rue could get them out. He snatched a quick look back but saw nothing, just a deeper blackness pressing after them around every corner. The breath was beginning to tear in his lungs, sweat stinging his eyes, so that at first he didn't see the line that seared the air between himself and Rue. He swerved aside as it blazed bright, stumbling into the wall. By the time he pulled himself upright again, Rue had vanished and the Margravine stood before him.

The howling and the dark narrow corridor were gone. He was standing in what looked like a wooden belvedere, with fluted pillars holding up a shingled roof. Great trees pressed in close on every side, obscuring any view of moon or stars, and there were leaves and vines tangled across the floor. The Margravine stood in a nimbus of pale light that cast a soft glow around her face and body. Like clouds around the moon, thought Sigismund, awed by her beauty in spite of himself. But her face, like that of the moon, was hidden in shadow.

She extended a hand and he was drawn toward her whether he wished to go or not. It didn't help, Sigismund found, to know that magic was being used against you if you could do nothing to stop it. He gritted his teeth, thinking of the long hours spent meditating on the tower roof and how he would not give in then either. Inside him, the serpent of power uncoiled, hissing.

Sigismund stopped moving forward and regarded the

woman in front of him. She was beautiful, he thought, detached now, but he remembered his mother's death, and the boar that had killed Wat, let loose in the forest of Thorn.

"Prince Sigismund," the Margravine said, "I congratulate you. You really have been quite clever." She was smiling and her tone was sweet, but he guessed that she was far from pleased. "Someone has taught you well, it seems."

Saying nothing, Sigismund decided, was the wisest course. He was certainly not going to tell her about Rue, and he could see no point in mentioning Balisan.

The Margravine took a step closer, and he saw that her blue eyes had turned so dark they were black hollows in her face. "Clever," she repeated, still smiling, "but discourteous to abandon my hospitality when we still have business to discuss."

"I have nothing to discuss with anyone who traps and then imprisons me," Sigismund said, his voice rusted metal against her sweetness.

She widened her eyes at him, stepping forward again. "So hasty—but can you be sure of that? What if I offered you peace in your father's kingdom, an end to the wars in the south?"

Sigismund stared at her, thinking how long those wars had bled his country dry, absorbing the energy of its kings. "In exchange for what?" he asked slowly.

Her smile deepened. "So you are interested," she murmured. "I thought you might be. And the exchange I ask is such a little thing." She was watching him closely and her voice crooned on a singsong note when she spoke again. "Such a little thing."

She was very close to him now, her perfume delicate yet dizzying, and Sigismund could feel the weave of illusion and magic. He blinked hard, trying to clear his mind. "Then ask it," he said, his voice hard, and something dangerous flared in the hollowed eyes—but was as quickly gone.

"In the west, where you grew up," the Margravine said, the timbre of her voice deepening, "there is another Wood, as you know, of which many tales are told. Mystery surrounds it, and fear, the fear that led your ancestor to place it under an interdict, forbidding any of his subjects to go there."

Sigismund's stomach muscles tightened as he met her eyes briefly and then shifted his gaze away, frightened of the wild ancient darkness he saw there. Her voice whispered close to his ear, like the wind in a midnight forest. "But there is a castle at the heart of that Wood, and in it a princess lies sleeping, imprisoned by magic for a hundred years." Her voice dropped lower still, a murmur on the surface of the night. "You think me your enemy, Prince Sigismund, and my purposes evil, but my sole desire is to release the princess from her long sleep. For me, that is worth as much as the peace of your father's kingdom."

Sigismund drew a ragged breath and forced himself to step back so he could see her face through the dim light. "And where do I come into all this?" he asked, wanting to hear her answer. "What have I to do with hidden castles and magic spells?"

The Margravine smiled. "Only one of your blood can lift the interdict that your ancestor placed on the western Wood. And only a trueborn prince may break the spell that holds the princess in sleep."

Sigismund's eyes narrowed, but he thought it wisest to pretend ignorance still. "So what is this princess to you? Why does breaking the spell matter so much?"

The Margravine's eyes opened a little wider. "Why," she said softly, "I thought you knew. The princess is my goddaughter, and the spell was cast upon her by another faie who is my deadly enemy. She does not care who is harmed, so long as her plotting hurts me. By the time I found out what she intended, it was too late to save my goddaughter."

She turned her face away from Sigismund, her voice sad. "And then your forefather took my enemy's part, closing the Wood and shutting out any who might have undone the spell. Your family have persisted in their enmity ever since, attacking my human kin and those known to be my friends, while my goddaughter remains trapped. Now you, Prince Sigismund, accuse me of taking you prisoner, when you know that I would never be allowed to speak with you openly." She paused, looking at him again, and shook her golden head. "Yet you are the last of your bloodline, so what choice had I but to resort to desperate means?"

There was a buzzing in Sigismund's head, like flies caught against a summer window, and he swallowed, shaken. It could be true, he thought. What actual proof do I have, other than Syrica's word, that it is she who is the good faie and the Margravine who is evil? But then he remembered Balisan and the buzzing cleared a little. He found it impossible to believe that Balisan would lie to him. And why, if the Margravine was acting in good faith, had Flor turned into his enemy?

He hesitated, not quite able to dismiss the Margravine's plea, and she reached out her hand to him. "You would be righting a great wrong, Prince Sigismund," she said.

Sigismund frowned at her, undecided, but it was hard not to be moved by her beauty and soft-voiced appeal, or the sweetness and distress in her expression. His head felt muzzy, and his tongue was thick, his speech clumsy when he spoke. "If I do help you and lift this spell, what then? What happens to the princess when she wakes?"

The Margravine looked puzzled. "What should happen," she asked, "except that my goddaughter will be free, and there will be peace in your father's kingdom?"

"And your enemy?" asked Sigismund. "Will she just let this happen?"

The Margravine smiled. "If you are with me, she will

have little choice. But I won't let you go into the Wood unguarded, or leave my goddaughter open to her influence again." She drew the blue ring from her finger and held it out to him. "This will repel any spells that my enemy may cast. And as soon as my goddaugther wakes you must place it on her finger, so that she is protected against any more ill-wishing." The ring gleamed against the whiteness of her hand. "Take it," she said, "as a token of my good faith and evidence of our bargain."

Sigismund watched his hand reach for the ring. There was something familiar about the whole scene, as though he had experienced it before. He hesitated, thinking he saw something move in the darkness behind the Margravine's head. Could it be the wind, he wondered, playing in the tangled vines, or had he glimpsed a pale face?

"Take it, Prince Sigismund," the Margravine urged him, sweet and low, "for my goddaughter's sake."

There was someone behind her, Sigismund was sure of it now. He could make out a figure, bound about by thick cables of vine, and a pale face lifting, the dark eyes fixed on his above a gag of thorns. He stared as the face moved slowly from side to side, just as it had in his dream, warning him, warning. . . . He heard the faintest of whispers, an echo of the Margravine's voice, speaking in his dream of the Faerie hall: *I will not let some grubby whelp, sired of the beggars this world calls kings, stand between me and my right.*

Sigismund shuddered, and knocked the Margravine's hand aside.

The ring spun toward the ground in a shimmer of interrupted magic, disappearing before it reached the floor. The faint nimbus that clung to the Margravine contracted, and the shadow on either side of her grew until it had wrapped huge batwings around the belvedere. The Margravine's form frayed with it, transforming into something primeval, raw with power. Dangerous too, thought Sigismund, his throat so dry that it was difficult to swallow. There was nothing human about what confronted him now: it was ancient, elemental, and fey.

"Shall I kill him for you now, Grandmother?" asked Flor, light-voiced, from behind him.

Sigismund shifted, trying not to turn his back on the Margravine, and saw that Flor had materialized on the topmost step, with a wedge of black-clad warriors behind him. The golden youth was smiling and a sword gleamed in his hand. The warriors behind him held drawn swords as well, but theirs were of glass and razor-sharp bone rather than metal.

"Really," said the Margravine, her voice sighing around them, "I almost think you should."

The moment hung in the balance, and Sigismund's mind cleared as though a wind had blown through it. He felt a familiar shift in the balance of energy around him—and recognized what it meant a moment before the belvedere shook beneath him.

"*Jump!*" said Balisan's voice in his mind.

Sigismund jumped, vaulting over the side of the belvedere as the floor rose up and buckled in two. He just had time to think that there must be something huge coming up beneath it, before he was falling and crashing down through a tangle of dirt, tree branches, and leaves, while the wind howled behind him. He clutched frantically at the branches, trying to slow his fall, but hit the ground hard anyway—only to have it give way beneath him. He tumbled and bounced down a long slope of dirt and pebbles to sprawl flat at the bottom.

Afterward, Sigismund could not say how long he lay there, but it seemed like a long time. He knew he was breathing, but his body felt like one great, aching bruise and he hesitated to try and sit up, in case he couldn't. The wind had died away again and there was no sound of pursuit, only the silence of stone and the soft steady drip of water. Sigismund groaned and rolled onto his hands and knees, then rose, still cautiously, to his feet. There must, he thought, be light coming from somewhere, because he could make out rough-hewn walls and a low rocky roof, but the origin of the light was unclear.

There was a hole where he had fallen through the ceiling, which seemed to be made of lathe and plaster rather than rock like the rest of the cavern. A mound of dirt was piled high beneath it, and Sigismund decided that he must have hit this first and then rolled to the bottom. "This place can't be a natural cave at all," he muttered. "It must have been dug out and some of the dirt left behind. Luckily for me."

He peered up but could only see darkness through the opening in the roof. "So where's the light coming from?" Sigismund murmured, and looked around the cavern again. He realized then that he had seen drawings of places like this before, in books that described the burial places of ancient rulers and heroes. If he was right, there should be an opening on the far side of this cavern, leading to a smaller cave where the dead had been laid to rest. "But am I back on the mortal plane," he wondered aloud, "or is this place still part of the Margravine's house in some way, or somewhere else entirely?"

Sigismund extended his inner awareness and decided that there was still much here that was of the faie, although with elements of the mortal plane—and possibly others—woven through it. But who, he wondered, would lie buried in a place that was of the human world but not of it at the same time? He swallowed, his throat tightening with a mix of anticipation and fear.

The aperture between the larger and smaller caves was so tight that Sigismund had to squeeze through sideways, before stooping to fit beneath an even lower roof. But he saw that he was right about this being a burial place: there was a sarcophagus, with light streaming up from it in a single beam. The light was so clear that it was almost white, but there was a ruddy glow along the outer edge of the beam.

Sigismund approached with caution. One could never be certain what powers or talismans had been buried in the tombs of old, or how they might respond to being disturbed.

He had thought, at first sight, that the sarcophagus was made of crystal, but now he decided that it was diamond, hard and cold. There was a body sealed in its center, the traditional figure of an armored knight with hands folded in prayer. The body shone with a faint radiance, similar to the way the Margravine had glowed in the belvedere, but the beam of light was coming from a sword resting on top of the diamond tomb.

Sigismund stood very still and for a moment almost forgot to breathe. He felt dizzy, but it was not the confusing muzziness that had filled his head in the belvedere. This was amazement mixed with excitement because he had seen this sword before, when he dreamed of the storm-darkened Wood. He remembered the white gleam along the blade's edge and the blood-red stone in the pommel. He recalled the sense of power too, like holding lightning in his closed fist.

The same power crackled in the air now, and Sigismund could see the fine red and white enamelwork around the guard and the dragon that rippled down the length of the blade. He wondered who the knight was and what would happen if he took the sword for his own. It had been his in the dream, and he needed a weapon now, but he didn't want to rob the dead.

"Please," he whispered. "I need a sword badly right now, even a borrowed one." He extended his hand and grapsed the hilt. "I promise that I'll return it, if it isn't meant for me."

Shock jarred Sigismund's arm to the elbow, but the hilt felt made for his hand and he lifted the sword clear of the tomb. A quick sighting showed him that the blade was true and he turned it this way and that, assessing weight and balance. It was a superb weapon. "The work of a master," Sigismund murmured, and wondered again who the knight had been, to bear such a sword.

There was a scabbard set into the tomb beneath the blade, with a broad sword belt wound around it. The belt was plain, but the scabbard was of crimson leather with a pattern of fine gold wires and white enamel flowers across its surface—and another dragon, cunningly entwined amongst the thorns and flowers. The scabbard was as fine in its way as the craftsmanship of the sword, like the richly worked casket that houses a priceless jewel.

Sigismund buckled the sword belt on. "Thank you," he whispered to the diamond tomb.

There was no answer but the feel of the sword in his hand, no reply but the way the belt curled around his waist and the scabbard sat on his hip as though born to it. Sigismund felt sure now that he had been meant to find this sword, despite the circumstances that had led him to the tomb.

There was a soft thud from the larger cave and a

grunt, as if someone had jumped down onto the same pile of dirt that had cushioned Sigismund's fall. It was followed almost immediately by a whisper of cold air and the scrape of a sword being drawn. Sigismund crept back to the opening, peering through. The cave was filled with a chill light that showed him Flor sidestepping down the dirt mound, the black-clad faie floating at his side. They still held their bone and glass weapons ready, but unlike Flor, who remained corporeal, their forms had begun to fray. They were only half substance now, half crackling energy and shadow, like the dancers in the Faerie hall. Their eyes, as they searched the cavern, were cold licks of flame.

Flor kicked at something with his foot. "Well, he can't be far away. He was carrying these saddlebags in the belvedere."

"Perhaps we should have remained there." The voice was cold as the light that filled the cavern, but Sigismund could not tell which of the faie warriors had spoken. "It was not wise to leave while the intruder remained undefeated, and we could have caught this princeling later. No human can elude us for long on this plane."

"My grandmother will deal with the intruder." Flor kicked the saddlebags aside. "And she wants this human caught and subdued, so that she can bind him to her will."

"Dead is safer." The faie voice was little more than a whisper.

Flor shrugged. "Will you explain a dead body to my

grandmother when she wants him alive?" He grinned at the silence that greeted these words, but without mirth. "Spread out and search the cave, and look for ways out."

A way out, thought Sigismund, looking around for one as he retreated from the narrow opening. He could see no physical escape from the smaller cave and frowned, one hand on the sword's hilt as his ears strained toward the outer cavern. A shadow stirred in the corner of the room and he turned, knowing that time was running out. A voice called sharply from the main cave and the shadow became a hand, beckoning. Sigismund could make out a dim form behind it and he took a step forward, drawing the red and white sword in case of treachery.

Light blazed from the blade and the shadow figure stepped away. Sigismund followed, the light from the sword showing him a line of energy curving through stone and earth: there were nodes of power strung along it, like planets or stepping-stones. Sigismund could see the shadow ahead of him leaping from one to the other, and there was a shout from behind as he sprang to follow.

It was like being caught in a flood, with currents of light and substance streaming past, and Sigismund was swept along like a leaf. Only the nodes were solid, islands in the main channel of the river, and he could feel the sword pulling him from one to the other, following a thread of mortal earth. The shadow figure darted ahead, but with every node they passed the shadow became a little more definite, until Sigismund could make out bare feet and a ragged skirt. Rue, it seemed, had found him again.

How did she do it this time? he wondered, before a roar from behind drove everything else from his mind. He saw Rue's head turn, saw her look of horror although she made no sound, and looked back himself. He could see earth and energy streaming away behind them, with layers of substance and shadow overlapping each other. The house in Thorn forest lay on top of the Faerie hall where elemental beings with firefly eyes had danced, and he could see the cupola of the belvedere as well, overlying trees that were tossing in a great wind. But the most substantial layer was the cavern tomb they had just fled and the thickening darkness within it.

There was something enormous moving in that darkness, heaving itself out of rock and dirt to pursue them. Sigismund could make out a flat head rising on an immense sinuous neck, then plunging down again as a first, huge loop of body uncurled from the earth behind it. It was a serpent, Sigismund realized, too shocked to move, except that its scales were of rippling stone, its eyes rock. The sword in his hand blazed brighter as he tried to lift it, but his body was frozen, disconnected from his will by the serpent's stare.

A hand closed over his left wrist from behind and jerked him off balance, breaking the contact with the serpent's eye and whirling him back into the torrent of power.

Rue was no shadow this time; Sigismund could feel the warmth and substance of her grip as he regained his balance and ran. She was terrified, he could feel that too as the earth serpent roared again. The energy river began to slow and Rue's hand tugged again, pulling him forward—but the flow beneath their feet was already sluggish, the serpent gaining on them.

Rue pointed ahead, to a break that had appeared in the energy pattern. Scarlet and gold flames circled the opening, shifting into a pattern of dragons flying on the wind. Sigismund blinked but followed the pull of Rue's hand toward the opening. Moving forward was hard work now, like wading through mud, and he felt sure that at any moment the current would reverse completely, dragging them back toward their pursuer.

Sigismund pulled his wrist out of Rue's grasp and stopped, turning to face the serpent. He made himself ignore how close it was now, and the looming immensity of its stone maw. Instead he concentrated on the sword in his hand and a memory of Balisan's voice, naming the heavenly conjunctions that opened the paths between different realms of existence—except that what Sigismund intended now was to close them.

He raised the sword and felt his own power answer as he turned his face away from the serpent's mesmerizing stare and cut into the energy current between them. As he cut, Sigismund named the last of the necessary conjunctions that Balisan had taught him, the one that would normally complete an invocation of opening—only the cut he made was against the flow of power. He did not look to see what effect it had on the serpent, he just raised the sword and cut again, continuing to name the conjunction of planets and powers in their reverse order. At the fourth cut he felt the node beneath his feet shudder, and the flow of energy back toward the earth serpent began to slow. Soon it was their pursuer that was struggling, fighting to make its way through disintegrating layers of reality.

Sigismund stepped back when his reverse chant was finally completed, breathing hard and looking round for Rue, who clapped her hands before pointing again to the fiery opening. Sigismund nodded and saw that the serpent was being pushed further back now, receding into whatever dimension of earth and stone had brought it forth. He shuddered, avoiding the baleful stare, and felt the pull of the flames from Rue's opening, reaching out to engulf him.

Rue must have already gone through, for she was nowhere to be seen as he turned and stepped toward the fire. He snatched another quick glance back, in case he had missed her, and stopped short as a huge red and golden dragon soared out of the twisting streams of energy and reality. Sigismund stared, sure he must be delirious—or really dreaming now—and then the dragon and everything else disappeared as fire roared around him. He stumbled forward into a warm, tapestry-hung chamber where two men were standing on either side of a large fireplace. Their somber, weary expressions were replaced by astonishment as Sigismund burst into the room, but it was the more familiar of the two who stepped forward.

"Sigismund!" exclaimed Master Griff, while the other man frowned at his shoulder. "How on earth did you get here?"

The Dream

Sigismund stared around the room, blinking at the rich colorful tapestries and the inlay of dragons above the door. They were worked in gold and bronze metal, inset with scarlet enamel, but Sigismund could not recall seeing either these particular dragons or the room before. He guessed that he must be in the Royal Palace and he looked hard at Master Griff's companion, who was still watching him from beneath frowning brows. This man's expression was grim, with lines carved deep into the bridge of his nose and around his mouth, and there was calculation in his eyes, as though he was accustomed to weighing men and their motives. The lines went deeper than in the portraits, and there was more gray than gold in the hair and beard, but Sigismund recognized his father's face.

The King looked past him into the corner of the room. "I take it," he said, "that despite his somewhat unexpected appearance, this is my son?"

Sigismund turned and saw Balisan standing in the shadows, although he was sure that the master-at-arms had not been there when he first plunged into the room. It was a moment later again before he recognized his own saddlebags slung across Balisan's shoulder. "So it *was* your voice I heard," he said, "in the belvedere. It must have been you they meant when they talked about an intruder."

"It was," said Balisan. There was a hint of a smile in his expression. "But you didn't seem to need much help, so I collected these and followed you here." His eyes gleamed as they rested on the red and white sword, but he said nothing more, just stepped forward and dropped the saddlebags onto the table.

Sigismund looked down at the sword in his hand and remembered the court etiquette that forbade anyone to come armed into the presence of the King. Reaction to the night's events, together with the shock of coming face to face with his father so unexpectedly, was starting to set in and his hands shook a little as he sheathed the sword and then unbuckled the belt, propping the weapon against the table. He shot a quick, covert glance at his father as he did so, wondering whether he should offer to embrace him, as father to son, or bow, as prince to king. The King's forbidding expression had not changed and he made no gesture of welcome, so Sigismund chose the safest option. He bowed low.

"I apologize, Sire," he said, "both for my unexpected arrival and for bringing a sword into your presence."

The King's answering nod was curt, his eyes narrow on Sigismund's face. "So," he said, but still offered no word or gesture of welcome. His eyes flicked back to Balisan again. "Is this really Sigismund?"

"It is," said Balisan. "But he would not know that an interloper, wearing the illusion of his face, came back to us from the forest of Thorn."

"An imposter," said Sigismund, remembering what the Margravine had said to Flor in the Faerie hall. "Let me guess—Ban Valensar?"

The King nodded. "It was a strong illusion, but fortunately Balisan saw through it." He shut his mouth hard on the last word, plainly reluctant to say more, and made no move away from the fire, just continued to watch Sigismund, the frown heavy on his face. The pause extended, becoming awkward, and was filled by Master Griff.

"It helped," he said, "that we had already become suspicious. Balisan found the body of your intended fencing master, buried in the lane between the herb garden and the old palace."

Sigismund looked from one to the other. "The one who never turned up, the day I met Flor?" He whistled softly. "They went that far, having him murdered so Flor had an excuse to draw me into his circle?" He frowned at Balisan. "But you were already suspicious. Wat said so just before he died."

Sigismund didn't ask why Balisan had let him go, if that was the case, but the master-at-arms seemed to understand the unspoken question. He shrugged, a very slight movement of his shoulders.

"We agreed, did we not, that you must live in the world? I knew the Margravine would move against you sooner or later, but not how soon—or where. I could not be sure that she would use the Thorn hunt, and if I had held you back, or accompanied you myself, she would only have found another opportunity. But once I found the body in the lane, I knew that she was moving."

"Besides," said the King, his voice still harsh, "who would respect or follow a prince who never stepped outside the Royal Palace, or needed a nursemaid when he did?"

It was not, Sigismund thought, a question that required an answer. He frowned again through his weariness. "And you suspected Flor?" he said to Balisan.

All three men nodded. "Although it seemed hard to believe," said Master Griff. "The Langrafon family has an unimpeachable record."

The King's laugh was short and hard. "No one is unimpeachable," he said. "The incentive has to be right, that's all."

"And the Margravine *zu* Malvolin," said Balisan, his tone meditative, "is a skilled purveyor of incentives."

"Flor called the Margravine his grandmother," said Sigismund. The firelight was blurring before his eyes and he found it hard to stand without swaying. He tried to focus on what Master Griff was saying, which seemed to be that he knew of no link between the *zu* Malvolin and Langrafon families. Besides, Balisan added, they only had the boy's own word that he was a Langrafon, given that all his kin were in the southeast. A Langrafon scion had been expected at court and a lad had turned up with a retinue, claiming that name and place, but who would even think of asking him to prove his identity? Balisan shrugged, leaving them to draw their own conclusions.

"Unfortunately," the King said heavily, "the Valensar whelp couldn't throw much light on the matter. All he knows is that Flor Langrafon asked him to masquerade in your place, pretending it was a jest that the two of you had planned together. And Langrafon, of course, disappeared after the hunt."

Sigismund forced himself to concentrate. "But that's what I don't understand," he said, looking to Balisan. "How can you know any of this, when the hunt was only yesterday? How could you possibly have discovered Ban's deception so soon, or known to come after me?"

He caught his father's headshake from the corner of his eye, but it was Master Griff who answered, his voice quiet. "Not yesterday, Sigismund. It's been almost two years now since the hunt of Thorn and your disappearance. Balisan has been gone nearly as long, searching for you."

Sigismund put out a hand, touching the reassuring firmness of stone and wall. After a moment he slumped into a high-backed settle. "Two years?" he whispered. "How is that possible?"

Balisan sank onto his heels beside the settle, so that their eyes were level. "The house in the forest was built where the mortal realm and Faerie overlap, and you were taken into a Faerie hill. Time does not move at the same speed on both planes, which is why two years could pass here in what seemed less than a day to you. But," he added quietly, "it could equally well have been twenty years, or two hundred."

Sigismund closed his eyes. "So I was lucky then."

"No," said Balisan, "you made your own luck. You resisted the Margravine's spells and fought your way clear. The way the realms function, that would tend to make the overlap work in your favor."

"Oh," said Sigismund. His bones felt like lead and he wondered if he could sit there forever and not move. Probably not, he decided, and opened his eyes again, focusing on Master Griff. "But you don't believe in magic," he said.

The King snorted, but both the other men smiled. "After the business with Ban Valensar," the tutor answered, his smile becoming a little wry, "I found I had to rethink my views—and then your father was so good as to take me more fully into his confidence." He made a little bow toward the King.

The King's smile looked as if it did not get much use. "Only because I had to," he said in his abrupt way, "to try and prevent more rumors of a curse at work. We gave it out," he added, with a quick glance that didn't quite meet Sigismund's eyes, "that you had gone on a tour to meet those who would be your fellow monarchs one day."

"And their eligible female relatives," murmured Balisan.

Master Griff cast him a repressive look. "So meanwhile," he said, "I have been shut up in the West Castle again with Ban Valensar, who I might add has no aptitude for scholarship at all." He shook his head. "But after two years we knew it was time to formulate another plan, and so your father called me here in secret."

Sigismund was sure that he was still taking in the sense of what was being said, but their words were starting to sough around him like wind along the boundaries of the Wood. There was something missing, though, he thought, something that was being overlooked. He sat up a little straighter and peered around the room. "Where's Rue?" he said.

They all looked at him strangely. "I didn't escape on my own," he explained. "Rue showed me the way here and then went through the opening ahead of me. So why isn't she here now?"

"Who is this Rue?" the King demanded, sharp and searching, but Master Griff shook his head.

"No one else came through, Sigismund. Only you."

Sigismund looked around the room again, half expecting to find Rue gazing back at him out of the shadows, then his gaze sharpened on the dragons above the door. "I'm sure we both went through the same opening, so where could she have gone?"

Balisan shook his head. "I do not know, but there is nothing we can do to find her, now that the opening has closed." His voice was calm, his gaze still intent on Sigismund. "We need to talk more about your whole adventure, including the part played by the young man that we know as Flor Langrafon—as well as how you came by that sword. But not now. You are exhausted and need to rest."

Sigismund nodded, too tired to pursue the question of Rue. Balisan stood up and turned to the King, who said something about safety.

"He will be safe," Balisan replied. His smile was grim. "No one will come at him, waking or sleeping, except through me."

Sigismund let his eyes close and the blur wash over him. When he opened them again he was in his own room and Master Griff was there, bending over the red and white sword and sketching the detail on the scabbard. "It's very old," he murmured. "And powerful, you say?"

"To Sigismund's benefit," agreed Balisan, from beside the fire. "The use he made of it was somewhat crude . . . but convincing." Sigismund was sure the master-at-arms was smiling, but his eyelids sank down again and he did not hear Master Griff's reply.

The next time he woke, sunshine was streaming in through the casement, with a hint of rainbow where it fell across the bed. Sigismund stretched, still half asleep, then remembered that it had been late autumn, almost winter, when he went hunting in the forest of Thorn. Almost two years, he thought, and twitched as though a fly had crawled across his skin, for both the hunt and his time in the Faerie hill were still yesterday for him. He flung an arm across his eyes, trying not to dwell on Flor's false friendship and subsequent betrayal, but he could almost taste the bitterness, sharp as bile in his mouth.

I did not see behind *his* mask, he thought, so how will I dare trust anyone again?

But then he remembered Wat, who had died to save him. The memory was still raw, and Sigismund found it almost impossible to comprehend that for everyone else it was now an old story.

And what about Annie, he thought, sitting up. There had been no formal betrothal between Wat and Annie, not even an official understanding, but Sigismund had seen them walking out together in the summer evenings. She would know of Wat's death, of course she would if Master Griff had been hidden away in the West Castle, but still—

"I must write to her," Sigismund said, and turned to rummage in the cabinet beside the bed.

Someone, Balisan he supposed, had put his saddlebags

there, still spattered with mud from the hunt. Sigismund's hand hovered, and then he was fumbling with the buckles, clumsy in his haste to find the treatise on boar hunting. It was still there, he saw with relief, and turned to the page where the sprig of rue had been, but all that remained was a few crumbled fragments.

Sigismund touched them with a gentle fingertip while his mind flashed to his first meeting with Rue, standing amidst a swirl of brown leaves in the autumn garden. Perhaps if he went there now and plucked a fresh sprig, it would bring her forth again. I hope so, thought Sigismund. He didn't want to think about what it might mean if she didn't appear. But it was only when he was pulling on his tunic that it occurred to him to wonder who had placed the herb inside the book in the first place. It was Balisan who had given the treatise to him, but Master Griff who had gotten it from the palace library— but that was before the tutor had come to rethink his views on magic.

"Besides," Sigismund said aloud, "even I didn't know about the connection between Rue and the herb until I was in the Margravine's power."

He stared into the mirror, thinking about those two lost years, and at first saw only what he had always seen: a square, open face with a smudge of freckles across the nose and cheekbones, rough fairish hair, and brown eyes. But the reflection had changed subtly since the last time he looked. The face was thinner, the line of the cheekbones and jaw a little more pronounced, and the arch of his eyebrows seemed stronger, more sharply defined.

Ageless, Sigismund thought with a slight shiver, not unlike the faces of the dancers in the Margravine's hall—proof, perhaps, that he was susceptible to their magic. He wondered exactly how time did move in that realm, and saw the enchanted hall again with its circle of faie dancers. And he heard the sweetness of the Margravine's voice while something wilder and darker moved in her eyes.

Sigismund's thoughts shifted to his father and he frowned at the eyes shadowed in the glass. The King hadn't seemed at all glad to see him, even after Balisan assured him that Sigismund was not an imposter. Is this how it is at every royal court, Sigismund wondered, or is it something particular about him? Or is it me?

He couldn't help hoping for a change in his father's manner, but the King remained distant when they met later that day, his attention focused on the implications of Sigismund's recent adventures. "I want to know everything about the part played by the Langrafon boy," he said, "and to understand more about the lineage and history of that sword. We need to know whether you stumbled on it by chance or if it was placed in your way—and if so, whether for good or ill."

They were in the King's private study, which was the room with the flight of dragons above the door. His father was standing by the window with his hands clasped behind his back, staring out into the sunlit afternoon. They had been going over every detail of Sigismund's encounter with the Margravine, from the time he realized that he had become separated from the rest of the hunt until the moment he burst through into the King's study. It was Balisan who asked most of the questions, patient as a hound casting for scent, while the King listened and frowned, and Master Griff scratched notes onto parchment.

The tutor looked up, however, at mention of the sword. "My research suggests that some of these weapons can be double-edged, for weal or woe or both. But the design on the scabbard is distinctive, so I should be able to find out more."

"There are dragons on the blade as well," Sigismund pointed out, his eyes going to the flight above the door. "And they are the symbol of our House."

Master Griff steepled his fingertips together. "True, but so far I have found no mention of such a sword in your family history. And I understand that the dragon symbol is favored in other lands, especially as one travels further east. Nor," he added, with a slight smile, "should we discount the possibility that the swordsmith drew on the old tales you enjoy so much—Arthur, Sigurd, and the like— simply to decorate his work."

"Master Griff may be right," said Balisan, checking Sigismund with a look. "Let him complete his research before we read too much into the dragons on the blade. As for this Rue of yours—"

Sigismund, out of the corner of his eye, saw his father's frown deepen.

"It is likely," Balisan continued, "that she is of the faie, but although she seems well disposed it is best to be careful. We cannot discount the possibility that the Margravine is playing a deep game."

"Web within web," agreed the King, his voice harsh, "that's her style. But whether this Rue is part of her schemes or not, faie or some human maid, I don't want you obsessing about the girl, Sigismund. If she had returned with you, then well and good—we would have thanked her in some suitable way. But you are the crown prince and I want to see you making friends with the other young people here, those of your own rank and station. And kind," he added.

Like Flor Langrafon and Ban Valensar? Sigismund wanted to ask. He pressed his lips together and said nothing, still determined to go to the herb garden as soon as the questioning and cross-questioning was over. Yet when he did finally get there and pluck a sprig of rue, nothing happened. Not even a breath of air moved to disturb the garden's peace, heavy with late-afternoon sunshine and the hum of bees.

Does this mean she's dead? Sigismund wondered, and felt cold, despite the warmth caught between the stone walls. He could hear Flor's voice, promising to hunt down all those who opposed his grandmother's will, and he felt afraid for Rue, who had put herself at risk to help him escape. Even, he thought savagely, if she is not of my rank, or station, or kind.

He chose to dream that night, deliberately defying his father and seeking a clue to Rue's whereabouts or fate. He hoped the dream would return him to the forest of Thorn and the house with the Faerie mound below it, but instead he found himself on a windswept hilltop. The green earth showed the outline of old ramparts and there were tumbledown foundations beneath the long grass. He could see a dark line of forest in the distance and the sky overhead was filled with gray hurrying clouds. The wind chilled him and his hand reached automatically for the hilt of the red and white sword, but closed on nothing.

"You must always carry it with you from now on," said Balisan's voice behind him, "even into your dreams."

The master-at-arms was standing on the crest of one of the ramparts, his hair and cloak blown sideways by the wind. He seemed sculpted out of shadow and bleached bone, and Sigismund shivered, remembering the warriors who had stood beside Flor in the Faerie hill. "Did you follow me here, or bring me?" he demanded. "And where is this place anyway? What happened here?"

"You did," said Balisan, jumping down from the rampart and walking toward him. "Once this would have been the *zu* Malvolin castle in the west, the one called Highthorn. It was built to overlap both Faerie and the house in Thorn forest where the Margravine trapped you. But you used the sword you found there to sever the planes and this was the outcome." He smiled, and Sigismund shivered again. "Your father will want to send a punitive expedition to put down the *zu* Malvolin here, but a ruin is all that they will find."

Sigismund stared around at the ruined hill, more shaken than he cared to admit. "You said I was gone for almost two years," he said, "but these ruins seem far older than that."

Balisan shrugged. "Time moves differently in dreams than in the waking world. But this is still your handiwork, Prince Sigismund—yours and the sword's. I thought that you should see it."

"The sword," Sigismund repeated, and shook his head. "It's one of those artifacts you told me about, isn't it? And its power is connected to mine, no matter what Master Griff says."

"Master Griff is a scholar," said Balisan, "and so finds it hard to trust in anything that is not set down in books. But you are right about the sword. It has power of its own, but it also focuses and extends the power of the one who wields it, as the Margravine has discovered to her cost."

Sigismund remembered how Balisan's eyes had gleamed when they first rested on the red and white blade. "You already know about this sword, don't you?" he said slowly. "Not just its power, but who it belonged to before?"

Balisan nodded, the gleam back in his eyes. "It is the

sword of Parsifal, the one he bore on the Grail quest. Its name is Quickthorn and you will need it when you go into the Wood."

Sigismund turned and looked at that dark, distant line of forest, remembering again how he had dreamed of the sword after his illness, before Balisan came to the West Castle. There were so many stories told about the sword of Parsifal: that it was twin to Excalibur, the sword wrought by the faie and given to Arthur; that it was a holy sword brought to the northern lands by Joseph of Arimathea; or that it was first found and drawn from a stone by Parsifal, outside the Castle Perilous. It was hard to believe that any human being could hold a blade of such power and live, let alone bring it out of Faerie and into the mortal world.

"But I have power too," he said, half to himself, and felt the dream wind touch cool fingers against his cheek. "And I'm stronger now, since I've been in the Faerie hill."

"That is what happens once you begin to use your power in earnest." Balisan rested his hand on Sigismund's shoulder. "Your talent for power is at least as great as your aptitude with a sword, but although you did every exercise I set for you, I still felt you were holding back at some level. Perhaps," he added, "because unlike swords, your power is not something you have been familiar with all your life."

"Perhaps," said Sigismund. He recalled that first moment when he knew he had been trapped and then all the events that followed. "I suppose need did drive me into it more fully," he admitted, and slid a suspicious glance at Balisan. "That wouldn't be one of the reasons you let me go off to Thorn without you, would it?"

He would not, he reflected privately, be at all surprised. Balisan kept his own counsel, but Sigismund was quite sure that he was capable of being devious.

The master-at-arms met his eyes, his expression inscrutable. "I have already told you my reasons," he said. "But you did seem to be managing on your own, once I caught up with you."

That was true, Sigismund supposed. He turned and studied the Wood again, thinking about the castle that lay at its heart and everything he knew about the hundred-year sleep. "If I am the chosen prince," he said, "then the Margravine will have to try and bring me under her power again. She won't have any choice." He frowned as he remembered her conversation with Flor. "And once she has what she wants, she'll go after everyone who's opposed her. Syrica and Rue. The sleeping princess. My father. People I care about," he added softly.

Balisan's answering tone was cool as the dream. "Then you will have to find a way to stop her."

Sigismund laughed, short and hard. "I will," he said grimly, then stopped, thinking he sounded like his father. He shook his head. "Of course, she'll try and kill me as well once I've served her purpose."

"Trying is one thing," Balisan replied calmly, "succeeding is quite another. You have already hurt her in this last encounter and now you have the sword, so the Margravine is not going to have it all her own way. And I am still here."

Yes, thought Sigismund, studying him carefully. But who or what are you? Where do you fit in? Are you of the faie as well, or some other power that moves in this world?

He supposed that his father must know, but was less sure that the King would give him the information he wanted. But a prince should know the truth, he thought, frowning again, about his friends as well as his enemies. He remembered, immediately afterward, that it was Balisan who had taught him that, but knew that he would get no answers from the master-at-arms. Balisan would expect him to work out any answers for himself.

The dream, Sigismund realized, was beginning to fade and Balisan had already gone. He expected the fading to continue into full sleep, but instead the dream shifted abruptly and for the first time in years he found himself inside the enchanted castle. He was standing in a hall that he had never seen before, with a dry fountain at its center and a drift of yellow leaves across the floor. Rose leaves, he thought, stooping to look at them, and when he straightened he saw the vines, twisting and scrambling their way through windows and along the wall. There was a stair at the end of the hall, curving upward with a cable of rose vine along the balustrade.

Sigismund walked up, following the vine until he came

to a landing where more roses had thrust their way through narrow pointed windows and were creeping down the walls. There was a door there as well, with a mosaic pattern in gold and lapis lazuli above the lintel and a thick carpet of rose leaves across the threshold. Sigismund tried to step through but was held back by an invisible barrier. The room was choked with briars, some of them as thick as his wrist and all armed with long cruel thorns, but he could just make out a bed through the tangle. There was a young woman sleeping on it, with golden hair so long that it spilled across the bed and down onto the leaf-strewn floor. It was held back from her face by a jeweled coronet and Sigismund stared, knowing that this was the most beautiful face he would ever see.

There was the slightest sound behind him, a flash of movement in the corner of his eye, and he whirled to catch a glimpse of ragged skirt and bare brown feet disappearing down the stairs. "Rue!" he cried, and sprang after her, but as is the way in dreams, he found himself stumbling out another door and into a wintry garden. There were weeds growing through the gravel paths and a small dilapidated summerhouse in the distance.

It stood, Sigismund realized, squinting at it, in the middle of a dry lake—but he was more interested in finding Rue. He called her name softly, but only the rustle of dry leaves answered him, and there was no herb to pluck and call her forth, only the ever-present rose briars.

"Rue," he called again, but the dream was fading now

in earnest. He could feel the familiar pull of his bed and the daylight world and this time they would not let him go.

"I'm glad you're still alive," he whispered, as the garden and the last of the dream slipped away. "And I won't stop looking. I'll find you, wherever you are."

Sigismund and the King

At first, Sigismund was haunted by his vision of the sleeping princess and his brief glimpse of Rue, but the urgency of the dream faded as the days passed, dissipated by events in the Royal Palace. Life with the King in residence was like stepping into the middle of a buzzing hive, with both the old and new palaces filled by what felt like a small army of courtiers, soldiers, and scribes. The center of the hive was the King's study, and Sigismund found that his opportunities to spend time with his father and get to know him better were limited. He struggled to put a name to all the new faces that came and went, and shook his head over the sheer volume of paperwork and the number of royal audiences that made up the business of being king.

He had been afraid, the morning after his dream of the ruined castle, that his sudden reappearance might give rise to fresh rumors of the royal curse, but no one seemed to doubt the story of his two-year tour of foreign courts.

"Although it is fortuitous," Master Griff said, when they next met in the King's study, "that my visit here has coincided with your return, since it will appear that we came back together."

Sigismund thought about the way magic power seemed to work and doubted that fortune played any part in his arrival at just the right moment. "But in secret? What reason would we have for that?"

The King's smile was mirthless. "We will say that your decision to return was highly confidential for reasons of state. Within a week any number of stories will be circulating without you, or I, or anyone close to us needing to say anything at all."

"But," Master Griff added, "I think we may safely rely on Wenceslas, who made the journey with me, to drop hints to anyone prepared to listen. He will suggest that we came back swiftly and without fanfare because you refused to like any of the ladies that your father had sent you to meet. So with unrest brewing in the south again, the King decided you had better make yourself useful here."

Sigismund shook his head over this duplicity but could not help smiling at the same time, thinking that Master Griff seemed to be enjoying his new role. The scheme worked too. People still whispered behind their hands and gossiped over the new list of prospective brides that the chamberlain was said to be drawing up, but at least there were no rumors about the royal curse or dark deeds in the forest of Thorn.

Any gossip around Sigismund's return, however, soon gave way to discussion of events in the southern provinces and reports that the unrest there might turn to outright rebellion again. Dispatch riders came and went and the King spent much of each day closeted with his generals. Sometimes he asked Sigismund to sit in, and these sessions were always about assessing and countering the *zu* Malvolin threat. Sigismund soon found that Balisan had been right in their dream discussion: his father was determined to put down any hint of insurrection, whether in the south or the west.

"I won't have the west go the way of the southern provinces," the King said grimly, on a day when early autumn rain was beating in grayly at the study windows. "I will take their holdings there into my own hands, or raze them to the ground if they resist." His generals murmured their agreement, one going so far as to add that the *zu* Malvolin were like cankered wood—you had to wipe them out, root and branch, before the rot spread.

Sigismund found out afterward that this particular general was a Langrafon, the younger brother of the present Count and in theory Flor's uncle. Except that he knew by then that the real Florian Langrafon, and all his retinue, had been ambushed and murdered on the way to the capital several years before, their bodies tipped into a mass grave on the edge of the forest of Thorn.

It was Balisan who uncovered this, pursuing the doubt raised in the King's study on the night of Sigismund's return. But as far as the court was concerned, the young man they knew as Flor Langrafon had remained at Thorn lodge after the boar hunt then returned south to answer an urgent summons from his family. All the Langrafons in the southeast knew was that Flor had sent word that he was coming home but never arrived. They made inquiries but no body was ever found, and in the end Flor's disappearance was put down to one of the many mishaps that could befall a young man traveling alone: brigands, a fall from a horse, or being swept away crossing a flooded river.

"Let them continue to believe that," the King said, when Balisan told them what he had discovered. "There is no need for the world to know how bold our enemy has become."

Bold indeed, Sigismund thought, remembering his own kidnapping. Not even Balisan could find out who the young man they knew as Flor really was, but the fact that he called the Margravine "grandmother" suggested that he must be one of the extensive *zu* Malvolin family. It was tempting, when faced with the real Florian Langrafon's murder, to agree that the whole *zu* Malvolin line needed to be wiped out.

The only problem with that, Sigismund reflected, is that my mother was related to the Margravine as well—and so am I. So nothing is ever simple.

He felt certain, when the reports of unrest in the south grew more frequent, that the trouble there was only a cover for the Margravine's true focus in the west of the realm. The real question was not what she would stir up in the south but when she would try and bring him beneath her power again. The uncertain situation reminded him of the times when he had trained blindfold with the sword: straining for the slightest whisper of movement, but not knowing where his opponent was or where the next attack would come from.

Restlessness drove him to seek out Balisan and train hard with Quickthorn, because then at least there was no time for thinking. There was only the thrust and counterthrust as they pressed up and down the hall, and the utter concentration required to hold his own against the master-at-arms. Sigismund had hoped this might prove easier with a mystical sword that answered to his power, but it didn't seem to make any discernible difference. He could sense the strength coiled inside the sword, but for the moment it lay quiet.

Sigismund was frustrated too by how little he could find out about Quickthorn's origins, despite spending considerable time reading through the books and scrolls that Master Griff had unearthed. There were numerous records of magical swords, as well as of heroes and ogres, faie and dragons, but few references to Quickthorn specifically or any definite connection to Parsifal.

"It's not even clear who made the sword," he complained to Master Griff, who had first been surprised, and then amused, to find him studying the records at all. "Although I like the story that it was twin to Excalibur."

"You'll notice that both swords were found in stones at different times," Master Griff replied, "depending on the story variant. But there are too many gaps in the record. It's unlikely that we'll ever know the truth of your sword's origins."

"There are a lot of variants," Sigismund agreed, "particularly around the Parsifal story. And sometimes I think it's become mixed up with the Gawain legend, with this part about the lady who is sometimes loathly and sometimes fair." He flicked over a few pages. "But I do like some of these other stories, especially the one about the princess chained in the cave as sacrifice to a dragon."

Master Griff looked taken aback. "I don't think I remember that one in particular."

"Quite a few of them do seem to be about girls being sacrificed to supernatural forces," Sigismund admitted. "Although that's not why I like this one, so you needn't look so worried," he added with a grin. "It's just that this girl doesn't sit around waiting for someone to rescue her. She distracts the dragon by telling it stories, and it enjoys them so much that eventually it lets her go. Later, the same dragon helps her defeat an invading army. It must have been one of the dragons that could talk," he said, putting the book aside and stretching. "Like in Wenceslas's stories."

"And fortunately for the princess, not particularly hungry when they first met," observed Master Griff, his tone so dry that Sigismund grinned again. Still, he couldn't resist mentioning the story to Wenceslas, the next time they were practicing archery together.

Wenceslas loosed his arrow, his expression interested. "I've never heard that tale before, but it sounds like a good one. I'd like to read it sometime."

Sigismund raised his own bow and took careful aim. "I'll ask Master Griff to lend you the book if you like." He narrowed his eyes at the target and shook his head. "Your shot beat mine. It's just a shade closer to the bull's-eye."

Wenceslas smiled, but his eyes held a faraway expression. "If I told that story," he said, "I'd make it so that eventually the princess kisses the dragon, and then it transforms into one of those dragonlords in the really old stories—you know, like the ones that spoke to the northern heroes, and to Parsifal when he was on the Grail quest."

Sigismund selected his next arrow with care. "Telling

stories I can understand, but why would the princess kiss the dragon? Especially," he added, thinking of Master Griff, "if she thought it was going to eat her? You'd think she'd want to keep as far away as possible, particularly from its mouth."

Wenceslas put another arrow into the bull's-eye. "Oh, I don't know," he said dreamily. "I'll think of a reason. But kisses are important, you know, magical *and* powerful. It's there in all the stories."

"There's no arguing with a storyteller," Sigismund murmured, but his lighter mood didn't last. The lack of real information in the books only added to his general frustration over the situation with the Margravine. He resented cooling his heels in the palace when he knew that she was out there somewhere, regrouping.

There must, he thought, be a way for me to force her hand or at least keep her off balance. It's what I would do if we were fighting with swords. I wouldn't stand around waiting for my opponent to make all the moves.

It didn't help when he found out that his father really had asked the chamberlain to prepare a list of princesses and noblewomen who might make a suitable crown princess. Sigismund protested, but his father cut him off with one of his quick abrupt gestures.

"As far as the world is concerned you're eighteen now," he said, "even if you don't feel like it because of the business in the Faerie hill. And it's traditional for the crown prince to marry once he turns eighteen, especially when he's the only heir the kingdom has."

Sigismund said nothing, but thought of the golden-haired princess in his dream and then of Rue. The princess was beautiful and that promised romance in every story Wenceslas had ever told, but Rue—despite the danger, she had found him inside the Margravine's hill and helped him to escape. She was brave, Sigismund thought, just like the princess in the old tale of the dragon, and how could any "suitable" young lady compare with that? As soon as his father left he tossed the chamberlain's list of potential brides on the fire, his disposition gray as the year outside.

Not for the first time since his return from Thorn, he was sharply aware of the gap left by Flor and his light-hearted friends. Adrian Valensar and others of that group were still in the palace but Sigismund felt no inclination to seek them out. From what he could see they were living much as they had two years before, with no idea of what had really happened after the Thorn hunt. He was amused, however, the day Adrian Valensar thanked him for taking Ban with him on his grand tour.

They had met by chance in one of the light-filled galleries in the new palace, and it was Adrian who initiated the conversation and the subject of Ban. "Our grandfather knew of his gaming debts, despite Flor Langrafon having paid them back. I think he would have disowned Ban if you hadn't taken him into your retinue. Our grandfather," Adrian said, with a wry twist to his mouth, "does not like gamblers."

"No," said Sigismund. Hearing Flor's name spoken so casually, as if he might come sauntering into the room at any moment, had hit him like a fist in the stomach. He saw the puzzlement in Adrian's gaze and tried to smile, although his face felt stiff. "I suppose you know that Ban is at the West Castle? My father felt he would benefit from training with Sir Andreas."

Adrian's puzzled expression vanished in a grin. "Of course, and our grandfather was hugely gratified by this sign of the King's favor. Ban actually wrote him a letter under Sir Andreas's seal—even his mother has never had so much as a note before." His grin faded. "But I suppose you were thinking about Flor just then. It was cursed bad news, what happened to him."

"Yes," Sigismund said, knowing that Adrian would never take the double meaning. "You must miss him here."

Adrian sighed. "It's definitely not the same without him, but we do our best."

Sigismund was not quite as diligent in avoiding Adrian and his former friends after that, and discovered new faces amongst them, young men who had served as squires with his father in the south. He soon learned too that those who had been in combat brought a new dimension to their weapons practice. As the weeks passed, he even found himself liking Adrian Valensar more. Adrian was a quieter and more thoughtful personality than Ban, and like many of the young men had been overshadowed by Flor's more flamboyant style. Sigismund began to see that he was well intentioned, but was still surprised when Adrian sought him out on the anniversary of the Thorn hunt.

Sigismund was alone in the gallery above the palace herb garden, watching rain and autumn leaves spatter against the windows. It was a day for thinking of lost friends, like Rue and Wat and even, in a twisted way, Flor. He heard someone come in, but didn't turn his head until Adrian stood beside him.

"It is exactly two years today," Adrian said, "since the Thorn hunt."

Adrian had been one of those who had fallen behind, Sigismund remembered, and come up just after the end. "Yes," he said, neither encouraging nor discouraging. He was wondering what Adrian wanted.

"Things happened so quickly after that," Adrian said. "You were gone, and Flor and Ban. But I always intended to say, when the time seemed right, that I was sorry for the death of your huntsman. I am not sure I could have acted with his courage, or yours, if I had been in either of your places."

Sigismund traced the lead between the panes and watched the rain splash into the garden below. "Thank you," he said, when he was sure his voice would be steady.

"There's something else I've always wanted you to know," Adrian said after a moment. "Flor was my friend and in most ways I admired him. But in Valensar we still hold to the old ways and do not hang or mutilate our people for taking game from the forest."

"Even when the forest belongs to the Crown?" Sigismund asked, remembering that brief conversation from two years before. He half thought Adrian might back away from this question, but the other's eyes continued to meet his.

"We do not encourage poaching," Adrian said quietly, "but in lean years, when the harvest fails, taking game may be the only thing that stands between the poorest people and starvation."

Sigismund nodded, because Master Griff had already taught him this, but he was pleased to learn that not all his companions were as unfeeling toward the common people as he had once thought. Perhaps that too had been Flor's influence at work, overshadowing those around him so that they hesitated to express a contrary view.

If so, thought Sigismund, then their reticence was unhelpful, since it gave me a false impression of who and what they were. He was certainly revising his opinion of Adrian Valensar, even if his ability to trust would never be the same as before Flor's betrayal. Wat and Rue had both proved that there were those who did and would keep faith, but he would always be more reserved from now on, a little less willing to accept friendship at face value.

And then word came that the southern provinces had flared into revolt again.

"You will ride with me," his father said. They were in his study and the table and floor were littered with all the maps and lists needed to get the royal armies into the field. "I'm not waiting for the spring. I'm going to take the rebels by surprise with a winter campaign and put the *zu* Malvolin in the south down, once and for all."

Sigismund looked at his harsh expression, and then away. "That's what she wants, of course," he said. "The Margravine, I mean. She wants us distracted in the south while she moves to achieve her ends in the west."

His father frowned. "You may be right, but there are still three years left until the spell reaches its hundredth year and can be undone. And the faie has no power base in the west anymore, now that her castle there has been destroyed."

"She may rebuild one while we are tied up in the south," Sigismund pointed out. "You should send me there to make sure that doesn't happen. I know the country and I know what the Margravine is after."

"Other than you?" his father inquired heavily. He had been leaning over his desk but now he straightened, his mouth a grim line. "If you are right, I would be sending you straight into her arms again. And I doubt there is much you could do there that Sir Andreas, as steward, cannot do equally well. Besides, you are the crown prince and my only son. This time I want you safe under my eye."

"But the danger in the west is real," Sigismund persisted, "and we can't afford to ignore it."

The King rolled up a map with a snap. "I am not ignoring the west or this old business of the Wood. We will deal with it in three years, which all our information suggests is the only right time, and with an army if that's what it takes to cut our way through." He held up a hand as Sigismund tried to speak again. "No arguments. You ride south with me and that's final."

Sigismund was tempted to demand how many years his father had been fighting in the south without success, or to simply storm out in exasperation. But even in their short time together, he had already learned that it was futile to argue once his father had made up his mind.

Yet if only, he thought, frustrated, we could deal with the Wood and the Margravine's ambitions there, I'm sure the situation in the southern provinces would resolve itself.

But he also knew that his father still thought of him as a boy, dreaming of Parsifal and high deeds of errantry, deeds the King saw as misguided in the modern world. Conflicts, in the King's view, were decided by the best-equipped and best-organized army, not by a single hero with a sword. It would be difficult, if not impossible, to persuade him otherwise.

Sigismund lay in bed that night, his arms behind his head, and thought about that long-ago day when he had stood on the very edge of the Wood. He remembered the listening quiet and how not even the wind had stirred beneath the canopy. The place had been heavy with magic, and he could not even begin to imagine what would happen to an army that tried to march its way through.

As for the Margravine, thought Sigismund, staring into the night, I have to either take her by surprise or anger her enough that she starts making mistakes.

There must, he reasoned, pursuing this line of thought, be some way around the hundred-year limitation on the spell, so that the Margravine isn't just sitting there at the appointed time and place, waiting for me. He frowned, trying to recall exactly what Balisan had said that night on the tower when he spoke of Sigismund's faie inheritance—that the flow of magic was two-way, that was it. And Syrica had said that no magic was entirely certain once a spell was set in motion.

"So if I am the chosen prince and therefore part of the spell, then perhaps I can influence the magic as well as be influenced by it—including changing the time when the spell can be lifted." Sigismund sat up in bed, unfolding the possibility out loud. "I should be able to go into the Wood *now* and shape the magic there to my will." He locked his arms around his knees. "And it's already very close to the hundredth year of the spell. That should help."

It was a course, Sigismund decided, that he had to attempt, even though it would be difficult without his father's support. In fact, the only reason he could think of for holding back was because to act meant deliberately disobeying his father.

We're only just starting to get to know each other again, Sigismund thought. If I disobey him now, it might damage our relationship beyond repair.

But what, he wondered, was the alternative? His father had been locked into the conflict in the south for so long that he couldn't see what was clear to Sigismund, which was that it was a symptom rather than the cause of their problems. And I must deal with the cause, Sigismund thought, no matter how much it angers or disappoints my father—especially as failure to do so is likely to result in his death as well as my own.

He sighed deeply, still not happy, but spent some time after that thinking of ways and means of returning to the west. He would have to go in secret, which meant acting alone, since anyone who helped him would have to face his father's anger as well as the Margravine's enmity. Besides, if no one else knew what he planned, then he could not be betrayed.

The best time to slip away, Sigismund decided, would be on the eve of his father's departure for the south, when there would be so much happening that his absence might not be noticed for some time. His plan was to head north first, disguising himself as a servant riding a common hack, and hope that the first pursuit would head west, searching for a prince on a fine horse. He would only turn west later, when the initial hunt had died down.

Sigismund knew that the likelihood of being found and brought back was high. But I'm still going to try, he thought. I'm done with dancing to the Margravine *zu* Malvolin's tune.

This spirit of resolve stayed with him over the next few weeks as he gathered together the things he would need, and was with him still as he crept out of the palace on the final night. His father was still closeted in his study, going over plans and supplies, and the palace was so full of soldiers and the noblemen who had answered the King's summons that no one paid any attention to one more servant, cloaked and hooded against the autumn cold. Sigismund picked up the saddlebags and travel roll that he had hidden earlier in the day and slipped into the stable where the palace hacks were kept. These were horses that could be used by anyone with a commission, or a servant with an errand to run.

It was dark between the stalls and Sigismund could smell horses and hay and oiled leather. The horse he had chosen was a strong bay, just ugly enough to discourage theft, but without being distinctive. It turned its head as he entered, ears flicking back and then forward again in doubt, but it stayed quiet as he drew on the bridle and settled the saddle on its back.

"Going somewhere?" asked Balisan, out of the darkness, and Sigismund jumped with shock. He said nothing until his heart calmed, letting his hands continue with the business of tightening and buckling the girth. "North—and then west," he said finally, turning his head toward the deeper shadows. "But I expect you've already guessed that, since you knew to be here."

"Your father told me what you said to him. And I know you." Balisan stepped out of the shadows and Sigismund's hands closed on the saddle.

"I'm not going to let you stop me," he said. "I'm going whether you and my father like it or not."

Balisan stopped at the entrance to the stall. "What makes you think I want to stop you?" he asked mildly.

Sigismund opened his mouth, then closed it. "I thought—well, you serve my father, don't you?"

"Do I?" Balisan's tone, like his shadowed expression, was enigmatic.

"Don't you?" Sigismund echoed, uncertain.

Balisan moved into the stall and Sigismund caught the gleam of his eyes across the horse's back. "I am pledged to guide and teach you," the master-at-arms said softly. "And since I believe that you are right in this case and your father wrong, I feel at liberty to honor that pledge by helping you."

"Oh," said Sigismund. He had not sought Balisan's approval or assistance, but his spirits felt lighter all the same. "So how are you planning to do that? It won't stop the hue-and-cry if we're both missing."

The bronze eyes shone like jewels, and the smile was back in Balisan's voice. "But we won't be missing. I thought we should put Ban Valensar to good use, since he's still wearing the illusion of your face."

The horse must have felt Sigismund's surprise because it shifted uneasily, tossing up its head. "Easy," said Sigismund, soothing it automatically. "Easy, boy. I thought that must have worn off long ago," he added, once the horse was quiet again. "Besides, isn't he in the West Castle?"

"The Margravine's magic is enduring," Balisan said. "And at first we needed to preserve the likeness for our own purposes, as you know. Once Ban was safely in the west there was no pressing need to lift it, especially while we were unsure when you would return and whether we would need to perpetuate his masquerade. More recently—" Balisan's shadow shrugged against the wall.

"You foresaw this, didn't you?" Sigismund said, shaking his head. "How soon did you send for Ban?"

"Soon enough," said Balisan, "to serve our purpose

now. He will ride south with me tomorrow, so as far as the world is concerned we will both be where we ought to be. And you are free to ride west tonight."

Sigismund shook his head again but had to admit that it was a clever plan. "How did you get Ban to agree to this?" he asked after a moment. "Why would he risk the King's anger a second time?"

"Let us say," Balisan replied, "that Ban Valensar hopes to redeem former errors and earn a place in your service, and I have persuaded him that it is worth enduring the King's displeasure in the short term. As for your father, I will tell him in due course, when it is too late for him to turn back or thwart your plans."

"He'll be furious," said Sigismund, thinking that was probably an understatement. "Aren't you afraid of what he might do?"

"No," said Balisan. "He will be angry," he added, as though sensing Sigismund's doubt, "but he has known from the beginning that I serve you, not him. He will not harm me, Sigismund."

Will not, Sigismund wondered, eyeing him across the horse's back, or cannot? "What about Ban?" he asked quietly.

Balisan's eyebrows flared. "Do you really think your father is the kind of man who would harm Ban Valensar for something he knows to be my responsibility? He is not vindictive, Sigismund, or even unreasonable. It is just that this long conflict in the south and his fear for you are clouding his judgment at present."

Sigismund was silent, sensing the truth in what Balisan said and knowing the ruse with Ban would give him a far greater chance of reaching the Wood undetected. He was grateful, although more than a little bit sorry for Ban, caught between Balisan and the King. "If we win through," he said, thinking out loud, "I really shall have to take Ban into my service. He will have more than earned it by then."

"It should not be too great a hardship," said Balisan. "The boy means well, even if he is not very bright."

Sigismund grinned, because it was an apt description of the Ban he remembered. But thinking of Ban meant that memories of Flor were never far behind, and that brought him back to the Margravine and all that lay ahead. For a moment Sigismund felt very much alone, but then his hand closed on Quickthorn's hilt and he felt the rising tide of adventure.

I've always known, he thought, that it's the chosen prince alone who must lift the spell. This is my quest. It always has been.

There was a burst of laughter and shouting from behind the stable and Sigismund's head turned. "I'd better go," he said, and Balisan nodded. Neither spoke as Sigismund led the bay horse out, and he half expected the yard to be empty when he paused at the gate and looked back. At first nothing moved, but then a deeper shadow stirred in the darkness cast by the stable door, and the night lantern caught the outline of a hand raised in farewell.

"Good-bye," Sigismund whispered, but there was no answer, just the echo of his horse's hooves as they passed beneath the gate and into the night.

The Road West

The Wood was bright with spring by the time Sigismund saw it again. There was a high pass where the road gave a fine view of the western provinces, all fading into the green mist of the forest. It was empty country, with vast stretches of wild land between scattered patchworks of farm and field, but the pass was too far east for Sigismund to make out the squat gray towers of the West Castle, even when he shaded his eyes against the spring sun.

His journey west had been slow, with winter blowing in hard in a series of snowstorms that blocked the road for weeks. Even when the weather cleared, the melting snow and backlog of travelers quickly turned the road into a quagmire, slowing progress even further. Sigismund found that it was a very different matter traveling the road as a serving man on a common hack, rather than as a prince for whom all the world gave way. He became used to being passed in a shower of mud and curses by young noblemen, and pushed into the ditch by merchant caravans anxious to reach home before the winter storms swirled in again.

The delays caused by the weather meant that every inn was full to overflowing with frustrated travelers, tempers were volatile, and rooms in short supply. Sigismund soon learned to count himself lucky if he could sleep in a stable or beside a forge fire, and he spent three days crowded into a drafty woodshed with his horse, waiting until the worst of the snowstorms blew itself out.

The inns where he did manage to find accommodation were frequently small and mean, little better than alehouses set at the crossroads between major towns. But whether the lodging was large or small, isolated or standing on a busy market square, the talk was always the same. Travelers reported an increase in outlaw bands, brought down from the hills by the severity of the winter, and there were darker tales too, of fell beasts and night creatures that lived on blood and human souls. Some said that the winter was behind this incursion, while others maintained that it was because the bulk of the fighting men had been drawn away to serve in the King's war in the south. The consensus was that it was only safe to travel the road in numbers, and it was this that led Sigismund to sign on with the horse copers.

He had seen them first in a town not far from the capital, two men who made their living traveling the countryside, buying and trading horses. He met up with them again after his three days spent sheltering in the woodshed, in a small walled town where the main road turned west. Sigismund was wet, cold, and hungry, and the horse copers were frowning over the stories of outlaws and night beasts. It was agreed, in the way that happens over beer and hot food, that they would take on extra men before the road became wilder and more isolated, and Sigismund was quick to put himself forward.

Martin and Bror, as the horse copers were called, were both middle-aged men and spoke with a recognizable northern burr. They had, they told Sigismund over a second beer to seal their bargain, spent most of their lives traveling the kingdom's circuit of horse fairs and markets. Although mainly taking on men for security, Martin made it clear that anyone who joined their party would be helping feed and groom their string of horses, as well as keeping them together on the road and clear of other travelers.

"Fair enough," said Sigismund. He took another long swallow of the beer. "I can mend harness as well, if you need help with that, and I know how to shoe a horse if I have to."

"Do ye now?" said Martin. "Well, that's handy to know, although we mostly do our own shoeing, Bror and I. You stick with the grooming and feeding for now, and we'll see how we go with the rest."

"Weather's clearing," said Bror, who had finished his beer first and gone to check the sky outside. He came back in on a gust of bitter air. "We'll be on the road again tomorrow, I reckon."

Another two men had joined their company before the night was out, and Sigismund guessed that they must be brothers, or at least close kin. They were both lean and ragged, with the red hair and blue eyes common in the western reaches of the kingdom, and said that their names were Fulk and Rafe. In the days that followed they would never quite meet Sigismund's gaze directly, looking away whenever he spoke to them. He suspected that they might easily turn cutthroat if opportunity arose and he wished that it was customary for serving men to carry swords. The only weapon he carried openly was his servant's dagger; and Quickthorn was trussed into a bundle on the bay horse's back. Martin and Bror had bows and staves, which made Sigismund feel a little safer, but he took to sleeping lightly all the same.

In the end they made it through the wild country without incident, although a flooded river and swept-away bridge held up their journey for several more weeks. The snow was melting in earnest by then and everyone agreed that it was spring. The milder weather meant more travelers on the road and news from the capital caught up with them as the snow disappeared. There was a great deal of rumor about the war in the south, although most stories agreed that the King had moved fast in the autumn, crossing the Vara river by night and occupying Varana citadel while the rebels were still recovering from their surprise. Prince Sigismund, it was said, was with the King, news that seemed to please most hearers.

"Here's to the Young Dragon!" one man shouted, in a wayside alehouse. "And to the honor of the west country, where we had the raising of him."

Sigismund raised his tankard with the rest; it would have been unwise not to. It was good news, he thought, that the ruse with Ban was working and that as far as the world was concerned he was still in the south. With luck, the Margravine would believe it too.

The alehouse was at the foot of the pass that led to the high saddle, and the view of the western provinces. The road dropped quickly after that and Sigismund lost sight of the Wood but was aware that it was there—like a sailor who smells salt on the breeze, long before he catches his first glimpse of ocean between coastal hills. Martin and Bror were planning a long circuit through the countryside and it would be several weeks before their route brought them close to the Wood. Sigismund contemplated leaving them and riding on alone but decided he was less conspicuous in their company. He doubted that the Margravine's agents would spare a second glance for a dirty, travel-worn groom working for an equally shabby band of horse traders. He felt certain too that there was no need to hurry. He was not yet nineteen and the Margravine would be biding her time, thinking she had three more years before he could make any move to lift the spell.

It was nearly summer before the horse copers' circuit brought them to Westwood, a half day's journey from the West Castle and just over a mile from the Wood. The town was small, but the mayor had ordered a riding horse from the capital and Martin and Bror thought that more business might be done there. They would stay a few days and then turn east again. Fulk and Rafe planned to continue further on, and the copers asked what Sigismund intended. He would be welcome to stay, they said, given that he knew horses and looked after them well.

Sigismund shook his head, unsure of his best course. He longed to go to the West Castle but suspected that it would be better to head straight into the Wood, making his departure from the horse copers as unobtrusive as possible. He was mulling over these thoughts, and a beer, in the dark reek of the local alehouse when Fulk and Rafe ducked in. Sigismund sighed inwardly, knowing that appearances would demand that they sat with him.

"Sleepy place," commented Fulk, when he had taken his first long draft of ale, and Rafe nodded. He rarely spoke, leaving any talking to Fulk. "'Cept for the knockin' down of some castle near here. Last year, that was."

"Magic," said Rafe, his eyes glancing off Sigismund and sliding toward the low door.

"So folk here say." Fulk took another deep swallow from his tankard, then wiped his mouth reflectively. "All they say, in fact. It's prob'ly the only thing that's happened here in a hundred years."

"What castle?" asked Sigismund, knowing what was expected of him, although he already knew the answer. The Margravine herself had told him that her castle of Highthorn was located near Westwood.

The upshot of the conversation was that they would ride out and see it the next day. Rafe and Fulk were fascinated by the prospect of a castle that had been brought down by magical energy, and it would have been unusual, Sigismund suspected, if he showed no interest in what was clearly a local phenomenon.

It was strange, he found, to look at a wreckage that was raw and new, with jagged walls and broken roofs gaping to the sky, rather than the ancient ruin that Balisan had shown him in his dream. The moat, where the Margravine had once told him that swans floated, was choked with fallen debris and the first weeds were springing up out of the scarred earth. If there had been swans, they were long gone, and it was hard to accept that he and Quickthorn had been responsible for so much destruction.

Sigismund shivered, but not just because of dark memories and the sight of the ruin before him. A cold wind had sprung up, and what had been a bright, sunny day quickly became overcast as clouds boiled up fast out of the east. They turned their horses into the gale, trying to return to Westwood, but the wind howled, blowing rain and then hail into their faces. The horses were forced backward, and then sideways, until they turned their tails to the stinging blast. Lightning slashed the sky as the full force of the storm struck. Thunder boomed overhead and the hail became torrential rain, plunging the day into darkness.

Sigismund could see his horse's neck and ears, but Fulk and Rafe had disappeared and the wind snatched his voice away when he called to them. He didn't see the Wood until he was in it, his horse stumbling and crashing its way through thick undergrowth and the canopy closing overhead. It shut out the worst of the wind and rain, but not the heavy crash of thunder or the lightning, which turned the understory blue-white. Every strike made Sigismund's horse shy and quiver with fear, then plunge deeper into the Wood.

The storm was driving them and for a while all they could do was run before it, helpless as a rudderless ship, until the wind's ferocity began to lessen. The thunder and lightning came at less frequent intervals and the rain stopped, but there was still no sun, just a deep twilight beneath the trees. Sigismund peered around, looking for a path or any clue to his location, but there was nothing except tree trunks in every direction and a tangle of undergrowth so thick that even the horse would find it difficult to force a way through.

Lost, thought Sigismund, and sodden to the skin!

He shook his head, aware that this was no ordinary storm, and wondered what had triggered it: whether the Margravine had become aware of his presence once he came to her fallen castle, or whether it was an automatic defense against any intrusion into the ruin. Either way, he could not see his danger lessening now that he had crossed into the forest, and there was a shrill note in the wind that made him uneasy.

The bay horse plodded on and the gloom beneath the trees began to thicken, heralding night. The whine in the wind had intensified, becoming urgent, and Sigismund thought he heard the faint distant winding of a hunting horn. It reminded him of the forest of Thorn, which was hardly reassuring, and he wished he had brought the bundle with Quickthorn in it, rather than leaving it at the inn.

The horse stopped with a snort and Sigismund blinked, then blinked again when the wall of blackness in front of him did not shift or fade away. It really was a wall, he realized after a moment, but one that stirred and whispered to itself as though alive. A hedge, he decided, straining his eyes to make out details through the thick dusk, but one that was high and thick as a castle wall. He stretched out a hand, then snatched it back, cursing. A thorn had pierced him through the leather of his glove. "A hedge of thorns," he muttered, and then, realizing: "*The* hedge of thorns. This must be the heart of the Wood."

He began to ride slowly round it, looking for a way in, but the ground was so thick with briars that it was difficult to move without being caught fast or slashed to ribbons by the long, vicious thorns.

If only I had Quickthorn, Sigismund thought again, I'm sure I could cut my way through. He cursed himself for leaving the sword behind, aware that the wind was strengthening and there were other noises in the darkness around him. He could hear a slithering from the under-growth as though some creature moved there, dragging it-self on its belly, and a beating like great wings in the trees overhead. He saw the white roll of his horse's eyes, the flare of its nostrils as it sidled, wanting to run—and the sound of horns was louder now, a rising clamor.

Lightning flashed, cracking the sky open, and a throng of ghostly horsemen poured through. They hovered above the treetops, twisting in and out of shape, and the eyes of both horses and riders flickered with the same lurid glow as the lightning. They reminded Sigismund of the dancers in the Margravine's hall, except that their appearance was wilder, fiercer, and he could see the glint of spear tips and the curve of bows. They cried out to each other in high cold voices as Sigismund stared up, and several of them put horns to their lips and blew. Then the whole hunt turned as one and swooped, a ribbon of fire and darkness hurtling toward him, down through the trees.

Sigismund's horse turned tail and ran, a headlong flight away from the thorn hedge with the faie hunt baying at its heels. An arrow hissed past Sigismund's ear and he crouched low against the bay's neck as it twisted and dodged, hoping that its maddened rush would save them both. But a quick glance back at the trail of light streaking after them, curving first one way and then another to avoid every obstacle, was not encouraging.

Another arrow zipped past him like a hornet. Sigismund wondered if these were followers of the Margravine, called up to defend her interest in the Wood, or another group of faie altogether, who only saw humans as prey. Either way, it seemed that hunting humans must be different from going to war against them, since the wild band behind him showed no signs of wanting anything but the kill. Sigismund could hear the exultation in their alien cries and the wild horns blowing as they gained on him with frightening speed. The bay must have heard them too, for its muscles bunched, gathering for a last frantic effort as Sigismund strove to clear his mind and tap into the power of earth and air around him, drawing it into a protective shield.

Something rose up out of the darkness ahead of them, a

black and jagged bar blocking their way. In the split second that it took Sigismund to realize that he was looking at a fallen tree, the bay horse had lifted itself in a wild leap. For a moment he thought they were going to make it, but the bay was no hunter, trained to jump. Its back legs caught the fallen trunk and it pitched forward, crashing down onto nose and knees, and threw Sigismund into the unyielding blackness of the forest floor.

Syrica

It was a dream, thought Sigismund, all a dream: the sickening plow into the ground and the crushing pain in his shoulder and arm. What else could it be but a dream when the trunk of the nearest tree yawned open and a hand reached out, hauling him inside? He heard the click as the trunk closed again behind him, and felt cold dry earth and the roughness of tree roots beneath the pain that was his body.

The strangest dream, he thought, as a hand rolled him over and a face peered down into his, a seamed and weathered face with bright blackbird eyes.

"Impatient 'ee is," husked a voice out of memory. He remembered the pipe too, the glow of bright coals in the small, flat bowl and the lazy curl of smoke. "Ye canna' stop an' think, or wait an' look afore rushin' in."

Sigismund tried to protest, but no words came out. The crone tilted her head to one side, unblinking as a bird, and a knotted hand reached out, cupping his face. Coolness flowed out of it, and a slow green peace.

"Bairn, 'ee is," the old voice said. "An' healin's what 'ee needs now—" She broke off, cackling around the pipe stem. "An' a mite more wisdom, if'n 'ee wants to find a safe way through these woods."

A dream, thought Sigismund again, drifting on that plume of smoke, but Balisan will find me. He always does.

"Dreams, is it?" Auld Hazel's tone was sly. "Is that what ye thinks? But ye be with Auld 'azel now, so don' go troublin' t' Lordly One, or worritin' 'is dreams."

The Lordly One? wondered Sigismund, and then reflected that dreams were strange by their very nature. You couldn't expect rhyme or reason to them, or things to work by the same rules as in the waking world. He thought Auld Hazel cackled again, but already the dream was changing, the trunk of the tree splitting open again behind her twisted head. There was a path there, flagged stone stretching into an infinite distance, pale with moonlight and dizzying with the scent of flowers.

Lilacs, thought Sigismund, and heaved himself up onto one elbow, biting back a cry as fire pierced the coolness left by Auld Hazel's touch.

"Hush now." The voice fell like silver through the pain and another hand clasped his. There was light, white and clear, but he couldn't see through it. Syrica's voice, he thought, and those are her lilacs, but what is she doing in my dream?

"Come to me," the silver voice said. "Don't struggle against the pain, just follow my voice with your mind."

"Thinks 'e's dreamin,' 'e does," said Auld Hazel's voice, from somewhere outside the white light. "Must 'ave fallen on 'is head, not just t' shoulder."

"Just the one step," Syrica said softly. "That's all it takes, exactly like a dream. A dream of my lilac walk and yourself lying on the bricks there, not amongst the roots of Auld Hazel's tree. Just one step, here to me."

The clasp on his hand tightened and Sigismund's fingers closed round it as he sought to focus on the lilac walk, the pattern of the bricks, and the pale shimmer of a skirt in scented moonlight. One step, he thought, just like following Rue when I was escaping from the Faerie hill.

Rue, he thought, Rue. . . . And then he wasn't lying on roots and earth anymore, but on bricks, and it wasn't Auld Hazel's face bending over him, but Syrica's, with a circle of stars like a halo around her head.

"Sigismund," she said. "That was a close-run thing." She shook her dark head and the stars danced. "But Hazel is quite right, my dear. You have been very rash."

Oh, thought Sigismund, and drifted away into a scent, not of lilacs this time but of roses: a familiar scent and comforting as sunshine on a summer's morning, with dew on the long grass and everything in the place where it ought to be. Safe, thought Sigismund drowsily, and reached out to touch the curtains of his old bed in the West Castle. There was light in the room but it wasn't sunshine, not yet, just the first hint of dawn turning night into shades of gray—and a deeper shadow standing between the bed and the drawn-back curtain.

"Who's there?" he asked, and the shadow shifted, becoming half silver, half rose, like the curtains. The hand that held the fabric back was translucent as a pressed leaf. "Rue?" he whispered, and the shadow head turned. He caught the hint of a smile as the hand reached out, tracing the curve of his injured shoulder and then the line of his sore arm, but without touching either. Rue shook her head.

"I know," said Sigismund, "it was silly to fall, even in a dream—although it was more like a nightmare. But soon I'll wake up. And when I do, I really will ride into the Wood and break that cursed enchantment."

Rue shook her head again, lifting one hand and making a sharp cutting gesture across her throat. She held his eyes, then made a gesture that took in the whole room before using both hands to indicate the floor. Sigismund stared, puzzled, as she repeated the gesture, then curled her left hand against her hip. Still holding his eyes, she brought her right fist across to the left and then drew it away again. It was almost, thought Sigismund, as if she was mimicking drawing a sword, but it was hard to think clearly through the pain in his shoulder and arm.

"I don't understand," he said, as she repeated the movement. "I wish you could talk. It would make everything so much easier—that and seeing you somewhere other than in Faerie mounds and my stranger dreams."

The bed curtain fell in a fragrant memory of pressed rose petals, and after that there was no more Rue, or anyone else for that matter. If asked, Sigismund would have said that he must have passed into a deeper sleep, but when he woke he was still in his bed in the West Castle. His shoulder ached as though someone had hit it with a battering ram, and there were salves on the bedside cabinet, and Annie dozing in a high-backed chair.

Sigismund closed his eyes, then opened them again, but the scene remained unchanged. He pinched himself, but to no avail. He was in the West Castle in his old bed, but it was the clothes of his serving man's disguise, stained and torn, that hung over the back of the chair. He stifled a groan, trying to ease his shoulder, and wondered what had happened to the bay horse and his bundle at the Westwood inn, the precious bundle with Quickthorn hidden inside it. Sigismund groaned again, and Annie sat up and said he should be resting after everything he'd been through. She shook her head when he tried to ask her questions, and gave him a draft that the apothecary had left, instead of answers.

It must have been a powerful draft, because when Sigismund woke again it was evening, with a sliver of new moon hanging in the open casement. It was Sir Andreas in the chair this time, but the first thing Sigismund took in was not the steward, but Quickthorn propped against the wall, together with the rest of his gear. He frowned, first at the sword and then at the steward. "How did that get here?" he asked. "It should be at the Westwood inn."

Sir Andreas smiled. "Two red-haired louts brought it to me this morning, after an hour banging on the park gates until someone finally let them in." His brows rose at Sigismund's expression. "You look surprised."

"I am," said Sigismund. He shook his head. "Fulk and Rafe. I thought they would have stolen anything of value, rather than bringing it here. But the last I saw of them was when the storm struck and I was driven into the Wood."

Sir Andreas's smile faded. "They did have some wild story about a storm and your being lost in the Wood," he admitted. "But the storm was over quickly for them and they were left on the forest fringe, not knowing what had happened to you." He shrugged. "They don't have an overly honest air, so it may be that they did intend to steal your possessions but changed their minds once they found the sword."

Or Quickthorn changed their minds for them, thought

Sigismund, even if they were unaware of its influence. "Did they say why?" he asked.

Sir Andreas nodded. "The sword convinced them that you were more than what you'd seemed up until then. The dragons on the scabbard and blade appear to have given your identity away."

And, thought Sigismund, they would have known from our time together with the horse copers that I am no thief. All the same, he would have expected them to leave his gear with a message, not beard the King's steward in his own castle. It just went to show how people could surprise you. "Did they want you to scour the Wood for me?" he asked.

Sir Andreas smiled again. "They did actually—were most insistent in their uncouth way—until I could reassure them you were already safe here." The smile faded as he met Sigismund's eyes. "Fortunately they took that at face value, so I didn't have to explain where we found you."

Sigismund shifted on the bed. "Not in the Wood," he said tonelessly. "It was in the garden wasn't it, by the lilac walk?"

Magic of the high kind, he thought, watching Sir Andreas nod—and I thought I was dreaming. He bit his lip, wondering whether Auld Hazel and Syrica had put themselves in danger, drawing the Margravine's attention by rescuing him. What had Syrica said? That he had been rash, that was it, and suggested that his rescue had been a close-run thing.

He blinked, focusing on Sir Andreas again. "Of course," the steward was saying, "I will have to inform your father that you're here."

"Of course," echoed Sigismund. It was what he had expected since realizing that he really was in the West Castle. He suspected too that he would not be allowed to leave until some word came back from the King.

"And you are not to get up straightaway," Sir Andreas continued. "The apothecary says you must rest awhile longer." He turned the hourglass on the table and they both watched the first sand trickle down. "Annie will bring you a meal in an hour, and the apothecary will come again in the morning—and then we shall see." His smile was encouraging. "But you look much better already. I thought we had lost you when I first saw you in the garden."

It was pleasant, Sigismund found, to doze while the hour trickled away, and then Annie came with his meal on a tray, swishing the curtains closed against the night and lighting the candles. She brought a bowl of lilacs too, their scent filling the room as she lingered, chatting while he ate. She seemed cheerful but did not giggle as much as Sigismund remembered; he supposed that was not surprising, given that they were both older now. Grown up, he thought, with a slight feeling of surprise. Annie kept her

chatter to general subjects as well, avoiding any talk of Wat and whether she had received the letter Sigismund wrote.

Keeping me at arm's length, Sigismund realized, uncertain how to breach her reserve. He watched her, trying not to frown, as she picked up the empty tray and moved toward the door.

"He saved my life, you know." His tone was more abrupt than he had intended and Annie stopped, one hand resting on the door handle.

"I know," she said. "It was in the letter you sent."

"I'm sorry," said Sigismund. "About Wat, and for taking so long to write. But you know the reasons for that."

Annie had been looking down at her hands, but now she looked up, meeting his eyes. "Yes," she said. "And we played our part, helping Master Griff keep the young lord Ban safely hidden." Her smile was a ghost of the old giggle. "The young lord didn't like it here at first, especially with all the lessons and being lonely for his friends, but I don't think he minded so much in the end." She hesitated, the smile fading. "He told me about the hunt . . . and everything that happened with the boar."

"Oh," said Sigismund. He hadn't given much thought to Ban being here, but it had been almost two years and it was a small castle. It made sense that he would have come to know everyone who lived here well. Sigismund frowned, trying to think what he wanted to say—how to

express what he truly felt. "If I could change what happened that day, I would. And what happened afterward, so that it was nearly two years before I wrote to you. But I acknowledge the debt, even if it's one that I can never repay."

Annie hesitated, her expression troubled. "I think," she said slowly, "that Wat would have been glad, not that he died, but that he saved you. He always dreamed of doing great deeds," she added, with a slight smile, "like the heroes in Wenceslas's stories. I don't think there's a debt, and I don't think he would either."

"Why not?" Sigismund asked, puzzled.

Annie's smile wavered a little in the candlelight, but her voice was firm. "Because it was Wat's choice to act as he did. You didn't compel him in any way. And if he risked his life freely, how can there be any talk of a debt?"

Sigismund bowed his head, unable to answer her, and after a moment he heard the door close. He mulled over the conversation as the candles flickered, their shadows growing first long and then short again. Wat *had* been brave, he thought, every bit as courageous as any hero in Wenceslas's stories, even if he wasn't a knight on a holy quest. He closed his eyes and saw the huntsman's gored and trampled body again, and the blood on the bo' tusks, dripping into the earth.

The image was as vivid as if he was still stan Thorn forest, and Sigismund knew that for F

would always be a debt. Anger burned too, deep and abiding, for part of that debt lay at the Margravine's door. She had made it clear, in her conversation with Flor in the Faerie hill, that she had been behind the boar's presence in the forest and that it was no normal beast. It had been too large and too fast, with a cunning and ferocity beyond even the rest of its savage kind.

"She doesn't care who dies or gets hurt," he said aloud, "so long as she gets what she wants. Even Flor will be just a pawn, to be played or swept aside."

"Yes," said Syrica's voice, cool and remote as the moonlight. "She is ruthless." But although Sigismund peered around the room there was no one there, just the scent of lilacs, heady as summer in the candlelit shadows.

The apothecary came early the next morning and clucked over the deep mottled bruising on Sigismund's shoulder and arm, but agreed that he was well enough to leave his bed. But not, the man emphasized, to ride or walk far, at least not on this first day. Sigismund got up as soon as he left and made his slow, stiff way down into the garden. The day was mild, without the fierce heat that would come later in summer, and the castle seemed full of life, with people laughing and calling out to each other over little things.

This is my true home, Sigismund thought, as he sank onto a sun-warmed bench. There was only the faintest breath of wind, riffling the lilacs, and he closed his eyes, reflecting that it was Syrica's home as well. She had dwelt at the heart of the West Castle for nearly a century now, maintaining the spells that made it a place where he could grow up in safety.

"I have doubted you in my heart," he whispered, "ever since Thorn forest. Wondered about what the Margravine said to me in the belvedere and whether you weren't the same as her in essence. Just another faie using human kingdoms and players as pawns on some greater board."

"Like a spider, sitting at the heart of my web." The whisper might have been nothing but the wind, stirring leaf and flower.

Sigismund nodded, still with his eyes closed, thinking about that. The Margravine had been so plausible, retelling the tale so that she was the wronged party, the sleeping princess's friend, rather than her enemy. Even afterward, when she sent Flor and the earth serpent after him, it had been difficult not to question whether the Margravine's ill intentions made Syrica's motives any better. Yet there was a mellow peace in the lilac garden, a kindliness that seemed part of the sunshine and warmth, that was entirely different from the mixture of wealth and shadow in the Margravine's hill.

"I do weave spells too, you know that." The breeze again, a lover's murmur in his ear.

"I know." But Sigismund was remembering the spiders' webs in the hedgerows, on the morning he left the capital for Thorn forest. He had marveled then at the delicacy of their beauty, the glitter and sparkle of the dew beading that would have outshone a queen's ransom in jewels.

"So you don't fear being trapped in my threads?"

It was important, Sigismund thought, to be honest. "I have wondered about your true motivation and that of your allies—Auld Hazel and Rue and even Balisan sometimes. But if you are a spider then you are trapped in your own web, since you are bound to this one place."

He thought for a moment that he might have offended her, for there was complete silence along the lilac walk; the sounds from the castle seemed unnaturally loud.

"I am." The silver voice was soft. "As are we all, until the larger magic unravels to its end—even the Margravine, although she would deny it." The silver shimmer could have been laughter, or a wind chime in some hidden corner. "As for allies, I crossed alone from Faerie to try and undo the Margravine's evil. But I have been fortunate in finding willing friends here, if only because many fear what will come if my opponent prevails. Auld Hazel is one such friend, and your great-grandparents also agreed to help, planting this garden and placing the interdict on the Wood."

Sigismund had opened his eyes by now and was frowning at the lilacs, but without taking in any detail of tree or blossom. "And Balisan?" he asked, finding that his throat was dry.

"Balisan's purposes are his own, in this as in all things." She paused, then added softly, "Although I seem to remember him saying that he was here for you."

Sigismund was silent for some time after that, reflecting on everything he knew of the master-at-arms. When he spoke again, to ask what she knew about Rue, there was no reply except the wind, which quickened into a little gust before fading away.

It was possible, Sigismund supposed, that Syrica didn't know who Rue was. Balisan had not known her either, or had not admitted it if he did. Rue, it seemed, was as great a mystery as the master-at-arms. Sigismund puzzled over her identity for much of the day and even spent some time in the library, looking through the older books there. But he could find no hint of any entity or power resembling Rue. The only thing of interest was a passage in a book titled *Dreams & Their Powers* that discussed the danger of shadows or sendings controlled by those who kept their identities and purposes secret.

Could Rue be a sending, Sigismund wondered, and if so, who is sending her? But she had proved his friend in the Faerie hill and he found it hard to believe that she could be someone else's tool. Despite his memory of Flor's betrayal, he still wanted to keep faith with her, even if it was unwise to be too trusting.

He was surprised, when he sent for Fulk and Rafe the next day to thank them, to find that they had no intention of leaving. They had, it seemed, decided to attach themselves to his service. Seeing the main chance and grasping it? Sigismund wondered. It was difficult to believe that these two were motivated by altruism or loyal fervor, although Fulk muttered something about service and the Young Dragon. But despite Sir Andreas's barely suppressed amusement, Sigismund could not bring himself to repudiate them. Instead, seized by inspiration, he sent them out to search for the bay horse along the forest fringe, in the faint hope that it might have survived the faie hunt—and to get them out of his way before he returned to the Wood.

He still felt that this was the right course of action, despite Syrica's belief that he had been rash. *I need to talk to her about the magic being two-way,* Sigismund thought that afternoon, as he cleaned and sharpened Quickthorn with careful precision. *The Margravine is almost certainly aware of me now that I have been in the Wood, but she may not know exactly what happened there or how much damage the fall has done me—if she knows even that much. But I need to make my next move soon, before she tries something herself.*

Which she will, he added to himself, turning Quickthorn to watch the dragons ripple and flow along either side of the blade. For the first time since he had returned from the Faerie hill, Sigismund felt the answering stir of its magic, like a tiny shiver up his arm. It seemed like confirmation, however slight, of his determination to act.

Yet resolve alone did not make a plan. Despite considerable thought, Sigismund could not see any alternative to riding into the Wood again and hoping for the best. As a strategy, it did not inspire him with confidence, and he remembered Rue's headshake when he first woke and the way she had drawn her hand across her throat. A fairly clear response to the charging headlong strategy, but she had been trying to tell him something else as well, perhaps suggest some alternative—but what?

Sigismund shook his head, thrusting the sword back into its scabbard with a small definite click. He wished again that he knew who Rue was and what hand she was playing in this game. I need to see her, he thought, and work out whatever it is that she's trying to tell me.

He plucked a sprig of rue in the garden that evening, rubbing it between his fingers as soon as he returned to his room. A shadow moved by the window and for a moment his breath caught, but then he saw the candlelight touch a coronal of flowers. "Oh," said Sigismund, and pushed the rue into his pocket. "It's you."

"Were you expecting someone else?" asked Syrica, her dark brows crooked as she watched him.

Sigismund shook his head, not wanting to raise the subject of Rue again, and Syrica drifted across the room. She paused by the bed and ran a hand down the old brocade of the curtains, as though her fingers could unravel any secrets hidden in the weave. Her frown was replaced by a slight smile. "Ah. I had forgotten these."

"Forgotten?" Sigismund echoed, and her smile deepened.

"Yes," she murmured, "forgotten. It has been a long time, after all, even for me. The spell of sleep did not take hold at once, you see. It came on the rest of the palace gradually. Some amongst the princess's attendants, who came running when she first fell, were adamant that she must be taken to a safe place and made comfortable. But they were distraught, panicked, and tore down the curtains from the princess's bed, laying one across the pallet they lifted her onto and covering her with another."

Her hand stroked the faded fabric again. "These two they thrust at me, thinking I was just another attendant, a bystander. Afterward I came straight here to speak with your great-grandparents, still with these curtains in my arms. It seemed right that something from that palace should carry on outside the Wood, but I never asked what your great-grandparents did with them."

"So these came from the enchanted palace," Sigismund said, touching the fabric himself. He was glad he had never let Annie arrange to have them replaced, and wondered if their presence might explain the clarity of his early dreams of the Wood.

Syrica gave herself a little shake, as though sloughing off memory. "It's why they smell of roses." But her voice was sad now and full of regret.

Sigismund studied her, his expression intent. "There's something," he said slowly, "that I've never really understood. I know the palace in the Wood is built on a node of great power, but why does a faie as powerful as the Margravine need it? Can't she just come and go and wreak her havoc wherever she pleases?"

Syrica went back to the window and looked out at the moon's slender crescent, rising above the castle wall. "It is the Margravine's nature to desire dominion," she replied quietly. "She longs to be free of the laws that trammel her here, especially those that prevent her from ruling openly or killing mortals who stand in her way. But to be free of these constraints she will have to be strong enough to withstand the Powers that govern Faerie. The Margravine believes that controlling the strongpoint in the Wood will give her the strength she needs, but unfortunately there is more to it than that."

She half turned to look at him again, and her voice deepened. "The worlds are changing, Sigismund, and have been for some time. The planes are drifting apart and the paths between this world and Faerie are becoming stretched, more difficult to follow; some of the weaker nodes have already begun to fragment. It may be that the worlds will come together again in some distant future, but no one knows, and the Powers have determined that it is best to minimize traffic between our two planes."

"But the Margravine won't accept that?" Sigismund asked, beginning to understand.

"Refuses to accept it," Syrica said, shaking her head. "She believes that if she can control the Wood, joining its power to hers, then she can hold the realms together. This would give her dominion here *and* continued access to the source of her power in Faerie, but—" Syrica paused, shaking her head again.

There's always a "but" to these schemes, thought Sigismund, always—and it's never good.

"What we fear," Syrica continued, "is that if the worlds are held together artificially, then the strain of the separating planes, concentrated through the node, may result in much wider damage. It is even possible that the ripple effects may become uncontrollable, destroying both this world and Faerie, and others we know nothing of."

"So why don't your Powers intervene?" Sigismund demanded. "Why don't they stop her?"

He thought Syrica smiled, but could not be sure in the shadowed light. "They sent me," she said softly. "But even the Powers are bound in terms of how they may intervene on other planes, or in our magic once it has been set in play. The Margravine has exploited this to full advantage."

Sigismund was silent, thinking about that. The scent of lilacs had grown stronger, dizzying rather than elusive, as though he stood in the middle of the lilac walk. "So I have to stop her," he said after a moment. "That's it, isn't it, part of how the spell is working itself out?"

Syrica bowed her head. "None of our magic, once cast, is ever entirely certain. And in this case there are two spells at work. My counterspell is bound into the Margravine's original working, turning it to another end, but the two magics have continued to act and interact within the one binding, increasing the element of uncertainty."

"And I'm part of the spell too," Sigismund said, coming to stand beside her at the window. "If Balisan is right and the magic is two-way, then that should give me some ability to shape it to my will and away from the Margravine's." He realized that he was frowning again and eased the expression out.

"So that is why you went into the Wood," said Syrica. "I did wonder."

"It wasn't exactly my choice, this first time," Sigismund said, and explained about the storm and how it had brought him to the hedge of thorns. It was encouraging, he supposed, that he had got that far, since it suggested that he was right—he did have influence over the spell.

"But what I don't understand," he said, "is how that faie hunt got in there if the Margravine can't? And despite what both you and Balisan have said about the law of the faie, they showed every sign of intending to kill me."

The moon was higher now, pale gold fading to bone as it climbed away from the earth. It reminded Sigismund of

Balisan's first night at the West Castle and another moon rising, half full above the garden wall. They had been waiting in the lilac walk, and soon Syrica had appeared to speak to them of the Margravine and a hundred-year spell. But it also reminded him of another conversation, earlier that same evening.

"You can't wall out what's already in," he said, before Syrica could speak. "The hunt must have been in the Wood when the spell took effect, and all this time it's kept them trapped."

Syrica nodded. "And unlike Auld Hazel, they do not belong there. From what she tells me, they are not the only ones caught in the Wood, a little like insects in magic's amber. They may not be the most dangerous either. But this particular hunt is known for its wildness, and now they are very angry." She paused, her expression troubled. "They may also be afraid of what will happen if the magic goes awry and the spell is not lifted at the end of the hundred years."

"Could that happen?" Sigismund asked, startled. "What would that mean?"

"If the chosen prince does not come, or if he fails—" Syrica sighed. "I'm not sure. The Margravine's original spell could take over. Or my spell could begin another hundred-year cycle. The hunt will fear that, and the possibility of being trapped on the mortal plane forever. Given this, I suspect they are beyond caring about the law, especially if killing a human might persuade our Powers to intervene—for at least then they would be free of the Wood."

Despite the terror of that wild chase through the forest, Sigismund could understand how the faie hunt felt. He shook his head, frowning. "So the chances are I'll meet the hunt again, or something worse, when I go back into the Wood?"

Syrica nodded. "I'm sorry," she murmured, as he let his breath out on a short sigh. "But there was no time, a century ago, to ensure an elegant solution. Farisie had already begun her working when I arrived here and I had no choice. I had to act."

They were both silent then, watching the moon. Somewhere in the night a cricket chirped, and beneath its voice Sigismund could sense peace unfurling its tendrils into every crack and cranny of the West Castle. Then his attention sharpened again. "What did you say?" he asked slowly. "Just now. You called the Margravine something, some other name?"

Syrica seemed lost in thought and for a moment he wondered if she would answer. When she did, her voice was no more than a thread, spun out of moonlight and the spring night. "Farisie. That is the name by which we know her on the other side." She moved slightly, the candlelight catching in her dark eyes. "*The* Farisie, she was called here once, before the word became general for our kind. But she likes titles, and the Margravine *zu* Malvolin is a useful mask."

Sigismund remembered the belvedere. "She said she was the princess's godmother. Is that true?"

Syrica smiled. "No," she said gently. "I am. It is one of the reasons I was sent across. As for the other—Farisie is my sister, my dark-hearted twin." She read his face and her fingertips touched his cheek. "It is an old sorrow, Sigismund. Do not let it grieve you."

She turned as if to go, but he made an abrupt movement and she stopped, her expression a question.

"A magic of twins," Sigismund said finally, struggling to come to terms with its implications. "Spell and counterspell twisted together but working in opposition. How could anyone outside of yourself and"—he hesitated—"the Margravine, hope to influence such a knot?"

Syrica considered this, her brows crooked together. "It is strong," she said at last, "but I feel you may be right in what you have argued tonight. You are part of the magic now and that will give you power over it. Action and reaction," she murmured, "ebb and flow. It is part of all magic, but especially ours—and you have power of your own. That too will affect the weave."

She paused, studying Quickthorn, which Sigismund had propped back against the wall. Her hand went out, but withdrew without touching it.

"The West Castle too stands on a strongpoint. It is

nothing to the one in the Wood, but it has concealed me from Farisie all these years. And you have this sword, the one the dragons made for Parsifal. Like you, Sigismund, it has power of its own. Use it," Syrica said, and vanished.

The Hedge of Thorns

Sigismund stared at Quickthorn, his eyes growing wide. "Dragons?" he whispered. "*Dragons* made you?"

He found it impossible to stand still and began to stride up and down the room, trying to understand what it all meant. Had Balisan known? he wondered. The master-at-arms had told him that the sword belonged to Parsifal, but would he have known who made it?

"And why," Sigismund asked aloud, "wouldn't he mention it if he did?" He paused, staring down at the sheathed sword. The dragon on the scabbard gazed back at him with the same enigmatic eye as the dragon above the fireplace of his suite in the Royal Palace. A breath of wind strayed through the open window, and Sigismund could have sworn the dragon's eye winked as the candlelight flickered. He drew a deep breath, steadying himself.

"Because I was supposed to find out for myself why the crown prince is called the Young Dragon," he said, dredging up the old memory. He began to pace again.

"That must have been what Rue meant, that gesture with her hands. She was drawing a sword. And the other part, pointing to the walls and floor—like Syrica, she was trying to remind me that this castle too stands on a place of power." Sigismund caught the blaze of his eyes as he passed the mirror, amber in the half-light thrown by the candles. He stopped, watching the eyes narrow and then flare as realization struck home. "Of course! I don't need to go into the Wood again and contend with whatever's been trapped in there. I am standing on a place of power and I have the sword." Sigismund drew another steadying breath. "I can use it to cross from one strongpoint to the other, just as Rue and I did when we escaped from the Faerie hill."

He picked up the sword and drew it, and this time the jolt of power was lightning up his arm. "So you agree, do you?" he whispered, turning the blade so that first ice and then fire glinted along its edge. Flame flickered from the dragon's jaw and burned in its eye as it caught the light.

Had dragons really made it? Sigismund wondered. Could possession of the sword, together with the dragon symbol of his House, mean that his power was connected to theirs?

He angled the blade again, remembering the dragon

that he had seen after his encounter with the earth serpent, just before he stepped back into his own world. "Is that why I could see it?" he whispered. "Because of Quickthorn, or my own power, or both?"

He went to the window and gazed into the night, wondering if it really mattered. The connection to the dragons was exciting—alright, very exciting, Sigismund amended with a half grin—but it didn't seem to have any direct bearing on the business at hand. He had the sword and the ability to use it; that was what mattered.

"And once we get there," he said, speaking as much to Quickthorn as himself, "then we'll find out whether I'm right about being able to influence the hundred-year spell—or not."

There was no reason to wait, Sigismund decided. His shoulder was already much better and he had his supplies from the road. The longer he waited, the more room he gave the Margravine to maneuver. "No," he said, buckling on the sword. "This is it. We're going tonight."

He waited until the castle was fully asleep, watching until the only lights were the night lanterns glowing above the hall and the main gate. There were guards on watch; he could hear their regular up-and-down tramp and low-voiced confirmations that all was well. Mist rose out of the damp ground and thickened as the night grew colder. Sigismund could see it lying in banks across the park as he finally drew his curtains closed, wrapped himself in a thick cloak, and let himself out of the room. He had decided to make for the topmost tower, because of its privacy and clear view of the Wood, and was confident that no one saw him as he traversed the dark silent corridors. Nothing moved and the only sound, other than the guards on their distant round, was the melancholy hoot of an owl.

The tower had a cool dusty smell, as though it had not been used at all since he and Balisan left the West Castle, but the trapdoor onto the roof opened without a creak. The mist was thinner here, the stars closer, and Sigismund could see the dark bulk of the nearby Wood, with the moon sailing westward above it. When he peered down, he could make out the sunken garden and the lilac walk, leached of color by night. The whole world was quiet, so still that he could imagine he heard the earth turning beneath his feet—but now he had to step outside that safe circle and cross the Wood.

Sigismund shivered and drew the sword, which glowed with the same pale light as the moon. He let his breath slow, attuning himself to the rhythm of the earth and the stately wheel of the stars. Quickthorn's power hummed, deepening until they became the pivot around which planes and time revolved. Sigismund stared straight ahead, eyes wide as he breathed in night and the darkness broke apart, reforming itself into the same herringbone pattern as the path through the lilac garden. This new path began at Sigismund's feet and flew, straight as an arrow through the wall of the castle and into the Wood. It cut across the tangle of magic like a sword, its hilt resting on the star-crowned tower, its tip piercing the hedge of thorns.

Sigismund lifted Quickthorn and extended it along the path of magic, one blade overlapping the other as he stepped forward into a great bending of energy and light. Substance and shadow rushed by him and he was blinded, the breath knocked out of his lungs and torn away. He felt impossibly stretched, little more than a ribbon of energy and thought extended along a rushing tunnel, spun out further and further between the place he needed to leave and the one he sought to reach. The pressure in his ears became a thunder and there was a sharp metallic taste in his mouth.

The tip of the red and white sword touched something solid and twisted. Pain lanced back up Sigismund's arm, but he tightened his grip rather than letting go. The thunder in his ears exploded and the tunnel became a wheel of spinning fragments. There was light, energy, and sound, with Sigismund spinning at the center, tumbled this way and that until he had no sense of up or down. It was all he could do to hold on to the sword: there was no more breathing, no more thinking, just a wild chaotic spiral—and then his whole body was flung down onto something solid, the last breath pushed out of his lungs.

He was still alive. That was Sigismund's first thought. The second was that he needed to breathe, and he sucked in air with a gasp. The first breath was fire, the second a little deeper, and by the third he could hear the wild pounding of his heart. He felt like he had run a race, but the surging of his blood was urgent, telling him there was no time to waste. Sigismund seized a few more ragged breaths, then opened his eyes. For a moment he thought that he was blind, then he realized it was still night and he was lying on his back, staring up into a thick canopy of trees.

When his eyes adjusted he could make out stars through the leaves, and when he tipped his head further back, he could see a sheer black wall behind him. His right arm was stretched out above his shoulder and Quickthorn was plunged hilt-deep into the wall—except that this was no wall, and Sigismund had seen it before.

"The hedge of thorns," he said, and scrambled to his feet, then swore as pain stabbed in his shoulder and arm.

Just the recent bruising, Sigismund reassured himself—and not helped by that last wild tumble. He pulled Quickthorn out of the hedge and swung his arm, rotating the shoulder joint. He didn't think there was any new damage, just the muscles protesting at more rough treatment, so he looked around. The sky through the trees seemed to be growing paler, but it was hard to be certain. Daylight would help, Sigismund decided, remembering the tangled briars and vicious thorns from his last visit, but the sense of urgency was still with him. If he was going to find a way through, he wanted to begin at once.

"But how?" he muttered, looking up at the soaring hedge. He had thought that Quickthorn might cut a way through, but now, facing the sheer size of the hedge again, he was not so sure. But it might be that there was an obvious point of entry, a gate or a place where the hedge grew thin. It had to be worth investigating, at least.

The ground here did not seem to be as thick with briars as he remembered, and the pale glow from the sword helped, picking out the worst patches. But neither the thickness nor the height of the hedge diminished, and although he circled it until the sky blushed pink, Sigismund was unable to find an opening. He stopped, studying the long, sharp thorns, and reflected that in any other forest the trees would be alive with birds by now, but not here. In this wood everything was utterly still, as though the whole world was holding its breath—and had been, he thought grimly, for nearly a hundred years.

"And I don't know about you," Sigismund said to the surrounding trees, "but I'm tired of waiting. It's time for some hack and slash." He raised Quickthorn up and cut into the hedge with a great, backhanded swing.

There was a clap like thunder and the ground shook so that Sigismund struggled to keep his balance. The rose vines in front of him curled away with a snap, and for a moment he thought they were going to whip back into his face, but instead they kept curling, rising and arching to form a tunnel though the hedge. Sigismund swallowed, be-

239

cause it was so deep, a good spear cast at least, and he could never have hacked his way through. But whether it was because of his influence acting on the spell, or some quality inherent in the sword, or both, it seemed he would be allowed to pass without challenge.

It worked, Sigismund thought, exultant. He wanted to punch the air and shout out to the sun, rising above the trees, but knew he needed to remain coolheaded. The magic was still far from undone, but even opening the hedge of thorns might be enough to lift the interdict and let the Margravine through.

Her appearance here, thought Sigismund, sobering, can only be a matter of time. He squared his shoulders and stepped into the shaded tunnel beneath the briar hedge, walking steadily through and out into sunlight and silence on its far side. He had hoped that the magic might work in his favor and the opening close again behind him, but it remained unchanged.

Not good, thought Sigismund, thinking of the faie hunt and whatever else might come out of the Wood, as well as the threat of the Margravine. I must hurry, he told himself, but found it hard to move. Everything was still and even the air appeared thick with sleep, the white towers of the palace shimmering like a mirage on the far side of the garden in which he stood. Sigismund wondered why his arm seemed so heavy, then realized that he was still holding Quickthorn, which felt as though it was made of stone. After another moment he sheathed it and stared around the garden, a puzzled frown on his face. It seemed familiar, but he couldn't remember it from any of his dreams.

It was certainly large and very formal, with manicured hedges and gravel walks, stone terraces, and trees in tubs leading up to the palace. There was an ornamental lake with a small green island at its center and a marble summerhouse reached by stepping-stones. The stones curved across the water like swans flying and the lake's blue surface was completely still, unmarred by a single ripple. Sigismund, staring hard, realized that the clouds mirrored in the water were motionless as well. He swallowed, glancing up at the unmoving sky and then as quickly away again, dizzied by the sheer scale of magic required to achieve such a thing.

"Must move," he mumbled, "find the princess, break the spell. No time to lose." But his legs felt numb as he forced himself forward and even his thoughts were slow, as though separated from each other by layers of cotton wool. Sigismund frowned, then dragged off his leather gauntlet and closed his hand around Quickthorn's hilt. There was no hum or crackle of power, but he found he could move and think clearly again.

There was another summerhouse further away, on a small wooded hill beyond the formal garden. Sigismund could see it as he climbed the terraces that led to the castle entrance, and supposed it must be part of a larger park. The whole place was a mixture of the cultivated and the wild, with the white palace floating above it like a cloud and rose vines scrambling down the steps and terraces to meet him. It was not until he stood in the palace gate, however, that Sigismund saw the full riot of briars that twisted and scrambled over the main courtyard and inner walls. They were the one thing, it seemed, that had not stood still but had thrived and grown rampant for the hundred years of the spell.

Sigismund stepped forward, picking his way across the briars and into his childhood dreams. It was all exactly the same, he thought, dizzy again—although the disorientation might not be magic this time, but simply the overwhelming perfume of the roses. Nothing moved and there was no sound, but in every room and around every corner he found people asleep. There were guards standing upright at their posts and courtiers slumped on chairs, some with sleeping hawks on their wrists or slumbering hounds at their feet. Sigismund peered into the silent courtyards where fountain water hung sparkling in midair, and stood for some time looking into the great hall where the King and Queen slept on their golden thrones. Their attendants lay sleeping around them and the birthday guests sprawled forward across the long tables.

But if this was the same as in his dreams, Sigismund thought, pulling himself away from that sad, glittering scene, then he already knew that the princess was not here, or in any of the rooms along these sleep-filled corridors. Instead he had to find the final staircase, the one that ended in shimmering impenetrable mist. Sigismund was not sure whether it was the same staircase he had climbed in his later dream, after his return from Thorn forest, but he was reasonably certain that he would find the briar-choked room at the top, with the sleeping princess inside it.

"So find one or both staircases, and then climb. It should be easy." He thought he spoke softly, but his voice echoed against the silence and a gong sounded once, discordant, as the echoes died away. It seemed distant, but Sigismund began to run anyway, fearing what it might herald. There was too much magic here, too many potential pitfalls, and he tried not to recall how the princess and her room had always stayed just out of sight in those early dreams, concealed at the top of the next stair or hidden around another corner.

I have to find her, he thought, his heart racing. I can't fail now.

There was no further sound but Sigismund could not shake the feeling of pursuit, a presence stalking behind him as he ran along corridors and up stairs, crossing through hall after empty hall. The silence became eerie, threatening as well as sleepy, and time blurred, so that he could not say how long it was before he finally stepped into another hall. There was a dry fountain at its center and a drift of leaves across the floor. Rose canes had crept in through the broken windows and down the wall, but the stair he sought was finally there. He recognized the wrought-iron balustrade, with the rose cable twisting up it, from his later dream.

Sigismund paused at the foot of the stair and peered up. It did not seem like a high tower, but it was hard to be sure when the staircase spiraled. He hesitated, listening hard, but everything remained quiet, unmoving, so he shrugged and began to climb.

It was not long before Sigismund decided that this must be the tallest tower in the palace, for the stair wound on and on, getting steeper and narrower with every landing he passed. The walls grew plainer too, shifting from paintings and tapestries to plaster, then undressed stone. The windows were high and narrow, little more than arrow slits in the walls. There was a full-length mirror on every landing, but these too became shabbier as Sigismund climbed, with ornate frames giving way to cheap gilt and then to unpolished wood. The quality of the glass deteriorated as well, so that the reflections thrown back at the world were increasingly cloudy and distorted.

Why so many mirrors? Sigismund wondered. Surely it was unusual to have a mirror on every landing, even in a palace of this grandeur?

He climbed for what felt like hours, but the staircase

showed no sign of coming to an end and finally he paused on yet another landing, staring at the inevitable mirror. The glass was mottled, with a ripple across its center, and at first it revealed nothing except a shadowy reflection of his own face, with gray stone behind his head. But as Sigismund continued to look the reflection began to break apart, fraying into an image of wind-tossed trees and a roof of curved wooden tiles.

"What—" he began, bending closer, but the trees had already boiled into clouds swirling around a tall white tower, then shifted again into a lover's knot of briars, crawling across tiles and through a door with gold and lapis lazuli above the lintel. Sigismund straightened, staring, then reached out and touched the glass, which undulated beneath his hand.

"It's the mirrors," he whispered, "not the stairs. You must get to the top by going through them, but how?" He pressed at the glass with his fingertips, watching it bubble and stir like liquid mercury. He frowned, then drew Quickthorn and touched the fluid surface with its point. Light rippled, red and white along the blade, and then the glass parted from top to bottom, creating a narrow opening.

Sigismund's mouth tightened but he turned the blade, holding the substance of the mirror to one side, and stepped into the gap. The glass pressed in on him, half fluid, half substance, and his skin crawled—but then he was through and standing on the same landing he had reached in his dream, after his return from the Faerie hill. When he looked back the mirror had gone, but there was a high, narrow door in its place, with the spiral stair twisting down to the world below. Sigismund shook his head, thinking that the magic that filled the palace was very strange, like an invisible maze designed to bewilder.

There was a door in front of him as well, with the blue and gold mosaic above the lintel and a thick carpet of rose leaves across the threshold. The rose vines twisted around and through the opening, and Sigismund already knew that they would choke the room beyond, climbing up the four posters of the bed and forming a living canopy above the sleeping princess. He also remembered that there had been an invisible barrier in his dream, preventing him from crossing the threshold. He raised Quickthorn again as he walked forward, but this time—whether because of the power in the sword or because the spell's magic was lifting—he was able to step across the drift of rose leaves and enter the room.

It took time and care to negotiate the jungle of briars between door and bed, but the sleeping princess too was as Sigismund remembered. Her long golden hair fanned out across the coverlet, spilling to the floor, and her sleeping face was perfect as a flower in its beauty. He found it hard to drag his eyes away, but knew he had to work out how to wake her.

"Or will she just wake up anyway?" Now that, thought

Sigismund, sheathing Quickthorn again, would be easier than having to shake her awake or shout in her ear. But the princess remained resolutely asleep, so in the end, feeling slightly foolish, he compromised and knelt beside the bed. "Princess," he said, taking her hand and keeping his voice level, "the spell of sleep is at an end. It is time for you to wake up."

Her hand was warm but did not stir in his, and her breast continued to rise and fall with the even breath of sleep. What next? Sigismund wondered, sitting back on his heels and looking for the slightest betraying flutter of her lashes. How do you wake someone who has been asleep for almost a hundred years?

He studied the room and the encroaching briars, thinking how they were everywhere in the sleeping palace, like the physical manifestation of the spell that had taken hold. He remembered how Rue could be summoned by plucking the herb of the same name and wondered if the magic here might work in the same way. He could at least try breaking off a rose and see what happened.

Sigismund chose the bloom that was closest to the princess's head and reached up, snapping it off. He was not sure, but he thought her eyelashes might have stirred. His other hand tightened around hers. "Princess," he said again, but this time he spoke in Balisan's tone, resonant with command. "The spell that binds you is done. By this rose that is your symbol, I bid you wake!"

And whether because of some alchemy of the rose, or

the memory of Wenceslas's voice assuring him that kisses were both magical and powerful, Sigismund leaned forward and touched her lips with his.

The briars retracted with a hiss, uncurling from the bed posters and canopy and slithering back toward the door and windows, clearing the room. Sigismund wondered if the same thing was happening all over the palace, but then the hand in his moved. The princess lifted the sweep of her golden lashes, gazing up at him with eyes that were the color of aquamarines, a shade between green and blue.

"But I was expecting a prince," she said, bewildered, "not a dragon."

Sigismund stared back at her, wondering what on earth she was talking about. He saw her eyes widen and caught a flash of movement, heard the whisper of a footfall behind him. Rue, he thought, remembering his dream, and began to turn—but something slammed into the back of his head and he slumped instead, meeting darkness.

The Belvedere

There was pain like an ax blade in the back of Sigismund's head and lights exploding behind his eyes. It was all he could do not to groan, but instead he lay perfectly still, trying to make sense of the voices and movement around him.

"So good of him to let us in," said Flor's voice, contemptuous. "What a fool! Did he really think we wouldn't know once he began lifting the spell?"

"The perversion of the Lady's death spell was clever. We would never have found our way here without this boy to lead us." It was a faie who spoke, in the light cold voice that Sigismund remembered from the Faerie hill.

"Even vermin have their uses. But now we have the princess, and my grandmother's ring is safe on her hand, so let the fools weep!" Flor's voice was a crow of triumph. "Their counterspells and chosen prince have all been in vain—my grandmother has still prevailed."

It was true, Sigismund saw, opening his eyes a crack. They must have flung him to one side after they struck him down, and he could look past a number of booted feet to where Flor stood by the door. The princess stood by Flor's side, the Margravine's ring blue against her finger. No one was holding her and her hands remained untied, but it seemed there was no need for restraint, since she was making no move to get away. She just stared straight ahead, her aquamarine eyes fixed on nothing—and seeing nothing either, or so Sigismund guessed.

They must have used the blue ring to ensorcell her, he thought, so that she has no will of her own. He felt sick to his stomach, and not just from the blow to his head. He wanted to believe that Flor must be under a spell himself, to do such a thing to another human soul, but the triumph in the golden youth's voice suggested otherwise.

Don't delude yourself, Sigismund told himself bitterly. Flor's face may be golden, but his heart is rotten.

He wanted to close his eyes again, but the blue jewel had begun to pulse on the princess's finger, like a small but brilliant star. It fascinated Sigismund, pulling his attention away from the rest of the room. It was hard to think clearly past the pain in his head, but he thought the ring was twisting the fabric of reality, sucking the room's light and energy into itself.

"We have delayed too long and now the Lady grows impatient." Sigismund was sure it was the same faie who spoke again. "We must do as instructed and bring the princess to her where she waits between the planes."

"What about him?" An ugly note crept into Flor's voice. "I want to finish him now."

"He must stay alive until the Lady's work here is done; she was adamant on that point." The faie's voice was without inflection, but it seemed to have an effect on Flor, who swore beneath his breath.

"Just as long as he can't escape. I want him here when we return."

"Without the girl," the faie replied, "he can do nothing to stop us. And the binding the Lady gave us will seal him into this room."

Flor hesitated, and this time Sigismund did close his eyes, trying to shut out the pulsating dazzle of the blue ring, but he could still see it through the darkness of his lids. He thought the pulse was faster now, the air in the room more warped, but still Flor hesitated. "Perhaps we should take his sword," he said, "just to be sure."

The faie's alarm was palpable, even to Sigismund. "Do not touch the sword!" he hissed, and there was a whisper of agreement from his companions, like a breath of cold wind through the chamber. "It is powerful and treacherous, and best shut up here lest it do us harm or interfere with the Lady's magic."

"Look to the ring!" commanded another voice, a rasp

beneath the chill tone. "It will destroy us all if we do not bring the girl to your grandmother at once."

"Alright!" snapped Flor. "But I'll leave this scum with something to remember me by!" He crossed the room as he spoke and kicked Sigismund in the side, a heavy vicious blow.

Sigismund had just enough time to force his whole body to relax, so that it stayed heavy and unresponsive as the kick landed. It was quite possibly the hardest thing he had ever done, but he needed Flor to believe that he was still unconscious. He nearly passed out in any case, from the pain and shock of the kick coming on top of the blow to his head. The darkness swam in until there was only a pinprick of consciousness behind his eyes, and when it cleared he was alone.

Sigismund lay where he was for some time, waiting until the pain from the kick subsided and staring straight ahead in much the same way as the ensorcelled princess had done. All they had to do was track me, he thought. I couldn't have made it easier for them if I'd tried. They just waited for me to lift every layer of protective magic, then seized the princess as soon as she was awake.

There was blood in Sigismund's mouth, but what he tasted was the bitterness of failure. How could I not have foreseen that happening? he wondered. And Syrica too—she must have known that was exactly what the Margravine would do. "Futile!" he whispered, and closed his eyes.

It was easy to give in and just lie there, drifting between the darkness and the pain, but something niggled, nudging at Sigismund's awareness. The lights behind his eyes coalesced until all he could see was gold, the color of sunshine and Flor's hair—the princess's too. He could see it still, spilling across the coverlet and onto the floor, and the coverlet was golden as well, with gold thread stitched into the cloth.

Sigismund's eyes flew open and he pushed himself up onto his elbows. *Gold*, he thought, trying to remember what Syrica had said to him the previous night. He frowned, because she had said so many things and his head hurt. *Something about curtains*, he thought, *and how those on his bed had been the princess's once, but her servants had removed them when the sleeping spell first took hold: They tore down the curtains from the princess's bed, laying one across the pallet they lifted her onto and covering her with another. . . .*

Sigismund raised his head and stared at the golden fabric on the bed. *Not gold*, he thought. Rose brocade with silver thread woven in, but definitely no gold. There had been no cover over the sleeping princess either, he realized, staggering to his feet. And there was no pallet in this room, just the four-poster bed. "Not here," he said aloud. "Not *her*. All—a trick."

Syrica, it seemed, had been cleverer than the Margravine anticipated.

It was amazing how his head cleared then, despite the pain and the blood in his mouth. He remembered the last mirror on the twisted stair, and his brief glimpse of some other place before the image shifted to show him the white tower and concealed chamber. There had been trees tossing and a curved roof with wooden tiles . . . or was it the tiles that were curved? Sigismund shook his head, reflecting that at least they did not have the real princess yet. And if what the faie had said was true, that meant he could still do something to thwart the Margravine's plans.

But I don't have much time, he thought. It won't be long before the Margravine realizes that she's been duped.

He felt a brief stab of pity for the substitute princess, knowing she would be unlikely to survive that realization. "So think!" he admonished himself savagely, and his hand clenched on Quickthorn's hilt.

Fire blazed against his hand, and for a split second he was no longer standing in the tower chamber, but in a wooden belvedere with trees pressing close on every side. It was night, a great wind howled, and in the darkness a pale figure stirred, gagged with thorns and bound about by cables of vine. Then the vision faded and Sigismund reeled back, one hand still fused to the sword hilt, the other flung out to retain his balance.

"Layer on layer," he gasped, "time and the planes overlapping each other at certain nodes. Strongpoints, beachheads—what a fool I've been, thinking I understood but never comprehending the truth. Until now." And then, very softly: "Rue."

He strode to the window and stared out. There were the two belvederes, the marble summerhouse on the lake and the second one further away, its wooden roof rising through green trees. And the roof, thought Sigismund, narrowing his eyes on that distant point, was curved at the eaves. But how to get there? His enemies had used a spell to seal him in, but he suspected that would prove ineffective without the real princess in their thrall.

"And I have Quickthorn," Sigismund said, still very soft, "and a sprig of rue in my pocket." He had put it there just before his last conversation with Syrica, and now he drew it out. The leaves had started to wilt, but the aromatic scent was strong as he held it to the light. "Rue," he said again, speaking in a clear, resolute tone, and crushed the herb between his fingers.

The world shivered, then shook, and Sigismund thought that the tower was falling, or perhaps it was *he* who was falling, and the clouds of plaster and dust and the voices crying out were just a dream, or someone else's memory. But the world was definitely spinning, although the masonry had become trees and branches now, the voices no more than the wind sighing. Sigismund drew a steadying breath and stepped forward, into the belvedere on its wooded hill.

The first thing he noticed was that it was very quiet. The world had righted itself again and there was no wind, just sunlight and leaf shadow speckled across the wooden floor. The second was the pallet, set in the middle of the belvedere, but it was empty except for a fall of rose brocade across it. Sigismund turned slowly, wondering, as the last of the herb slipped between his fingers and something stirred in the deeper shadows. He blinked a little, because the light seemed so bright after the tower, but decided that the movement was just another shadow. Then he blinked again and saw a silhouette against his closed lids, an outline that was still there when his eyes opened. Leaf and shadow stirred as a young woman stepped forward, her dark eyes lifting to meet his.

"Welcome, Sigismund," she said, and held out her hands to him.

He did not recognize her at first, she was so richly dressed. Her gown was velvet over silk, and there was a golden fillet around her brow, a net of jewels and gold wire lying across her hair. Sigismund thought that the hair curled, though, the brown touched here with red lights, there with gold—and there was something elusive and familiar and bewildering about that tangle of lashes, and the gold flecks glimmering in the dark eyes.

It must, Sigismund thought, be the blow to his head, because his vision had blurred again and the outline of her outstretched hands wavered, becoming brown and scratched. He could see bare brown legs now too, and feet shoved into wooden clogs below a ragged hem. Then a sparrow flew into the arched roof and clung there, chattering at him, and the world cleared. The hands held out to him became smooth, the ragged skirt was a sweep of silk again, and Sigismund realized that what he had thought was a mantle, draped over one arm, was in fact a curtain of rose brocade.

He must, Sigismund thought, seem very stupid just standing there, staring at her. After a moment her hands fell, but her smile remained warm, her voice low.

"Don't you recognize me, Sigismund?" She stepped close, lifting her hands to frame his face, and kissed him.

The touch of her lips was soft as rose petals, their taste rose water as Sigismund folded his arms around her and returned the kiss. He could feel the wing beat of her heart against the rapid hammer stroke of his own as he tightened one arm and lifted the other, tracing the fall of her hair beneath the jeweled web.

"Rue," he murmured, struck by the wonder of it, when for so long she had been little more than a shadow. She smiled and answered him with another kiss.

"I feel as though there are stars," she murmured, "shooting in my blood."

The flecks in her eyes, thought Sigismund, unable to look away from them, were like torchlight on midnight water. Deep water, he added, feeling slightly off balance, as if he might fall in. He thought that he could stand like this forever, that he would never let her go.

"And you can speak," he said, feeling the wonder of that too.

"I can now. I tried before, but the magic was too strong." Rue's tone was soft with regret, her eyes shadowed, remembering. "I could never quite break through it."

Sigismund shook his head and realized that the pain from the blow had eased. "All these years I've thought of the sleeping princess as someone remote, distant as a dream, when all the time it was you." He kissed her again, slowly, and they smiled into each other's eyes. "That *was* you, wasn't it, standing in the ditch the very first time I saw the Margravine? You did something when she tried to give me the blue ring?"

Rue nodded. "Syrica worked loopholes into her counter-spell, to give me a chance to remain aware of the world outside the magic and to work against Farisie's ambitions— if I could."

It was strange, thought Sigismund, to hear the Margravine referred to by name. It made her seem less re-mote, if not less dangerous. Rue's expression was turned in-ward, looking back at those dark days. "But we didn't know how the loopholes would work, so Syrica placed objects in the world that could act as reference points for me."

"Like these curtains," said Sigismund, touching the brocade lightly, "and the rue planted in the palace herb garden."

"Yes," said Rue. "Your great-grandmother planted that, I think, with cuttings from our garden here, and scattered the briar seeds in the ditch where you first saw me. But initially, when the spell took hold, I was completely disoriented, lost beneath the weight of enchanted sleep. It was many years before I could locate any of Syrica's reference points, let alone find my way to them, years in which Farisie had been busy building her strength. I had to be very careful that she never suspected my presence, even for a moment, or my small workings to thwart her will." She shivered, although the sunlight streaming into the belvedere was warm.

Sigismund remembered the blue ring spinning into the white dust of the road, and their flight through the Faerie hill. "What would have happened if she had suspected?"

Rue looked away, a slight frown beneath her slim brows, then she shrugged. "She could have trapped my spirit, so that I would have been hers, body and soul, as soon as I woke up. Or she could simply have extinguished me, like someone snuffing out a candle flame. But," she added, the frown easing, "I was both careful and fortunate, and she never found me out."

"And now we've won," said Sigismund, and felt joy break inside him, like a bubble. "I've undone the spell, and the Margravine has lost." He shivered, thinking that it seemed too easy after so long and bitter a contest. He could not help wondering how long it would be before the Margravine tried to seize another strongpoint, and if he and Rue would ever truly be safe. Then he frowned, re-membering Flor and the blue ring.

"They still have your friend," he said, "the young woman who slept on the bed in your place. Flor knocked me out as soon as I woke her, and then put that cursed ring on her finger." Sigismund threaded his fingers through Rue's, watching the sun dapples on her skin. "We must do something, make him let her go."

To his surprise, Rue smiled and shook her head. "She's not real, Sigismund. Do you think I would allow anyone to run such a risk, knowing Farisie's malevolence? The princess you woke is a simulacrum, woven of sunspells and daydreams and the roses that are the symbol of my House. She will dissipate before the rest of the castle wakes." Her fingers tightened around his. "The only connection be-tween us was that once you woke her, I too began to wake."

But she spoke to me, Sigismund thought, amazed at the intricacy of Syrica's working. "So when did the last knot unravel?" he asked. "Was it when I found my way here?"

Rue nodded, but her face clouded, the happiness of only a few moments before draining away. She turned to study the dreaming palace, a crease between her brows.

"But—" She pressed her fingertips against her lips, and Sigismund saw the slow dawn of fear in her expression. "That *wasn't* the last knot. It will still be some time before the others wake, just as it took longer for them to fall asleep when the spell took hold. Until they do . . ." She stopped, shaking her head.

"The magic won't be fully undone." Sigismund spoke slowly, every word falling like a weight. "So we haven't won yet."

"No," said Rue. "But the Margravine will still have to move fast." She looked around, her expression intent. "This hill is at the heart of the power that fills the Wood—that is why I was placed here when the sleep took hold. To win, Farisie will have to seize it before the last of the magic dissipates."

A wind had sprung up, cold off the surface of the lake, and the day was growing dark. Sigismund shivered, feeling the wind's chill. "Surely Syrica must have foreseen this," he said. "She must have had some kind of plan."

Rue's smile was a little crooked. "We are her plan, Sigismund, the hope on which she based her counterspell. She foresaw that the blood of the Wood and the blood of the dragon, brought together and drawing on the strongpoint here, could thwart even Farisie's power."

"The blood of the dragon," whispered Sigismund, wondering if that was simply a figurative way of referring to his House or meant a great deal more. But clouds were beginning to pile up above the towers of the palace so he forced himself to focus on more immediate concerns. "I suppose she's still bound by the law of the faie, but that didn't help you last time round."

Rue nodded. She was frowning too as she continued to watch the sky. "But things are different now," she replied, low-voiced. "Last time she still had her strongpoint at Highthorn, but you destroyed that with the sword." Her fingers found his and squeezed briefly. "And there's no time for her to try and gain control of the West Castle node, not with all the wards that guard it. So she will have to cross fully over to this side if she wishes to move against us, either that or use an agent that is part of the mortal plane."

The look that Sigismund slanted at her belonged to Balisan. He could feel the familiar lift of his brows as the first lightning crackled across the sky. "Do you really think we can withstand her?"

"An excellent question," drawled Flor's voice, out of the air, "although I'm surprised you have the wit to ask it."

Quickthorn

ightning seared again, and when the dazzle cleared Flor was standing outside the belvedere, a sword held ready in his hand. Gold light swam along its blade, turning to indigo flame at the edges, and blue fire blazed on his gloved hand. The ring again, thought Sigismund, unsurprised, as he stepped into the entrance.

Flor smiled, his blue eyes bright. "You have outlived your usefulness, Prince Sigismund," he said. "So now I have the pleasurable task of killing you."

Sigismund watched him carefully, making no move to draw Quickthorn. "Only you?" he inquired. "Do you think that will be enough?"

Flor shrugged, still smiling. "If not—" he said, and let the words hang as ten black-clad forms unfolded out of the trees, floating down behind him. Their faces were bleached bone in the lurid light, their pupil-less eyes elongated and black. Two of them held nets, Sigismund saw, while another bore a long narrow pipe on his back.

"But I think," Flor continued, "that I should be more than a match for you, Prince Sigismund. What are you, after all? Little more than a bumpkin, raised by a provincial steward."

"There was also Balisan," Sigismund pointed out quietly. "Be careful," he added over his shoulder to Rue. "This is probably a distraction of some kind."

"No," said Flor, "it isn't. My grandmother has instructed me to kill you, and as I've already assured you, and her, it's going to be a pleasure. As for your Balisan, you yourself told me that he was not one of the paladins, wherever he may come from. And I, after all, was taught my swordsmanship by the faie." He made a few cuts with his sword, making it whine against the wind. "Now are you going to continue to hide in there, or come out and fight me like a man?"

Sigismund did not allow his expression to change, knowing what Flor was trying to do. "We don't have to fight," he said calmly. "This is the Margravine's battle, not yours. And since we both seem to be related to her, that must make us cousins of some sort, which is another reason not to fight."

Flor laughed on a wild mocking note, his eyes brighter

than ever. He thinks I'm afraid of him, Sigismund realized, and that excites him. He believes he's the cat, playing with a mouse.

"Florizal *zu* Malvolin," the golden youth said, with a flourish. "At your service," he added, with a sneer that gave the lie to his words. "And second cousins, as it happens—but with no reason at all not to fight, or for me to hold back from the kill once I have you at my mercy."

"If," Rue said, speaking for the first time. Her voice was clear and very cold.

Flor turned his smile on her, his tone all silk. "My grandmother will deal with you afterward. You'll sing a different tune once you wear this jewel on your finger." He held up the blue ring, then tugged the glove from his other hand, hurling it to Sigismund's feet.

"I challenge you to meet me in single combat, Prince Sigismund, to answer for the wrongs your family has done to my grandmother and the *zu* Malvolin family. Meet me," he cried, his voice rising, "or be named a coward as well as a fool."

"Don't!" whispered Rue, standing at Sigismund's shoulder. "Farisie just wants him to draw you out and kill you."

Sigismund shook his head. "I must," he said gently. "There is no knight or prince sworn to the code of chivalry who could refuse such a challenge. You know that, and so does Flor."

Rue looked from Flor to the faie with their nets. Her

lips were compressed, her eyes bleak. "Just don't let them get you away from the entrance to the belvedere," she whispered, "or they will use those nets to trap you. And you need to be able to retreat in here if *she* comes."

Sigismund glanced at the faie. "I imagine they'll only use those if Flor can't best me outright. He wants the pleasure of the kill."

Flor too was looking around the half circle of faie behind him, a sneer twisting his golden face. "This prince is a coward. He won't even pick up my glove." He turned back to Sigismund, the sneer becoming a jeer. "Shall I help you, Prince Sigismund? If knightly honor is not enough, what about family feeling? Don't you want to avenge yourself on the person who poisoned your mother?"

For Sigismund, it was as though the day had grown very still again, despite the gathering storm. He felt his heart begin to pound as he stooped and picked up the glove. "What had you to do with my mother's death?" he asked, keeping his voice quiet.

Flor threw back his head, his laugh a crack of satisfaction. "My father and your mother were cousins, so of course my mother visited yours in the Southern Palace. She was always closely watched, but who pays attention to a child playing, or whining around his mother's chair? No one was even looking when I worked the poisoned thorn into your mother's glove."

Sigismund shut his mouth hard on the rage that surged

through him. Beneath and above it he could hear Balisan's voice, reminding him that there was no room for emotion when facing an opponent: frustration, fury, fear—all would kill him more surely than any enemy.

In his mind Sigismund stood again on the West Castle tower at midwinter, counting the numberless stars. He breathed in the snow-chilled air and felt it curl into his stomach; he released the cloud of his anger and watched it dissipate against the frosty black of the sky. Only then did he toss the glove back to Flor, smiling faintly as their eyes met. He drew Quickthorn from the dragon scabbard and walked down the belvedere steps.

Now, thought Sigismund, we shall see.

He never took his eyes off Flor for a moment. Nor did he allow himself to consider the handicap of an already injured shoulder, or the limitations imposed by having to defend the entrance to the belvedere. Instead he slipped into the familiar oneness with the red and white blade and felt its energy course into his hands. There was no light, no sound, just that fiery ripple up and through his body as he shifted on the balls of his feet and watched Flor.

He shifted again as Flor took a first step forward, feinting a thrust and trying to draw him out. Sigismund parried but refused to be drawn, watching Flor's eyes for the tiny flicker that presaged a second attack—and then red and white fire crackled, crossing blue-edged gold. The clang of the blades followed a split second later and then the fight was on in earnest, sword hammering on sword as both combatants strove for the advantage.

The first flurry of blows seemed even in skill and strength. Flor was good, very good even, but this was not fencing and Sigismund had been trained by Balisan, who was a master. He remembered Flor's temperament too, from their lessons together, his desire to finish quickly and his love of flashy moves. Sigismund's main weakness was his injury, especially since his inability to move away from the belvedere meant close-in work, slugging it out toe to toe.

Flor's faie companions were hanging back for the moment, waiting to see if their champion would prevail, but Sigismund had no doubt that they would use their nets if things went badly. They were here to serve the Margravine's interests, not play by chivalrous rules. He parried as Flor pressed in again, locking Sigismund's blade against his own and trying to push through by sheer brute force. The blue eyes snarled into Sigismund's but there was strain there too, and the first flicker of doubt as Sigismund hurled him back.

Flor hesitated, but only for a moment, before blazing in again, raining a fury of blows against Sigismund's defense and forcing him to retreat into the shadow of the belvedere. The black-clad faie rolled forward a step, then retreated as Sigismund countered, pressing Flor back in his turn—but once again, he could not advance too far and leave the access to the belvedere unprotected.

Flor smirked as he withdrew, knowing what constrained Sigismund. Sigismund registered the expression, but from a distance, parrying any attendant emotion like a blow. He settled into a grim defensive pattern, fuelling Flor's impatience and luring him into doing something rash. In the end it worked more quickly than he expected. Sigismund could almost feel the moment when Flor's patience snapped and he came charging in with a wild flurry of blows, only to cry out and reel back as Quickthorn slipped through, opening his right side from shoulder to hip.

Flor staggered further back and out of Sigismund's range, dropping his swordpoint and clutching at his wounded side. Blood streamed red through his gloved fingers and his face twisted, something ugly and dangerous snarling out of it as he turned on his followers: "Don't just stand there, fools! Rush him!"

The faie warriors, however, seemed to have their own ideas about the best approach. They spread out in a loose half circle, with both sides closing on Sigismund in a pincer movement. The two with the weighted nets shook them out as they stepped forward, and Sigismund took a step back. He could not hold off ten, and these faie looked like they knew their business. There were no wasted moves or breath; they advanced steadily and in silence, black shadows reaching out for him across the grass.

He had no choice, Sigismund thought, except to retreat into the belvedere or be entangled. He guessed that they would leave killing him to Flor, who was crouched over his wound at a safe distance, watching with a fixed, glittering stare. Sigismund moved back again and placed his rear foot on the lowest step of the belvedere. He could feel the sweat, hot on his face and body, but he realized now that the day had grown even colder while they fought, and the clouds had spread out to cover the sky.

The faie warriors paused, and now the one with the long narrow pipe unslung it and lifted it to his lips. Quickthorn thrummed, fierce in Sigismund's hand, and behind him Rue uttered a whispered cry: " 'Ware the dart! They dip them in a venom that freezes their victims."

The trees on the hill were tossing and bending now, the way they had when Sigismund confronted the Margravine in another belvedere. His eyes remained intent on the pipe as he retreated again, uncertain whether even Quickthorn could parry a blown dart. A half second later a horse crashed out of the trees and bore down on them at a gallop.

It was his bay horse, Sigismund saw, startled, the one he had thought killed by the faie hunt. Its saddle was empty, the whites of its eyes showing, and the faie warriors scattered before its wild rush. Even so, the bay veered away from the closest warrior at the last moment, turning back into the trees on the other side of the belvedere. The black-clad warriors were already regrouping when two more horses, both with riders on their backs this time, burst from the trees and thundered toward them. The riders wore breastplates and helmets, but Sigismund caught a glimpse of red hair as one of the horsemen lifted a bow and shot from the saddle.

Sigismund would have called it an impossible shot, except that the faie warrior with the blowpipe crumpled to the ground while the others ran for cover, dragging Flor with them. Sigismund stared in disbelief, recognizing Fulk and Rafe, then leapt aside himself as Fulk's horse slid to a halt in front of him. "How—" he demanded, and for a fleeting moment he was sure that a knot in a nearby tree had twisted into Auld Hazel's face, and that she winked at him.

"What—" Sigismund began again, recovering his balance. Rue reached out from behind and dragged him fully into the belvedere as Fulk and Rafe struggled to stay on their horses, which were rearing and bucking as though they had suddenly gone mad.

"There's no time," Rue said, her voice tight. Her eyes were darker than the clouded sky. "She's here."

"A meeting long overdue," said a voice Sigismund remembered from that other belvedere. It beat around them like a great wind and darkness pressed in thickly from every side. Fulk's and Rafe's horses bolted, their ears pressed back flat against their skulls and their riders clinging on desperately as they were borne away toward the palace in the distance.

Sigismund looked up and saw the Margravine floating in the air above them, her hair streaming out like a banner and billowing into the growing storm. Shadow flared on either side of her like the batwings he remembered, and the clouds rolled close, dark as nightfall with lightning at their heart. The Margravine's hair was bone-white against their darkness, and her eyes had narrowed and lengthened into feline slits; her gaze was indigo fire. The wind gusted down, whipping at Rue's hair and skirts and tearing their breath away.

"You will not keep me from what is mine," the soughing voice said, cold in their heads.

"It is not yours," Rue said clearly, projecting her voice above the howl of the wind. "You have no right or claim here, Farisie. Leave now, while you still can."

"Or you will do—what?" mocked the Margravine. "You are powerless to stand in my way."

"Not so," Rue said to Sigismund, but quietly, never taking her eyes off the hovering faie. "Otherwise we wouldn't be exchanging these pleasantries." The wind whipped a strand of hair across her face.

The Margravine floated higher into the sky, the clouds boiling and lightning flickering all around her. "She can't have many choices left," Rue whispered, but she sounded far from certain. "Not now that Flor has failed her. And surely she won't dare come against us herself?"

Sigismund glanced toward the place where Flor had found shelter, just inside the first line of trees. The blue ring had begun to pulse, and magic and the storm broke around them at the same time. Lightning leapt down and hail drove in through the open sides of the belvedere as the Margravine floated closer. The bone-white hair had fanned out around her head, wildfire crackling along every strand. Fissures appeared in the mask of her face, flickering like the lightning as her eyes widened, deepening into twin pits that opened onto a void. The wind howled back toward her, filled with dirt, leaves, and branches, as well as wooden tiles from the belvedere.

"I will not be denied!" It was hard to tell where the storm's voice ended and the faie's began. "I will have what is mine, or destroy it all!"

"We can't hold—against this—for long!" Rue shouted into the devouring wind. The faie warriors had disappeared, abandoning Flor, who was flattened into the ground at the base of a large oak, his fingers trying to dig into its roots as the tree streamed into the wind's vortex. Not much further away, a sapling was wrenched up and sucked toward the abyss that was the Margravine zu Malvolin.

Sigismund took a step forward, struggling to keep his

footing against the wind. "Yes, we can," he said. "We have the sword, and we have each other."

He raised Quickthorn, extending the red and white blade toward the faie, and let his mind and heart grow clear as the sky that follows a storm. He could feel the earth turning, and the rumble and crack of rock and fire deep beneath its crust. There was a taproot of strength that went down, far below the hill on which they stood, and then spread out, in a network of roots and fiber, across the vast expanse of the Wood. Through it, Sigismund could sense the shy presence of all the strange and wild creatures that inhabited the forest, and its cool green power flowed into him like a tide.

Rue was part of that power, and it of her. Sigismund could see it without having to look at her, and feel her power joined to his without having to ask. It twisted its way round and through the green flow like a rose vine, tenacious as the herb for which she was named. They reached out together, north and south, east and west, tapping into the layers of energy until the belvedere crackled with a power to answer the Margravine's.

Sigismund felt as though together they had encompassed the world. He had a fleeting vision of Auld Hazel, her flat-bowled pipe clamped between her teeth and its spark reflected in her blackbird eyes. A moment later the air was filled with the scent of lilacs, subtle and tranquil as moonlight falling on herringbone brick. Sigismund let the calm fill him and flow into the sword in his hands. It was living fire, answering the Margravine's lightning, and at first the bolts of power writhed and strove together, red and white against lurid indigo. But slowly, the red and white fire forced the lightning to retreat.

Calm, thought Sigismund, and the debris on the wind began to fall back toward the belvedere. The flow of power was reversing, just as it had done in the energy river between the planes. Gradually, the wind died away, and the fissures into the void closed as the Margravine coalesced back into human form. As she did so a bell rang out, sweet and clear from the white palace, to be answered by another, and then another after that, all pealing in joyful chorus. The faie hunt that had pursued Sigismund through the forest winked into view and wound their horns, then as quickly disappeared. Sigismund threw a quick, questioning glance at Rue.

"The sleepers in the palace are waking," she said, low-voiced. "Farisie has lost." But she didn't sound exultant, just kept watching the Margravine, her lower lip caught between her teeth.

Sigismund reached out his free arm and drew her close. "Surely she must accept it," he said, speaking to Rue's doubt. "The terms were bound into the spell, at least part of which came from her own magic."

"I, accept?" The Margravine's voice echoed in thunder, filling the sky. "I am *the* Farisie, not some sprite to let myself be hedged about by petty rules." There was nothing human remaining in the eyes that glared down at them.

"We held against the storm," Rue began, then stopped, looking toward the lake and the palace beyond. All color drained from her face, and her voice sank to a whisper. "But we can't hold against that."

Blood Price

igismund followed Rue's gaze, and for a moment he thought his heart had stopped, until it slammed against his chest again. The surface of the lake was boiling, reflecting the clouds overhead, and then the water parted, spinning outward as an enormous head broke through and reared skyward. The eyes that gazed down on them were stone and Sigismund looked away just in time, avoiding their mesmerizing effect. The serpent's head plunged down again as more body looped up behind, curving out of the lakebed as it had pulled itself out of rock inside the Faerie mound.

The Margravine's laughter echoed with the thunder overhead. "See, Prince Sigismund, I bring you an old friend. And this time you have nowhere to run."

"No running," said Rue, but her expression was pinched, her eyes strained. "Running won't save us, not if she gains control of the belvedere."

Sigismund tightened his grip on Quickthorn, but thought that nothing was going to save them anyway. The earth serpent was a monster, at least half as high as the palace when it reared up, and the best they could hope for was to do it some damage. The next downward plunge of that rock-eyed head was going to be right on top of them, and the huge mouth was already gaping wide.

It'll swallow us whole, by the looks of it, Sigismund thought, as the belvedere shook. The floor buckled, as though there was an earthquake directly beneath them, and both he and Rue struggled to maintain their balance while the serpent's head reared high, and higher again— then whipped back, recoiling on itself.

"What—" began Sigismund, then flung up a hand to cover his eyes as the sun rose directly in front of him, a huge flaming ball of carnelian and gold. There was light and heat and fire that burned without consuming, and then the sun exploded—or he thought it did, except that there were no flames falling from the sky, just a giant dragon hovering where the sun had been. Its scales were red and gold, with light rippling over them like water, and its wingspan was immense, filling the sky. The Margravine had already retreated, dark cloud and lightning pulled in tight around her, but the dragon was watching the serpent, its eyes flame.

"I've seen this dragon before," Sigismund said, finding it hard to breathe. "Just for a moment, the last time we met the earth serpent."

Rue's hand found his. "It's going to speak," she whispered.

The dragon's voice filled their minds and the air around them, much as the Margravine's had done except that it was deeper, and with a curious sibilance that came, Sigismund realized, from breathing fire. "Go back, Brother of Earth," it said. "This is no battle of yours." The flames roared, red gold as the sun that had exploded and white-hot along the edges.

"How dare you, Dragon!" The Margravine's wind voice boomed, cracking around them, and the trees on the hill bent almost to the ground before its force. "This is no affair of yours!"

"Oh, but it is, Faie," the dragon replied. "I find it necessary to offer advice to my brother of earth, on behalf of our younger kinsman here."

"Balisan?" breathed Sigismund, staring. He recognized the hum in that fiery voice now, like bees swarming, and the flicker of humor beneath the flame. It can't be, he thought, a little wildly, except that it is. He found that he wanted to laugh, but the Margravine did not seem to be amused.

"This boy?" she sneered. "Kin to either of you? As well call a pig kin to a king!"

The fire in the dragon's eye blazed hotter, as though an

inner veil had lifted. Its other eye remained fixed on the earth serpent, which had withdrawn to a safer distance. "He and his father are the blood of the dragon," the sibilant voice replied, in a long gout of flame. "And now, thanks to your plots and poisons, they are the last of that line. We are not pleased, Lady Farisie."

The storm wind boomed again, but with a new note in it now. Could it be uncertainty? wondered Sigismund, and caught a gleam of hope in Rue's expression. Then the Margravine laughed.

"The blood of the dragon," she said. "How quaint, but forgive me if I find it hard to believe—given your tender care for that line over the past thousand years."

"The affairs of humans," Balisan replied, "are rarely the concern of dragons, even when they bear our blood. But some things we do notice, like the hand of the faie at work picking off our kin, one by one. You might say, Lady Farisie, that you attracted our attention."

The lightning had died as soon as the dragon arrived, and now Sigismund was sure that he saw a patch of blue above the palace. The Margravine was silent, studying the dragon, and the earth serpent's head swung slowly, looking from one to the other. "But still," the faie said at last, "you may not aid your kinsman to lift the spell. That is forbidden by the terms of the magic."

"Ahhh," said the dragon—a long, outward sigh of fire. "I think you know, Lady Farisie, that he has already lifted

the spell, fulfilling all the requirements of your faie magic."
He stretched like a cat in midair, extending scythe-like
claws on every foot. "But regardless of that, there is still
the matter of kin right to be resolved with my brother of
earth here. And that, Faie, is no business of yours."

"Do you know what he means?" Rue asked, her voice
low.

Sigismund shook his head, but he was remembering
the rumbling, hissing voice that he had heard talking to
Flor, when he was trapped in the Margravine's house. The
voice had said that it would need gold to kill him, because
Sigismund was kin of a sort. He had not understood then,
but it was beginning to make sense at last.

"Will you claim a blood price for this one then, Balisan
the Red?" The earth serpent's voice was the dull roar of
earth sliding, the grating of rocks beneath the earth, but
Sigismund thought the tone was respectful. The enormous
head was still now, a flat-as-stone eye studying the dragon.

"I will," said Balisan. "But I will not accept gold, firedrake though I am. The blood of the dragon is at stake, so I
will claim your life for his, as is my right."

The Margravine howled. "We have a bargain, Earth
Worm! I have already paid you a fortune in gold for this
boy's blood, more even than you asked for!"

The serpent's head drew back, and the stone gaze
turned toward the faie. "I will return your gold," it said. "It
is not worth the bargain that my red kinsman here would

drive, which is of a harsher kind." Its body had already begun to slide back into the mud of the lakebed.

"A prudent course," Balisan murmured, a sibilant hiss. He rose higher into the air, fire washing across his scales, until he was on the same level as the Margravine. "You might be wise, Faie, to reflect further on yours."

In the distance, people had begun to spill out of the palace onto the terraces, and Sigismund could see the small figures of Fulk and Rafe, who appeared to have mastered their horses. He was aware too of Flor, pulling himself up from the ground, but he did not take his eyes off the Margravine. She had retreated further from the dragon's path, but lightning forked behind her head. "Do you think me done?" she hissed. A fireball began to spin between her hands.

"I'll kill him for you!" Flor had pushed to his knees and now wavered there, uncertain. Blood was still flowing from his wounded side, and his good arm shook as he drew it back and hurled a dagger at Sigismund. The dagger fell short.

"You!" the Margravine snarled. "You promised me you could kill this whelp—easily, that was your boast. But instead you fail me at every turn!" The fireball burst from her hands and exploded into a torrent of lightning spears that rained down on the hilltop. Quickthorn flamed in answer, throwing a protective circle around the belvedere, but one of the lightning bolts struck the pulse of blue on Flor's hand. He screamed, an inhuman sound, as the blue stone exploded, and both ring and wearer disintegrated in a blast of cobalt fire.

Sigismund reeled back, appalled, and Rue had both hands pressed hard against her mouth, as though suppressing a scream. The next moment, the air in front of Sigismund split apart and Syrica stood on the topmost step of the belvedere. She extended both arms toward the Margravine, and her silver voice rang out. "Desist, Sister!" she cried. "You have warred directly against humans on this mortal plane and defied the terms of the magic set in place one hundred years ago. And now you have taken a human life. In the name of the Powers that rule the faie, I bid you cease!"

The Margravine's laughter cracked across the sky. "I, yield? To you? I defy you and your puling power, *Sister*." The last word was a sneer.

"Do you defy mine?" The voice that spoke was cold, but wild, and like the Margravine's laughter, it filled the sky. A woman on a white horse rode out of the trees beside the belvedere and sat, looking up, as the wildfire died away.

Was it a woman? Sigismund wondered. There was a shimmer around the edge of her form and he had to keep blinking, trying to focus on a shifting shape of energy and light. But she certainly looked like a woman whenever his vision cleared. He could see the great fall of her green sleeves, webbed over with gold, and the sweep of a green kirtle against the horse's white flank. She did not move or extend a hand skyward as Syrica had done, but the figure of the Margravine dwindled and was drawn inexorably toward the ground.

"Who is that?" Sigismund whispered to Rue, but it was Syrica who answered.

"She is first amongst the Powers that rule the faie— what you would call our Queen."

A long line of riders was emerging from the trees, materializing somewhere behind the hill. Most were armed as knights, with glittering helms and weapons, although the light wavered and bent around them, much as it did about their Queen. They rose into the air and surrounded the Margravine, escorting her to the ground. Defiance glittered in her expression, as well as fury, but it warred with fear as the Queen gazed down at her.

"So," said the Queen. "You have overreached yourself at last, Farisie, and allowed me to intervene." She looked around at the devastation caused by the storm and the passage of the earth serpent. "Which is just as well, since you have already done great harm here—and would have done more if left unchecked. You were a threat, in fact, to both our worlds."

"It's a pity then," Sigismund muttered, "that you couldn't have done something about it sooner."

A ripple ran through the faie, and even Syrica looked alarmed as the Queen turned her golden head toward him.

There was something about the way her head moved, and the fathomless green of her eyes, that reminded Sigismund of the dragon.

"Do not look into her eyes." Balisan's voice was a whisper in his mind.

The Queen laughed, a wild icy chime. "Hark at the Lord Dragon," she said. "Who here would dare look into your eyes, Balisan the Red?" She did not, however, seem to expect an answer, but studied first Sigismund and then Rue. "So this is the Young Dragon and the heiress to the Wood, standing together as was foretold. As for the rest— once spell and counterspell were cast, one against the other, we had to let the magic find its own path. That too is part of our law. And until now, Farisie has always been careful to use human tools, or other agents that are part of this world, to avoid giving us cause for intervention."

The Margravine's defiance flashed as she faced the Queen. "You let this mortal *dare* question you? You should strike him down, rather than finding fault with me. What have I done, after all, but champion the rightful cause of the faie, trying to maintain our rights and dominion here in the mortal realm—something *you* should have done, but would not!"

Perhaps she's mad, thought Sigismund. She doesn't seem to realize—or care—that others don't see things the same way that she does. And she killed Flor without a second thought because he was no longer of use to her.

He shuddered, still hearing Flor's scream, and felt Rue

draw closer to him, but her eyes remained fixed on the Queen of the Faie.

The Queen was studying the Margravine, her expression as fathomless as her eyes. "Do the faie have rights on this mortal plane?" she asked at last, her tone reflective. "It is not our world, Farisie, and you know the way our law has evolved: we have had the ability to travel at will amongst the planes but not to exert dominion over them. To do so would be to become Other to the core of what we are. Our law reflects that—and it may not be broken, either by you or by me, Farisie."

She leaned forward so that her eyes met the Margravine's. "But you should be grateful that we intervene. Have you thought what your fate would have been, if your grand plan succeeded and the planes had torn apart, trapping you here? All your power would have dwindled to a candle flicker, no more than a will-o'-the-wisp seen in the forest by night." The Queen straightened, sitting back. "So you might say that you have been saved from yourself, although whether you deserve saving is another matter." She nodded to the knights surrounding the Margravine. "Take her," she said, "and return to Faerie."

"As easy as that," whispered Rue, "after all we've been through."

Sigismund thought about his fear that the Margravine would never give up, whatever the outcome of the spell. "It does seem to be over," he murmured. "Really over . . . at last."

He stood back while Rue went to greet Syrica, and watched as the Queen turned to Balisan. Sigismund could see their two heads inclined together and the flicker of their eyes, but any communication between them was silent. The faie knights behind the Queen maintained their line, but those surrounding the Margravine had already disappeared, taking her with them.

Above their heads the storm clouds were breaking up, letting through a pale watery sunshine. There were more people now, gathered on the terraces outside the palace. They were all looking toward the belvedere, but no one seemed to want to come over. Well, he would hesitate too, Sigismund thought with a wry grin. A dragon and a small host of faie knights were a situation that needed to be fully understood before rushing in, especially after having been asleep for nearly a hundred years. He wondered what it would be like waking up after so long. Would the sleepers feel bewildered and disoriented, or simply take up their lives as though rising from an afternoon's nap?

Sigismund sighed and sheathed Quickthorn, he hoped for the last time that day, and when he looked up again he saw that Fulk and Rafe had started making their way back toward the belvedere. The rider in the lead had taken off his helmet, but his appearance kept shifting, so that at one moment he looked like Rafe and the next like . . . "Wenceslas?" Sigismund wondered aloud, staring hard as the second rider drew off his helmet too. The red hair that Sigismund was familiar with had become as fair as his own, and after another long, incredulous moment, he recognized Adrian Valensar.

"Shape changing and illusion," muttered Sigismund, still finding it difficult to believe—but it certainly explained why neither "Fulk" nor "Rafe" would ever look at him directly. They must have been afraid that he would see through the illusion.

And I know who to thank for casting that, Sigismund thought. There were definitely questions he wanted answered, and not just by Adrian and Wenceslas. He caught Syrica's eye, watching him over Rue's shoulder. She smiled, but Sigismund thought she looked tired, rather than triumphant.

"It worked out," he said, a little awkwardly. "Your counterspell and the end to the Margravine's plotting."

"Thanks to you, Sigismund." Her smile was as sweet as his first memory of it, her voice a shimmer of silver. "And to Rue. No magic is ever certain, as I told you long ago. It takes courage and commitment to bring it to a good end."

"Although not an entirely happy one for you," Rue said softly, and Syrica sighed.

"No. Farisie had to be stopped, but she will always be my twin. And there were long ages, both in this world and the realm of Faerie, when we were closer, each to the other, than to our own shadows."

"What happened?" Sigismund asked. She had said in

the West Castle that it was an old sorrow, but looking at her face now he wondered if so deep a grief could ever fade. Syrica sighed again, her expression pensive.

"Is it ever possible, in cases such as this, to point to one specific incident or moment and say—there, that was it, it was then the change began." Syrica shook her dark head. "We followed different paths, Farisie and I, but as to when the first small steps were taken—that I do not know."

They were all silent, and Sigismund suspected that he was not the only one reflecting on where the Margravine's path had led and the grief it had brought to so many. "I thought," he said at last, "that she might be mad."

Syrica's mouth twisted, as if she had tasted something bitter. "When pride and the lust for power grow to such an extent that a person disregards all law, and cares nothing for the consequences to others, then that may well be a form of madness."

"Yet in the end," Rue said quietly, "it was Farisie's undoing. She allowed her rage to govern her, blind to everything but the fact that we dared to thwart her will."

Sigismund nodded, and saw that the sky had grown blue again. The last of the thunder was rumbling away westward and there was a rainbow above the white towers of the palace. "Well, it's done now," he said, and stretched, sighing. When he dropped his arms again, he saw that Syrica was watching him, the rainbow reflected in her eyes. She smiled from him to Rue.

"From the beginning," she said, "I had the highest hopes for both of you. You have disappointed none of them."

Rue smiled too, but shook her head. "If you had not come here, a century ago—" She broke off, then added quickly, "They've finished speaking. The Queen's coming over here."

They all watched, silent again, as the white horse approached the belvedere. "Our work here is done," the Queen said to Syrica. "Do you stay or ride with us?"

Syrica held out one hand to Rue, the other to Sigismund. "If I stay," she told them, "I too will dwindle, as Farisie would have done." She turned to the Queen and bowed. "I ride with you."

"It is well," said the Queen, and one of her knights led forth a dappled horse, garlanded with lilacs. Syrica took the rein he held out, then turned back into her goddaughter's embrace.

"Thank you," Rue said. The words were simple, but her expression, and the clasp of her hands, said a great deal more.

"It is well," said Syrica, echoing the Queen. Already, thought Sigismund, she seemed less human, her form growing translucent and beginning to fray.

"Do not be sad," she said, kissing them farewell in turn. "I have done what I came here to do, and now you may live out your lives untroubled by Farisie and her plots."

Her smile was sunshine and shadow at the same time. "Use the years well."

The Queen had already turned her horse and the cavalcade was moving. Syrica mounted too, and the dappled horse followed the rest of the faie as they flowed to either side of the green hill. There was a shimmer around them, a glow, and it was hard to tell whether the horses were touching the earth or floating through the trees. Syrica waved once, smiling, and then they were all rising up, much as the faie hunt had done on the night of the storm, and riding into the face of the sun. Sigismund suspected that Balisan could still see them for quite some time after that, tracking their path with his dragon's sight, but for everyone else there was just the sun's dazzle and a residual brightness in the air.

Everything was so fresh, even the air felt clean and new. Sigismund could see raindrops sparkling on every leaf, brighter than the jewels in Rue's hair, which had become tangled again during the storm. There was a twig caught in the golden net and leaves plastered against her skirt. He reached out and removed the twig, and Rue turned her head, smiling. From the corner of his eye, Sigismund saw that Adrian and Wenceslas had finally arrived. They must have walked up the hill, leaving their horses well away from the dragon.

Soon, Sigismund thought, it would be time to speak with Balisan and thank him, but also to insist on answers to his many questions. He smiled a little crookedly as he looked from Adrian to Wenceslas and back again.

"I imagine," he said, "that the two of you have some kind of explanation for your masquerade?"

"*I thought that you could use some company on the road.*" Balisan's voice was a hum in his mind. "*And I didn't want you to send them away. Besides, Adrian was also the person most likely to see through Ban's illusion.*"

Adrian smiled, and spread his hands wide as if to say that he was not to blame. "It was an adventure," he said, then seeming to recollect himself, he bowed low to Rue. "Princess," he murmured, a courtier's hand over his heart. Wenceslas, however, was still staring in the direction that the faie had taken.

"I've seen the Queen of the Faie, She-of-the-Green-Gold-Sleeves, with my very own eyes. And you've spoken with her, Sigismund, yet still live." Wenceslas squared his shoulders, the dawn of a story in his eyes. "So what happens next?"

Ever After

A great deal, Sigismund thought later that evening. The rest of the afternoon had been turmoil with the whole palace woken from sleep. The first thing Sigismund noticed was the noise. The silent castle had become a cacophony of voices as everyone greeted everyone else, and hugged and cried and kissed. And absolutely everyone, it seemed, had wanted to hug and kiss and cry over Rue. Except that they didn't call her that.

That was the second thing Sigismund had realized as they made their way through the outstretched hands and all the smiling, crying faces outside the palace. There was no Rue. All around him people were calling out to their princess, but the name they cried was Aurora. Shortly afterward, when the tide of people swept them into the great hall and the heralds there had blown a triumphant blast on their silver trumpets, the whole awakened gathering had cheered for the Princess Aurora Elisabeth Irina Anne, Heiress of the Wood.

They had cheered for him too, Sigismund recalled, leaning his elbows on the parapet of the tower to which he had retreated and gazing east toward where his own gray castle lay. His bruised shoulder was aching again from being thumped so often, friendly-wise, and having to shake so many hands. The King and Queen of the Wood had been both gracious and grateful, but Sigismund had seen the way they clung to Rue when she first reached them, and how their eyes kept going to her even while they were talking with him. It was plain that they wanted time with their daughter alone, and Sigismund had understood that. It had been hard, in fact, not to compare their welcome, a little wistfully, with the stern remoteness of his own father.

"But," Sigismund said aloud, "does she have to have quite so many cousins and schoolmates and childhood friends?" They had kept coming forward, all eager to introduce themselves and to thank him, as well as to hug and cry over Rue—except that they all called her Aura—before her parents swept her away.

"Aura. Aurora." Sigismund sighed deeply. He couldn't help feeling that somewhere in the noise and press of people he had lost Rue. It was like watching someone carried away from you by a current, except what could you do when the river was the love of family and friends? He had been disconcerted, as well, to find out just how many of those cousins and childhood friends were young men.

And in all the noise and excitement, it had been some time before he realized that Balisan had disappeared.

It made sense, Sigismund supposed. There had been more than enough uproar without those in the newly awakened palace having to try and come to terms with the presence of a dragon in their grounds. But sensible or not, he couldn't help feeling doubly abandoned, given what had happened with Rue.

How like Balisan, he thought, to turn up, reveal that he's a dragon, and then depart again without a word. But his feelings were definitely mixed, because there was awe as well as pride that a dragon had been protecting him all these years. Sigismund grinned and shook his head. "And I used to think that my life in the West Castle was completely ordinary."

He would, he supposed, have to go down soon. The King and Queen had ordered that the old feast be cleared away and a new celebration prepared for that night. Sigismund and his friends, they said, would be the guests of honor, and there would be music and dancing as well as feasting. But then they had taken Rue away, and although the courtiers treated Sigismund with every courtesy, he felt very much the stranger and rather in the way of all the preparations. He had also begun to feel extremely tired, which was not surprising, given that he had begun the crossing of the Wood the previous night, and the day itself had been filled with magic and violence.

As soon as Sigismund mentioned feeling weary, he, Adrian, and Wenceslas had been taken to rooms where there was food and drink on trays, clean clothes and soft beds, and hot water for bathing in. Sigismund even slept for a while, in a shaft of warm sunshine stretched across the bed, but woke filled with restlessness and the desire to keep away from other people for as long as possible. In the end he had found himself here, in a narrow tower with a curved balcony near the top, and a clear view over the palace grounds to the deepening shadow of the Wood. Sigismund suspected that the tower might have been built as a folly, simply for people to enjoy the view, since the few rooms it contained were small, and no one had come there to disturb him.

The sunset was coral and fire along the western horizon, but the sky overhead was already dark blue and there were a hundred lights streaming out across the lawns and terraces below. The air was mild and Sigismund could hear the first strains of music from the hall. It floated out the open windows with the lantern light, the notes mingling with laughter and the clamor of children playing hide-and-seek along the terraces.

"So this is where you're hiding," said Balisan, stepping

out onto the balcony so quietly that Sigismund jumped. Balisan leaned against the balustrade beside him, and Sigismund relaxed as he recognized his usual quizzical smile. It was hard, he thought, to see the immense firedrake in the man—unless it was in the eyes: not just their slanting shape and the flared brows, but something in their unfathomable expression and the way they shone like molten metal, even in the dark.

"I thought you'd gone," he said.

Balisan's brows rose, and Sigismund was surprised at just how good it felt to see that familiar expression. "Without saying good-bye?" The voice too was exactly as he remembered, the tone mild beneath the faint sibilance. "I would not do that."

"I'm glad," Sigismund said. He studied the dark cloud of the forest, thinking that soon it too would be filled with sound again. The roads would open up and traders like Martin and Bror would begin to come further west—and no doubt there would be negotiations and treaties to establish a clear boundary between his father's realm and the Kingdom of the Wood. There was, Sigismund reflected, going to be a great deal to do. "But I suppose you'll be going soon, now this business with the Margravine is done?"

"In time," Balisan replied. "But I do not have to go straightaway."

"I would like that," Sigismund said. He let his breath

out on the tiniest of sighs. "I've just realized how different everything is going to be."

Balisan nodded, slanting him a sideways look. "More than you know perhaps. Your father is on his way here from the south."

Sigismund straightened, all the confusion and lethargy of the day's aftermath falling away. "Why? How far away is he? When does he arrive?"

Balisan held up a hand, smiling. "Why?" he echoed. "That is easy enough. No one could have held him back once he knew that you intended to venture the Wood on your own. And I did not try." The sibilant voice was soft. "He loves you, Sigismund, although he is not the kind of man to show such emotion easily and will probably never say the words. The resistance in the south collapsed as soon as he occupied the Varana citadel, and he realized that this must be because the Margravine was no longer there to fan the flames—that you were right, in other words. So he left matters in the hands of General Langrafon—although with strict instructions, I believe, not to put all the *zu* Malvolin to the sword—and came north with the royal bodyguard. He has been pressing hard and should reach the West Castle in the next few days."

I had better return there before that, Sigismund thought. He suspected that the reunion was going to be awkward, because Balisan was right and his father's personality wasn't going to change. "Well, at least we should have plenty to talk about. Not just what happened with the Margravine, but formally lifting the interdict and establishing relations with the King and the Queen of the Wood." He frowned, thinking. "And there's still the south. Even if the rebellion there has died out, we still need to reestablish a tradition of peace."

Balisan nodded. "There will be a great deal to do. Your father will need your help, and be glad to have it."

"Even if he doesn't say so." Sigismund straightened and peered down at the terrace below. A lone flautist had come out and was playing a sweet merry air that had drawn the children like moths to a candle. Sigismund could see their attentive half circle and feel the joy expressed in the music, a joy that was reflected throughout the castle. But he felt outside it all, like the knights-errant in the stories, who having achieved their quest, accept the thanks of those they have helped . . . and leave.

But I don't want to leave, thought Sigismund. He turned his head and found Balisan watching him. "I hope," he said, "that this means an end to Ban Valensar wearing the likeness of my face."

The bronze eyes gleamed. "As far as the world is concerned, Ban Valensar has never left the West Castle, and you have been at your father's side throughout this past winter and spring." Balisan shrugged. "It will not be difficult to make the switch without anyone being the wiser. It is a very small glamour to manage."

"For a dragon," Sigismund said, and Balisan raised an eyebrow.

"Does that trouble you?" he asked.

"I'm not sure." Sigismund pushed a hand through his hair, trying to decide what he felt. "Perhaps. Or perhaps it's just that I didn't know, although I suppose that my father must have." A memory flashed, the boyhood vision of his father in a lantern-lit campaign tent and Balisan entering on a gust of wind.

"He knew the old story, of course, but only as one of the legends of your House." Balisan's tone was thoughtful. "I do not think he believed it was anything more than that, until he sent into the Paladinates for a champion and I answered his call."

Sigismund felt a shiver creep across his skin. He wondered how his father would have felt, hearing Balisan speak of that long-forgotten kinship and offer help that might level the odds against the Margravine.

"At first," Balisan said, as if reading his thoughts, "he thought he was dreaming, fallen asleep over the war reports. More than a thousand years had passed, after all, since we made the sword for Parsifal."

Sigismund shivered outright then, and his hand closed around Quickthorn's hilt. The sword was quiet again, except for a tiny answering flicker. "A thousand years," he said. "No wonder the Margravine was surprised when you appeared today."

"What are a thousand years to a dragon?" Balisan's tone was reflective. "She should have known better than to discount our interest. And your father is not the man to refuse a bargain when it is offered to him."

The flautist had changed to another tune, a plaintive melody that spoke of regret, of love lost and roads not taken. Sigismund shifted, tracing the pattern of the stones set into the balustrade. "But you never told me," he said quietly, and caught his companion's headshake from the corner of his eye.

"I dared not," Balisan replied, "in case doing so upset the balance of magic in the hundred-year spell. I knew that Syrica's influence over the Margravine's original working was delicately poised, and if I intruded too far . . ." He shrugged. "And the magic was specific—the chosen prince alone must lift the spell. I needed to teach you how to access your own power in order to do that. If you had known that I was a dragon, then you might, even at a subconscious level, have relied on me."

"Yet in a way," said Sigismund, thinking it through, "I had already drawn you into the spell, because I was the chosen prince and you had a kinship link to me."

"It is possible that I could have intervened further than I did." Balisan shrugged again. "But it seemed best to leave you free to find your own path."

The flute music was still melancholy, and Sigismund felt a great deal older than he had that morning. He didn't want to think about the Margravine anymore, or to go down into the great hall and see Rue again—but only at a remote and glittering distance. Now the quest that had driven him for so long was over with and done, all the paths ahead of him seemed flat and gray.

If only, Sigismund thought, I could stay here forever, talking with Balisan in the old way, and delay taking the first inevitable step into that future. He sighed, watching the western sky fade from apricot to a clear pale lemon. "You said it was a thousand years since you made the sword. Is that when the blood of the dragon came into our line? And are the dragons where our power comes from?"

Balisan reached out and clasped his shoulder, a brief touch but oddly comforting. "Yes to your last question," he said, "although your family already had a deep connection to the land. Adding in the power of the dragon was like a successful graft onto the original stock. But how and why it came about is an old story, older by far than Parsifal." He paused, smiling faintly. "Do you remember the tale that you told Master Griff you liked, the one about the princess who spun stories to the dragon to stop it from eating her?"

Sigismund nodded. "Was that you?" he asked, his interest quickening. "Were you going to eat her?"

To his surprise, Balisan laughed. "It was not me. I have a brother who is much fonder of hunting than I am, but of a solitary disposition. He was hunting in the northern regions of what is now this kingdom, and news of his presence came to the people who dwelt there. They were ignorant and thought that a dragon must be appeased lest it prey on them, and the princess had enemies amongst the king's councilors. It turned out later that some of them were already in the pay of their kingdom's enemies, and the princess was old enough to be a threat. So she was taken and chained in my brother's cave when the watchers saw that he had flown out. And no," he added, reading the question in Sigismund's face, "he would not have eaten her. But he was annoyed because his solitude had been disturbed, so he thought he would let everyone suffer a bit longer before he let her go and then departed the region himself."

Balisan paused, the slight smile on his lips reflected in his eyes. "He has never been entirely sure whether the princess guessed that he was intelligent and not just a brute beast, or whether she began telling the stories just to keep her spirits up. But like you, Sigismund, he loves stories, and the princess quickly realized that he was listening and began to offer more storytelling in exchange for her life."

Sigismund was smiling now too. "Wenceslas was sure that there must have been a kiss in the mix somewhere."

"I think there were many kisses," Balisan observed dryly, "and considerably more than that, since he ended up taking his human form for her sake, and their children were the ones that brought the blood of the dragon into your family line. Their son," he added softly, "was the first to be known as the Young Dragon."

"And the sword?" asked Sigismund. "Where does Parsifal come into this?" He raised his own brows at Balisan's look. "What?"

"You know the story well," the dragon said. "You should be able to work it out."

Sigismund shook his head, thinking that he was too tired to work anything out. The evening star was out and the moon rising, its crescent a little fuller than it had been the previous night. If you looked at it from a certain angle, Sigismund thought, it could almost be a question mark. He felt the ache of the flute's last song, like an answering question in his throat.

"I think he has worked enough things out for one day." Rue's voice spoke from the darkened room behind them, and then she too stepped out onto the balcony, looking from one to the other. "The Parsifal story has many variants, but all have threads in common: the lady who is both loathly and fair, the presence of a sorceress and also of a woman who acts as a wise counselor. Perhaps it is my faie inheritance, but I have always understood this to mean that the knight Parsifal was loved by a dragon, who at times took human form."

Balisan pressed his hands together and inclined his head gracefully. "You are right, Princess," he said, "and the sword Quickthorn was her gift to him. There is much of our power in it, which means that it has a will of its own and is an ally to the one who holds it, not a servant. It did not come to Sigismund at my request, but of its own free will."

"So you see, it is exactly like one of those old stories," Rue said, smiling at Sigismund. "Only better, because you are in it."

Sigismund felt his heart quicken and was almost certain that Balisan was smiling too, somewhere behind his enigmatic expression. Rue looked from one to the other through the dusk.

"You do look alike," she said slowly. "It's something about the shape and color of your eyes. But," she added, speaking to Balisan, "you told me that you would not keep him long."

Balisan's smile reflected the moon's curve. "He had a lot of questions, despite having worked out so many answers today. But I will leave you both now and pay my respects to the King and Queen."

"I have told them you are here," Rue said, "and in what form. They are expecting you." She sank in a curtsy, answering his bow, and then came to stand beside Sigismund. She had changed her clothes, he saw, and was wearing something even richer and more formal than the dress in the belvedere. It had a velvet surcoat and cobweb sleeves, and a brocade skirt crumbed with jewels. Her hair curled and twisted down her back beneath a coronal of golden flowers.

Sigismund thought she looked very beautiful and every

inch a great princess, not at all like his ragged Rue. He could smell the familiar elusive rose of her perfume and was trying not to remember kissing her in the belvedere, for that brief dizzy time when they thought they had already won against the Margravine.

Perhaps that was all the kisses had been, he thought now, just part of the excitement of thinking the spell had been lifted.

Rue rested her arms on the balustrade. "I am sorry," she said, "for leaving you like that. But there was so much happening, such a jumble of people, and my parents—"

"You had to be with them, I know," Sigismund said, determined to be reasonable despite the tightness in his throat. "And I don't want you to think that you owe me anything for undoing the spell, chosen prince or not." He kept his eyes fixed on the evening star, trying to focus on that and not her warm presence so close beside him. "The truth is that I always wanted to be the one to lift the spell, ever since Syrica first told me the story. It was my free choice," he added, thinking about his conversation with Annie.

"So I don't owe you anything. I do see that." Rue's tone was so thoughtful that it took Sigismund a moment to realize that she was laughing at him. She put her hand out and rested it on top of his. "Oh, Sigismund, don't you see that I owe you everything? We all do. But that"—she put the fingertips of her other hand against his mouth before he could say anything—"isn't why I love you."

After that, neither of them said anything for quite some time. Drowning, thought Sigismund, and sank further into the deep water that was his mouth on hers, her arms twisted close around his neck and his twined beneath the fall of her hair. When he finally raised his head, Sigismund thought the moon looked considerably less like a question mark. The music from the palace below was louder now, viol and harp joining merrily with flute and horn and drifting into the night.

"We'll be missed at the feast," Sigismund said, but he did not step back or make any move to let her go. He caught the ghost of her smile.

"My parents will not be there yet," she said. "They wished for private speech with Lord Balisan, and said that they would wait afterward for me to bring you to them."

"Ah." Sigismund let her hair run through his fingers like water. "I suppose," he added after a moment, "that I had better call you Aurora now, since that's your real name."

"Aura," said Rue. "I could never manage Aurora when I was small, so I called myself Aura instead, and the name stuck."

"Aura then," Sigismund murmured. "But I'll miss Rue."

She leaned back a little, her hands still linked behind his neck, considering this. "I think I will too, a little. But I have to learn to be Aura again now and live in the waking world."

Sigismund nodded, recognizing the truth in this. "Aura," he said again, letting her name hang on the night air. "It suits you." But he knew that she would always be Rue in his heart. He paused, struck by a sudden thought. "So did Balisan know about you? Did he put the rue in that treatise on boar hunting, or was it someone else?"

The slim straight line was back between Aura's brows. "I don't know. I took the herb as my personal emblem when I was old enough to understand the Margravine's curse. That's why Syrica took rue from the gardens here to be one of my anchors in the world." She shrugged. "But I have no reason to believe that Lord Balisan knew that, or about my limited ability to move and act within the boundaries of the spell."

But you never really know with Balisan, thought Sigismund. He's very good at keeping his own counsel.

Aura was right, he thought. They had been part of exactly the kind of story that Wenceslas would tell on a summer evening in the West Castle stable yard. There had been good faie and evil, a faithless friend and others who stood true, an enchanted princess and a magic sword, and a dragon that took human shape and walked amongst men. And although that story was over, the days ahead no longer seemed colorless and dull.

"Right now," said Sigismund, sharing this thought, "I feel that the next part of our story could be even more extraordinary than the beginning." He took a step back, slipping an arm around Aura's waist so they stood side by side, watching the constellations flower overhead.

"But I suspect," she said, after a time, "that the beginning is the part that the world will remember. People may even tell of it for another hundred years, the story of the Prince and the Wood."

"They will if Wenceslas has anything to do with it." Sigismund let his arm tighten, just for a moment. "But he's bound to embellish the original." He smiled, remembering the tower of mirrors. "He'll insist that the sleeping princess is woken by a kiss."

Aura turned and brushed her lips against his. "And you?" she murmured. "What will you insist on?"

Sigismund tilted his face to the moon, which could never, he decided, have looked anything like a question mark. "Only that they live happily ever after. That's the ending I want."

And they went down from the tower together, to the lights and the laughter and the friends who waited for them there.

Helen Lowe won an inaugural Robbie Burns National Poetry Award in 2003 and was the recipient of a NZ Society of Authors/Creative New Zealand award for emerging writers. Helen has had short stories and poetry published and anthologized in New Zealand, Australia, and the United States, and currently fronts a regular poetry feature for a local radio station (Plains 96.9 FM). *Thornspell* is Helen's first novel, and she is already hard at work on her next one.

In addition to her writing life, Helen is a second-*dan* black belt in aikido and represented her university in the sport of fencing. She lives in a ninety-year-old house with a woodland garden in Christchurch, New Zealand, which she shares with her partner, Andrew, and two cats.